"Saying I love you—it's l   **promise." S**

"But making prom...   ...e."

"Can't or won't?" s...

"I don't want to stay... ...want a house in the suburbs. It's al... ...e. Too much sameness. The monotony, the boredom scare me."

"It doesn't have to be that way," she said.

His hand moved to the back of her neck, pulling her closer. "I've never forgotten you, Meg. I dream about you. When I was in California I'd look up at the night sky and think, these same stars are shining down on Meg. When I was on the water, I felt the ocean currents connecting us even though we were apart. When we're together, I want to be *with* you. I want to make love to you...."

The ache inside her was part physical need, part emotional connection that defied time and logic. But could she handle a relationship on his terms? Yes, she could, she would, yes, yes—

Davis. She'd forgotten what her involvement with Spencer could do to her son...*their* son, though Spencer still didn't know it. Her blood cooled. Her eyes opened. She pushed on Spencer's shoulders, clumsily trying to move him off her.

"I can't do this, Spencer." Another meteorite blazed across the sky and was gone. "I've had enough. Please take me home."

Dear Reader,

Before I became a writer, I was a marine biologist. Although *Spencer's Child* is a fictional story with fictional characters, I drew upon my experiences living and working on the west coast of British Columbia to give it authenticity. I never studied killer whales, but in researching this book I've learned so much about these wonderful animals I almost wish I had one.

Through the Vancouver Aquarium, I became the proud adoptive parent of Takush, a northern resident killer whale. The names of the whales Spencer and Meg work with are taken from records of whales identified on the B.C. coast, although the whales don't all belong to the same pod in real life.

As for my characters, Spencer is one of my favorite kinds of hero—a brilliant but flawed loner, untamable and unattainable. Loving such a man could haunt a woman all her life—especially when she's borne his child. It was a great pleasure for me to create a heroine, Meg, whose vulnerability is balanced by inner strength, and whose abiding love ultimately heals Spencer and brings them together, forever, with all the joy they so richly deserve.

I hope you enjoy reading this story as much as I enjoyed writing it.

Joan Kilby

SPENCER'S CHILD
Joan Kilby

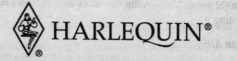

TORONTO • NEW YORK • LONDON
AMSTERDAM • PARIS • SYDNEY • HAMBURG
STOCKHOLM • ATHENS • TOKYO • MILAN • MADRID
PRAGUE • WARSAW • BUDAPEST • AUCKLAND

ISBN 0-373-70873-4

SPENCER'S CHILD

Copyright © 1999 by Joan Kilby.

All rights reserved. Except for use in any review, the reproduction or utilization of this work in whole or in part in any form by any electronic, mechanical or other means, now known or hereafter invented, including xerography, photocopying and recording, or in any information storage or retrieval system, is forbidden without the written permission of the publisher, Harlequin Enterprises Limited, 225 Duncan Mill Road, Don Mills, Ontario, Canada M3B 3K9.

All characters in this book have no existence outside the imagination of the author and have no relation whatsoever to anyone bearing the same name or names. They are not even distantly inspired by any individual known or unknown to the author, and all incidents are pure invention.

This edition published by arrangement with Harlequin Books S.A.

® and TM are trademarks of the publisher. Trademarks indicated with ® are registered in the United States Patent and Trademark Office, the Canadian Trade Marks Office and in other countries.

Visit us at www.romance.net

Printed in U.S.A.

To my father, for instilling in me the belief that I could accomplish anything I set my heart on and making sure I had the discipline to achieve my goals.

And to Nan, for giving me the gift of time.

ACKNOWLEDGMENTS

I would like to thank Volker Deeke for sharing his expert knowledge in the field of killer whale bioacoustics and for patiently answering my many questions.

Meg Pocklington (who has the same name as my heroine purely by coincidence!) of the Vancouver Aquarium was of great assistance in helping me gather information on killer whales.

Any technical errors are mine.

PROLOGUE

MEG PEERED THROUGH her microscope at the marine polychaete curled on its side in the petri dish. With one hand she held open the identification guide to marine invertebrates of the Pacific Northwest; with the other she used a probe to count the bristles arranged in paired sets on each segment. She'd almost finished when the chair next to hers scraped back and someone dropped into the empty seat.

Her concentration broken, Meg glanced up. And her heart beat a little faster.

Spencer Valiella. His brown hair was long and unkempt, as though permanently ruffled by the wind that blew in off the Pacific. He wore khaki pants and a faded black sweatshirt with the sleeves cut out. On the crest of his tanned biceps rode the tattoo of a leaping killer whale.

No one knew much about Spencer. He was a loner. Also a fourth-year honors student here at the University of Victoria and reputed to be brilliant. Yet not the kind of boy her parents would approve of. But she'd noticed him around the building, found him wildly attractive and now he was sitting right beside her.

"Hi," she said. "I'm Meg."

"Spencer." Barely glancing her way, he hauled his

beat-up leather satchel onto the table and began to rummage inside.

Her gaze slid back to the killer whale tattoo. She'd been fascinated with the sleek black-and-white marine mammals ever since she was eight years old and one had leaped straight out of the water not fifty feet from her father's cabin cruiser. She'd gone into biology with the sole intention of studying them.

"Are you sure you're in the right class?" she asked, trying to engage him in conversation. "This is Marine Invertebrates 301—a third-year course."

His features were clean and straight, his sea-green eyes so dark that when she gazed into them she swore she could hear things that went bump in the night.

He took in her styled blond hair, miniskirt and designer top and smiled briefly. "I'm where I have to be, princess."

Meg turned up her nose and pretended interest in the worm.

Spencer pulled a laboratory manual out of his satchel. A folded square of paper came out with it and slid across the table. From the corner of her eye, Meg saw it coming and stopped it with her hand. She recognized the pale greens and blues and dotted curving lines of a navigation chart.

"Are you into boating?" she asked, sliding it back. "My dad has a cabin cruiser. We go over to Port Townsend all the time."

"I have a kayak."

For a second she thought he was being apologetic. But the look that accompanied his words withered that notion and made her cheeks flush. Spencer Valiella was not impressed by clothes or looks or wealth.

Meg had brains, too, but she doubted he was interested enough to find out.

He tucked the chart back into his satchel and leaned closer to her microscope. "What have you got there—a polychaete?"

He seemed oblivious to the fact that his knee was now touching hers. She found it hard to focus on anything but the heat generated by the point of contact. Or the wild clean scent of salt air on his skin. "I'm almost finished the ID," she said without looking up. "You can have the worm when I'm done."

With a flick of his finger, Spencer turned the worm onto its dorsal surface. *"Abarenicola pacifica."*

Meg blinked. It had taken her twenty minutes just to get the family name. "Are you sure?"

"Positive."

"How many segments is it supposed to have?"

"Twenty," he said, sounding bored. "Three pairs of branched gills containing hemoglobin on the anterior segment."

"Wait a minute." She flipped through the pages of the identification key to the species' descriptions. "You're right."

Meg wrote the name in her notebook beside her pencil illustration of the worm. "Thanks," she said, and gave him her most brilliant smile. "I'm interested in killer whales, too. Are you studying them for your honors thesis?"

One corner of his mouth curved slowly upward. Above his high cheekbones, his dark eyes gleamed. "Only one thing you need to know about me, princess. I'm here for a good time, not a long time."

"Oh, really." She started to close her notebook,

annoyed with herself now for even trying to get through to the guy.

"Wait a minute." He reached for the notebook and took a closer look at her drawing of the worm, which was accurate and detailed, down to the very last segment and bristle. "This is good."

Pride put a bloom in her cheeks. She whipped her notebook away and stuffed it into her bag. She didn't need approval from Spencer Valiella.

With the eraser end of a pencil, he pushed back the lock of hair that hid her face. "I'm studying communication between maternal groups of resident killer whales, Meg."

Reluctantly, yet irresistibly, she raised her eyes to his.

"I'll take you along sometime if you're seriously interested," he said.

"Oh, yes," she replied as casually as she could. "I'm interested."

CHAPTER ONE

FROM THE TOP FLOOR of his rented house, Spencer gazed out over the tiled roofs of Monterey Bay. Beyond the rocky shore lay the Pacific, blue and wrinkled, darker in patches where kelp forests swayed beneath the surface. The ocean stretched northward, its currents linking this temporary home with another he'd known in Victoria, British Columbia.

In his thirty-one years Spencer had moved thirty-five times. Victoria was one place he'd sworn never to return to. He still thought about Meg. Still felt the tug on his soul across the miles, across the years. A tug he'd resisted seven years ago and finally fled.

But Doc Campbell, his honors supervisor, had just suffered a stroke. Doc, his good friend and mentor, wanted Spencer to take over his marine mammals class until he could return to work. Christmas, at the latest, Doc had promised. The plea had been followed up by a formal request from Randolph Ashton-Whyte, the head of the biology department.

Spencer paced the sparsely furnished living room. His postdoctoral fellowship at the Monterey Aquarium had wound to a close. He'd applied for another research position in Bergen, Norway, but it could be months before he got word on that.

He didn't want to go back to Victoria and memories of Meg. But for Doc he'd do it.

Two days later Spencer roared through Victoria in his beat-up Camaro with the California plates and muffler full of holes. He had a kayak strapped to the roof rack, and the back end was loaded down with boxes of books, electronic gear and the few personal effects he'd hung on to over the years. He'd come straight up from Monterey, driving all day and all night, stopping only for gas and coffee and microwaved burritos that tasted like the cardboard they were served in.

It was eight in the morning when Spencer turned onto the potholed ribbon of asphalt that led to his father Ray's beach cottage in Sooke, west of Victoria. A patchwork of brightly colored wooden houses lined the beach. Across the road, towering Douglas firs spilled their resiny scent into the mid-August heat where it mingled with the salt of the ocean. Spencer rolled down the window and his fingers tapped out the bass of an old Queen song on the hot black roof of the Camaro.

He slowed as he came around the bend, an eye out for the cottage his father had bought twenty years ago with the proceeds from the sale of his first record album. Ray's flirtation with domesticity had been brief, coinciding with the birth of Spencer's younger sister, Janis, and lasting only until the next big gig lured him across the continent. Except for the two years Spencer had spent at the university, the cottage had been inhabited off and on by itinerant musician friends of his father's. His mother had split long ago, taking Janis and Spencer south to her native San Clemente, where she'd eventually settled down with, of all people, an investment banker. Spencer guessed he couldn't blame her. Some people needed stability.

Around a bend he spotted the mailbox carved from driftwood and slowed to pull into the gravel driveway beside the tiny wooden house with peeling blue paint. The yard was overgrown with weeds and a wind chime of oyster shells clattered in the breeze that drifted around the porch.

He unfolded his limbs from the car and sucked the strong salt air deep into his lungs. Across the grass-strewn sand dunes, the ocean beckoned. The seemingly limitless expanse made him breathe easier. *Home.* The thought made him laugh. Like the tortoise, his home was on his back. Or more precisely, in the Camaro.

Yawning from lack of sleep, he pulled his duffel bag and laptop computer from the trunk and deposited them on the porch. The house appeared to be empty, as he'd hoped. He reached into a side pocket of the duffel for his key ring. Not the one with the brass killer whale that held his car keys, but the plain steel circle that held the keys to the cottage. And the keys to Doc's laboratory and office. He'd never returned those when he left. If he believed in fate, he might have thought it was because he was meant to return.

Spencer opened the torn screen door and put the key in the lock knowing it wasn't fate that had made him hang on to the keys. The research vessel he'd worked on that last summer had set sail early to follow a bumper salmon run that was drawing the killer whales north of their usual habitat. He hadn't had time to drop off the keys. Or to say goodbye to... anyone.

The screen door banged shut behind him. Inside, the cottage wore the somnolent air of endless summer that seemed to inhabit all beach houses. Before his mother's defection to southern climes, she'd hung curtains of sand-colored handwoven cloth shot with strands of aqua. The detritus of beach-combing expeditions littered the windowsills: shells, bits of twisted and polished driftwood, colored glass fishing floats washed ashore after perhaps decades at sea.

The plain board floor creaked beneath his feet, the sound muffled by a large oval rag rug. He crossed to the far wall, drawn by an enlarged black-and-white photo of Subpod C3: Kitasu, the matriarch; Geetla and Joker, her two grown sons; and Takush, her daughter. Takush was old enough to have a calf of her own by now. Spencer could still recognize individual killer whales by the shape and size of their dorsal fins and the scars on their sleek black-and-white hides. They seemed more like old friends than the subjects of his honors thesis.

He wondered if their dialect of calls and whistles had altered in the years he'd been gone. He planned to paddle out to see them for old time's sake, but there was no point starting a research program when he'd be leaving again so soon. Doc had sounded robust in spite of his slurred speech when Spencer had called the hospital from Seattle. He'd surely be back by Christmas.

Dropping his duffel bag next to a low bookshelf crammed with tattered paperbacks, Spencer carried his laptop into the kitchen. His head was fuzzy with fatigue but he wanted to check his e-mail—the closest thing he had to a permanent address—before he hit the sack for a few z's. He set the laptop on the table, plugged it in, then attached the modem to the phone jack on the wall beside the fridge. As he flicked the switch he realized belatedly there might not be any electricity or phone connection. To his surprise, numbers flashed across the screen as the system booted up. He dialed his service provider in California, waiting for the dialog box that would tell him he couldn't connect...

Brrrinnng.

So the phone was on, too. He hit "receive messages" and got up to look around while the in-box filled.

A used coffee cup sat in the sink. An empty milk carton peeked out of the garbage bin. *Damn.* Someone was here, after all.

Spencer strode back to the living room and stood at the entrance to the short hall where the two bedrooms were. "Hello? Anybody home?"

Silence.

He knocked softly on the door to the main bedroom and when there was still no answer, pushed it open. The bed was a tangle of thin wool blankets and forest-green sheets. A pile of dirty clothes sat on the floor beside the open closet.

Who was staying here? And where were they now?

Then Spencer noticed the battered guitar case propped against the wall behind the door. The medley of souvenir stickers from cities across the continent spoke of decades of life on the road. He knew that guitar case. A grin spread across his face. His father was in town. He hadn't seen Ray for a few years, not since he'd driven down to San Francisco from Seattle to catch the Brass Monkeys in concert. Ray had been riding high, a new record deal and a promotional tour in the offing.

Spencer had a flash of memory of doing school-work in a bus seat while music blared and his father and the guys in the band played cards or wrote songs. As a kid, he'd loved going on the road with them. Pulling out of the hotel parking lot at dawn, a new city every night, the excitement of the unknown—all were magnified in his young mind. As an adult he still got a kick out of moving on. As if maybe *this* time he was going to find the Holy Grail, whatever that was. Victoria was a step backward, but seeing Ray would make the trip worthwhile.

Where the hell was he? Spencer shut the door to his father's room and went back to the kitchen. Ray would turn up sooner or later. Meanwhile, at the top of his in-box was a message from the head of the biology department at University of Victoria.

Dr. Valiella,
Did I mention that Angus Campbell has an honors student? Please give her a call ASAP. Her name is Meg McKenzie, phone number...

Spencer rocked back in his chair, his pulse thrumming. *Meg.* Could this be *his* Meg McKenzie? No way. She'd only been one year behind him. She would have finished her degree long ago and gone on to either graduate studies or a job somewhere.

Spencer got up to pace across to the window overlooking the tiny backyard. Meg's image, tucked away in his subconscious, surged forth. Impish smile, bright eyes the blue of a robin's egg, hair the color of sunlight. The memory of her laughter rang in his ears, the careless confident laughter of a girl possessed of talent, brains and wealth.

He shut his eyes and the blackness behind his lids pulsed with pinpricks of light. They were the stars above a campsite on Saltspring Island. Sleeping bags zipped together, bare limbs entwined. The wonder of their first time together.

And their last. For a few short hours he'd been able to give her what she wanted.

If only she hadn't said what she'd said.

He'd known then he'd never be able to give her what she needed.

Spencer ran a hand through his hair. It was years ago. Time he forgot about her.

But he had to call.

His hand hovered over the phone. Even if it was Meg, she might not remember him. The weekend imprinted in his memory was probably just a blip on her busy social schedule.

He picked up the phone and dialed the number, annoyed to notice his palms were damp and he had trouble taking a breath.

ABOVE THE INCESSANT squawk of Noel, her son's golden cockatiel, Meg heard the ringing telephone. She ignored both and cocked an ear toward Davis's bedroom. His cry of frustration stabbed straight to the "mother" center of her brain. God, she hoped this was only a phase. But it was one phase after another.

With a sigh, she turned off the heat under the pot of oatmeal and strode down the narrow hallway that linked the kitchen with the bedrooms. As she passed the bathroom she could hear Patrick warbling Gilbert and Sullivan over the roar of the shower. At least Patrick's noise was cheerful.

She paused in her son's doorway. Davis, in his little white Jockeys and socks, was struggling to do up the buttons on an inside-out shirt. At the sight of her, his cries rose a decibel.

"Mom! It won't do up." Angry tears spurted from his dark green eyes. Eyes that were a daily reminder of the best, and the worst, period of her life.

"Come here, sweetie." Meg dropped to her knees and held out her arms. From the rumpled bed, Morticia, the black-and-orange cat, looked up sleepily.

A lock of straight brown hair fell over Davis's scowling forehead, but he didn't budge. Sometimes he reminded her so much of his father it made her heart ache.

With a grunt, Davis jammed the button through. "I did it!"

"Do you know why it was so hard?" Meg asked, her tone carefully matter-of-fact. "Your shirt is inside out."

"I know that." He started to jam another button through its hole. His smooth olive skin stretched tight over his cheekbones and once again turned crimson with frustration.

Shaking back her long hair, Meg ignored his protests and pulled his shirt over his head, then quickly whipped the sleeves right side out. "Now, show me again how you can do up those buttons."

A few minutes later Davis's buttons were fastened and he was proud to bursting.

Meg pulled him into a hug. Small progress for most kids perhaps, but for Davis, some things had to be learned over and over again. He could build complex Lego structures without instructions, figure out how simple machines worked and knew almost as much about the insects he collected as Meg, who'd done three years of university biology. But he couldn't sit

still for more than two seconds at a time, had diffi-
culty putting thoughts into words and forgot instructions as soon as they were given.

He was the most exasperating child in the universe,
and if she didn't love him desperately, she'd surely
have strangled him before he'd turned three. But here
he was, six years old, and weeks away from starting
school.

"Put your pants on," she said, handing him a pair
of navy corduroys.

Davis grasped the pants by the elasticized waist and
raised a leg. He lost his balance, so he moved to lean
against the bed. He got one leg in, then paused to
study a fly cleaning its forelegs on the windowsill.

Meg waited. "Your pants, honey. Davis. *Davis*."

"What?" His eyes were innocent, inward-seeing.

"Your pants." She must have done something
gravely wrong in a past life. She, who at the best of
times battled her impatience, now required the pa-
tience of Job.

Davis gazed blankly at his corduroys. Then, "Oh."
He thrust his other leg in and hopped up and down
to settle the waistband around his skinny hips. When
he got them on, he kept on hopping. "Look at me,
I'm a bunny."

Meg grabbed him and tucked in his shirt.

He squirmed in her arms, turning mutinous. "I
don't want to go to day care. Kids are mean to me."

Meg's heart sank. She'd been afraid of this even
though the woman who ran the day-care center had
assured her she'd be discreet when she gave Davis
his tablet at lunchtime. How much worse would it be
when he went to school? "There's nothing wrong
with having to take medicine."

"It's not that," he said, his small hands clenched into fists. "Tommy said…he…I couldn't go to…to big kids' school if I didn't have a daddy."

"Oh, Davis." Meg gathered her son into her arms. Over his shoulder, she glanced at her watch. He had to be at day care in half an hour if she was going to be on time to register for classes at the university. But even though they'd been over the subject of his father what seemed like a million times, she never begrudged him the opportunity to ask questions. Maybe it was her sensitivity. Or maybe it was guilt. She just wished she had better answers.

"You do have a daddy," she said. "He's just not like other dads. He's…special."

"Because he studies killer whales?" Davis jiggled his legs.

"That's part of it."

"What else?" He picked up a car and began running it across the floor.

"He's…" *A lover. A loner. A modern-day Ulysses. He's a genius. A bastard. And my poor heart's desire.* "He can take the peel off an entire orange in just one strip."

"Really? Wow." Davis paused momentarily to give the feat its due. "But why doesn't he…you know?"

"What?"

"Live with us. Doesn't he like us?" Davis dropped the car and picked up a toy sword. He began banging it on the floor.

"This isn't his home, sweetheart, you know that— Please stop banging. I don't think he's ever had a real home. But if he knew about you, I know he'd love you just as much as I do." She mentally crossed her fingers and wondered, as she often did, if that was true.

"How come you didn't tell him about me?" There was just about as much hurt as there could be in his small voice. Bang, bang, bang, went the sword on the carpeted floor.

She took the sword off him. He picked up a plastic baseball bat and started banging it, instead.

"I tried to tell him, years ago. I...couldn't get through."

The first time had been the summer after her third year, on the ship-to-shore radio. But when she'd realized bored fishermen all over the Pacific Northwest were listening in, the words had choked in her throat. Then, when she was eight months along, she'd called him in Seattle where he was doing his masters degree. Before she could mention the baby, he'd started talking about scholarships and a Ph.D. at a prestigious university. It wasn't the thought of screwing up his life that had held her tongue, although that had been a consideration. It was the excitement in his voice when he talked about moving on. New location, new research topic, new everything. Girlfriend, too, undoubtedly. Meg had guts but apparently not enough.

It wasn't Spencer's fault that her family, particularly her mother, had never forgiven her for dropping out of university to have his baby. Nor was it his fault Davis was growing up with only her gay housemate for a male role model. None of it was his fault. And all of it was.

Not a day went by when she didn't think of him. Not a trip to the university when she didn't look for him around every corner even though she knew he'd left the country years ago. Hopeless. Futile. Pathetic. It was a good thing she was over him.

The banging of the plastic bat tore at her nerves. "Stop."

"I want to learn to play baseball," Davis said, grudgingly relinquishing the bat. "Tommy's dad plays catch with him."

"*I'll* teach you. When we get home tonight we'll toss the ball around, okay?" She gave Davis another hug and got to her feet. "It's just you and me, kid, better get used to it. Come on. Your oatmeal is almost ready."

"First I'm going to see Charlie."

Charlie, the lizard. Meg watched Davis race down the hall, through the kitchen to the laundry room, his socks flapping loosely in front of his toes. *Pull up your socks,* she wanted to shout, but didn't. The time would come soon enough when Davis had no choice but to pull them up, figuratively speaking. *Please, God, give my boy an understanding teacher.*

She was stirring the oatmeal again when Patrick sailed into the kitchen. His brush cut was shiny with gel, his shoes spit-shined to a high gloss, and his beige navy uniform pressed to a knife-edge. "Good morning, sweetcheeks," he said, giving her a peck on the forehead. "Davis all right?"

"He's fine. Just a minor skirmish with his buttons."

"Good. Now, how do I look?" Patrick spun on his toes, arms outstretched. "I've got an interview with the selection committee today, and I'm *that* far away from promotion." He held his thumb and forefinger a quarter of an inch apart.

"You look terrific." She put down the wooden

spoon to tweak his tie a little straighter. "I just love a man in uniform."

"So do I, sweetie. So do I," he replied with a waggle of his eyebrows.

Meg laughed. "You're terrible. But I don't know what I'd do without you."

"Probably slit your little wrists." Patrick turned as Davis came into the kitchen with Charlie cradled in his hands. "I'm in the galley tonight, champ. What would you like for dinner?"

"Hot dogs!" Davis opened his hands and the reptile began to crawl over his sleeve toward his neck.

Patrick planted his fists on his hips. "You simply *must* expand your repertoire, mister. But discipline's your mom's department. Hot dogs, it is. I'll make Caesar salad for us," he added to Meg.

"*Patrick.* You know I'm trying to establish a pattern of one meal for all."

Patrick turned puppy-dog eyes on her. They always made her cave. As he well knew.

"Oh, all right. Since you're cooking, you get to choose."

They might as well be married the way they argued over Davis's upbringing. She had the final say of course, but she couldn't squash all of Patrick's many indulgences.

"Davis," she said, turning to her son, "get Charlie out of your collar and back in his cage. Then run and wash your hands. You don't want lizard slime in your oatmeal."

"Lizards aren't slimy, Mom. Sheesh!" But he plucked the reptile off his neck and returned to the laundry room where the less socially acceptable of his pets were housed, his feet dragging in exaggerated slow motion. Just to let her know he was complying under duress.

Through the open door, Meg watched him put Charlie away. "Keep going," she said, stepping across to where she could see the hall to make sure he didn't get sidetracked on the way to the bathroom.

Patrick clucked his tongue as he put the kettle on to boil. "Ease up on the boy," he said, measuring ground Colombian into the coffee plunger. "Watching his every move like a hawk won't teach him self-reliance."

Meg dropped a handful of raisins into the oatmeal and turned down the heat. "Oh, Patrick, you know what he's like."

"Vividly. But you can't be the earth, moon and stars to the child. You need a break before school starts. Why don't you let me look after him for a couple of days while you pamper yourself with a weekend at the Empress Hotel?"

"You know I can't afford that."

Even if she could afford a weekend at the Empress, she wouldn't go. It wasn't that she didn't trust Patrick's life-style; he was just way too lenient. Davis constantly pushed the limits. He needed a firm hand. He needed stability, continuity and routine. He needed to know where he stood every moment of the day. She could just imagine how spun out her son would be after a couple of days with Patrick giving him whatever his heart desired. If only she could call on her mother.... But there was no use wishing.

The telephone began to ring again.

Meg reached for the cordless phone and, still stirring the oatmeal, tucked it under her chin while she opened the fridge to get some milk. "Hello?"

Noel hopped out of his open cage above the kitchen counter and onto her shoulder. "Hello?" he squawked in her other ear.

"Get away." She brushed at the bird and it flew to the top of the fridge. "Sorry, not you," she said into the receiver. Behind her she could hear Davis rummaging through the cupboard. The kettle began to hiss. "Hello? Is anybody there?"

A man cleared his throat. "May I speak to Meg McKenzie?"

Her hand froze on the wooden spoon. *Spencer.* She'd know his deep voice anywhere, anytime. The pale yellow walls of the kitchen seemed to swirl. The sounds around her faded away. Without warning she was snatched from the mundane activities of breakfast and dropped, like a stone through water, into the past. She was sinking, fast.

"Who is this?" she whispered hoarsely, buying time. What could he be calling for now, after all these years?

"Spencer…" He paused. "Spencer Valiella."

A prickling chill ran from behind her ears and down her arms. Glancing up, she saw Patrick's round hazel eyes regarding her avidly. She turned away so he couldn't see her face, which she was sure must be pale.

"Dr. Ashton-Whyte from the university asked me to call you," Spencer went on, as though speaking to a stranger. "I'm taking over Dr. Campbell's position—I assume you know he had a stroke?"

His words caused a roaring in her ears. *Spencer, it's me you're talking to.* "Yes. I—I went to see him in the hospital."

There was a pause, then he said slowly, "I used to

know a Meg McKenzie—about seven years ago. She did the best biological illustrations I've ever seen.''

He *did* remember. If she shut her eyes she could almost imagine she was hearing his voice in the dark—

''Mom! Can I have my oatmeal? I'm starving.''

Davis. Meg felt her spine go cold. Spinning around, she held a finger against her lips to shush him, then hurried over to spoon oatmeal into his bowl.

With her free hand pressed to her other ear, she walked back into the kitchen and said quietly into the receiver, ''Thank you. Spencer.''

Silence while she listened to the sound of her thudding heart and shallow breath.

''Meg,'' he said at last, ''so it *is* you. I couldn't believe it at first. How are you?''

''Fine. Just fine.'' Unexpectedly anger coursed through her, bringing the blood back to her cheeks. She was *not* fine. He'd made love to her, then left town without even saying goodbye.

''I had no idea *you* would be taking over Dr. Campbell's position,'' she said, covering her anger with an artificially bright voice, taking refuge from hurt by reverting to her preppy self of seven years ago. Before Davis. Before poverty. Before the falling out with her mother.

''I've kept in touch with Doc over the years,'' Spencer said. ''He knew I was available and suggested to Ashton-Whyte I'd be suitable for the job. I'll be an assistant professor, not a full professor like Doc, but I can live with that.''

He'd kept in touch with Dr. Campbell. But not with her. Meg gripped the telephone, trying not to weep with anger and frustration and hurt. When she thought of all the nights she'd lain awake and fantasized about an emotional reunion. *Idiot.*

"Well, you certainly know your cetaceans," she replied, still in that overbright tone reminiscent of her mother's garden-club voice.

"Have you decided on a topic?"

"Topic? Oh, you're talking about my thesis." She didn't mean anything to him. Never had. "I've got some ideas I was going to discuss with Dr. Campbell."

"I guess you'll be discussing them with me, instead."

It hit her then. She was not only *talking* to Spencer, she would soon *see* him. And not only see him, but work with him on a daily basis. Meg groped for a chair and lowered herself into it. Davis spooned oatmeal into his mouth and watched her, wide-eyed. Patrick set a cup of coffee in front of her.

"So *you'll* be my honors supervisor?"

"If you have no objection."

"Do I have a choice?" She laughed to show she was joking, but it sounded thin.

"Not if you want to work with killer whales."

Nothing was going to stop her from working with killer whales. Not even Spencer Valiella. Then she thought about why he'd said that, the reason he was there at all. Dr. Campbell had been the only marine mammalogist in the department. "Won't Dr. Campbell be coming back to work?"

"The doctors don't know yet how permanent the damage is. Right now, he's got some paralysis down his right side, but he's recovering well. I only expect to be here until Christmas."

"Oh." *Dear God.* Did she feel hope or disappointment? Where Spencer was concerned she'd known too much of both.

"Meg, why are you doing your honors now? Seven years later?"

The answer was sitting there at the kitchen table, licking milky droplets from the side of his mouth. She was going to have to tell him about Davis. But it wasn't something she could blurt over the phone. After all this time of wishing he could know his son, and vice versa, she was suddenly terrified of them meeting.

"I guess we'd better make a time to discuss my thesis," she said, evading his question. "I'll be up at the university today to register."

"I just got into town. I need some sleep before I can think coherently. How about this afternoon in Doc's office? Say, three o'clock?"

"Two o'clock would be better. I've, uh, got something I have to pick up around three."

"Fine. I'll see you then."

The phone slipped from her cold fingers into its cradle. She wiped a hand across her forehead and felt the perspiration. She was *not* disappointed he hadn't declared his long-lost love.

Over at the sink, Patrick was rinsing his bowl. "What was *that* all about?" he said. "And don't you tell me 'nothing' sweetcheeks, because I *know* it's something. Something *big*."

She frowned and tilted her head toward Davis. "Later."

Patrick's eyes widened. "Say no more. But I'll be home early tonight and I'll expect a full report."

Meg rose shakily. "Time to wash up, Davis. We're late."

To her relief, her son complied without argument for once and went roaring down the hall doing his White Rabbit impression. ''I'm late. I'm late. For a very important date. I'm late....''

CHAPTER TWO

SPENCER TURNED LEFT off the ring road that circled the campus and swung into the faculty parking lot tucked behind the biology building. He parked away from the handful of other cars that dotted the lot and sat there a moment, picturing himself as a permanent member of the department. If Doc decided to take early retirement, Spencer'd have a good shot at the job.

But when he tried to imagine coming here every day, month after month, year after year, the thought sent a cold shiver down his spine. He had to fight the urge to restart the car and head down to the bay with his kayak. To be on the water, alone with the cormorants and the killer whales and the thing inside him that kept him moving.

Spencer pulled his keys out of the ignition. It was too late to run. He'd committed himself, if only temporarily. He threw on a black suit jacket over his T-shirt and jeans and grabbed his battered leather briefcase from the back seat. Kicking the door shut behind him, he strolled along the path to the biology building.

Spencer pushed through the heavy glass doors. Doc's office was on his immediate right, but he continued down the wide empty corridor, his footsteps echoing as he walked past doors that led to classrooms or labs or offices. His eyes narrowed and the hall seemed to swarm with ghosts of students past, as distant and separate from him now as they were then.

At the end of the corridor he turned right and continued along the L-shaped passage. From somewhere came the sound of a radio. The classroom to his left jogged more memories. Thursday afternoons and Meg McKenzie.

He paused in the open doorway, his gaze seeking out the second table from the back. He saw her there, thick blond hair curving around an oval chin. Trying to keep her face straight and her perfect nose in the air while he told some outrageous story just to hear her laugh. He wondered if she'd realized how hard he'd tried to impress her.

Spencer pushed away from the doorjamb. She'd probably married a stockbroker and lived in Uplands, just down the road from Mommy and Daddy.

"May I help you, young man?" a pompous male voice said from behind him. "Classes don't start for two weeks."

Spencer recognized the department head's plummy English tones from their phone conversations. He turned to the portly figure in the pristine white lab coat and full gray beard. "Dr. Randolph Ashton-Whyte, I presume." He held out his hand. "Spencer Valiella."

Ashton-Whyte's bushy gray eyebrows climbed his forehead as he took in Spencer's clothes and wayward hair. Slowly he extended his own hand. "A...pleasure to meet you, Dr. Valiella."

"Likewise. 'Spencer' will do."

"I've heard a great deal about you from Angus. He spoke so highly of you I expected—" Ashton-Whyte broke off and patted the row of pens in the breast pocket of his lab coat as if assuring himself they were still there and all was still right with the world.

Spencer grinned. He could just imagine what this tight-ass had expected. "Doc told me all about you, too."

The department head rubbed his hands together, his manner brisk and important. "Now that you're here, come along to my office. We have paperwork that needs to be completed."

Spencer glanced at his watch. "My honors student will be along shortly. And I want to get my gear stowed away in the lab."

Ashton-Whyte smiled coldly. "Ah, but for that you'll need the keys to Dr. Campbell's office and lab."

"Got 'em right here." Spencer pulled the key ring from his pocket and jangled it in front of Ashton-Whyte. "Never got around to returning them when I left."

He grinned, just to let Ashton-Whyte know what kind of reprehensible character he'd hired. Spencer blamed his father for his habit of baiting what Ray still referred to as the establishment. He and Ray saw eye to eye on a lot of things.

Ashton-Whyte's lips tightened, causing his mustache to meet his beard in a double row of raised bristles. "Well, do stop by and fill out the forms when it's convenient, won't you, old chap? We'll need your details—" he paused significantly "—*before we can put you on the payroll.*" Then he spun on his heel and strode off, white coat flapping, confident, no doubt, he'd had the last word.

Spencer chuckled to himself and retraced his steps

to Doc's lab. As he put the key into the lock, again a weird feeling came over him, as though the last seven years had somehow been leading to this day—when he'd step into the shoes of his mentor. He shook his head. Crazy New Age stuff was his mother's thing, not his.

He swung open the door. The familiar smell of a biology laboratory hit him. Its pungent bouquet of chemical reagents, marine organisms, cleaning fluids and old books felt like home. Especially to him, a man *with* no other home.

He'd expected to walk into the untidy disorganized lab of yesteryear. To his surprise, the workbenches and shelves were scrubbed, the glassware clean and put away, and plastic covers protected the microscopes. A new computer with a wide-screen monitor sat on a side table with a digital audio tape recorder next to it for analysis of killer whale vocalizations.

Spencer walked around the central workbench to open Doc's office. A desk faced one wall with a table catercorner along the window and a floor-to-ceiling bookshelf on his immediate left. The window slanted outward at the base and overlooked the biology pond, where an endless succession of first-year students dipped their nets to study pond organisms.

He dropped his briefcase and went back to the car for the box containing the hydrophone equipment he used to collect and record killer whale calls. It was old and pretty basic, dating from his honors year when Doc had "retired" it from his own use. Catch 22: if Spencer wanted new equipment, he had to get a research grant and stay in one spot. He'd thought about that on more than one occasion and always decided it wasn't worth it.

Another trip to the parking lot brought in his collection of killer whale teeth and bones. He was arranging these in a glass-fronted cabinet when he heard a knock at the door.

Meg. She was early.

His heart hammering, he turned.

Through the doorway came a young man of Asian extraction, not more than nineteen or twenty years old. He wore gray slacks and a crisp white shirt with a narrow tie, which he'd loosened. He moved quickly and his gaze darted from Spencer to the bone collection.

"Hi," Spencer said. "Can I help you?" Some lost soul from the faculty of business, no doubt.

"I am Lee Cheung." He strode forward and pumped Spencer's hand. "Very pleased to meet you, Dr. Var...r..ierr...a." He threw his head back and laughed. "Very hard name for Chinese to say."

"You can call me Spencer. How do you know me?"

"I am Dr. Campbell's research assistant. He did not tell you about me?" Lee grinned and shook his head. "Doc and I collected data over summer from stationary hydrophones. My job will continue, yes?"

"I guess. I don't know what arrangements have been made for transferring Doc's grant monies to me." Another thing he'd have to take up with Ashton-Whyte. Spencer dropped the empty box he was holding to the floor and flattened it with the soles of his boots.

Lee flipped his briefcase up on the lab bench and popped open the lid. "If you would like to review transcript of my last year's biology grades—"

"That won't be necessary," Spencer said, amazed

anyone would carry that information around. Still, Angus Campbell surrounded himself only with people who had a consuming passion for killer whales. Besides that, there was something very engaging about Lee's wide smile and enthusiasm.

"Tell you what, Lee. I'll hire you out of my own pocket if necessary—as long as you're not in a hurry for a paycheck—until I can see about Doc's money situation."

"Okeydokey, thank you very much." Lee reached out and pumped Spencer's hand again. "I appreciate your confidence."

"Don't thank me, thank Doc. Now, I've got a trunkful of equipment and books to bring in. Want to give me a hand?"

Together they brought in the rest of the boxes and equipment, and with astonishing speed and efficiency, Lee organized everything. Two o'clock approached and Spencer glanced at his watch with increasing frequency. To distract himself, he went down the hall and got a coffee from the vending machines located in the lounge area at the corner of the L. The staff room probably had better coffee, but he might encounter Ashton-Whyte and say something really rude.

He was walking slowly back to the lab, sipping his coffee, when he felt the change in air pressure and the gust of air that accompanied the opening of the heavy front door.

In slow motion he turned around—and there was Meg. Blue eyes startled. Textbooks clutched to her chest. Looking as unprepared as he was to meet unexpectedly. Time became fluid and the present turned into the past. So many things they *hadn't* said. She looked different. She looked *good*. Her hair had grown. But...jeans and a T-shirt? Where were her designer duds?

"Hi." He couldn't think of anything else to say.

"Hi." Self-conscious, Meg pushed her hair over her shoulder. She'd stopped ten feet away from Spencer and couldn't seem to close the distance. She made herself keep her eyes on his face, keep the smile on hers. His youthful features had matured into sharp cheekbones and a strongly defined chin. Warm coloring, warm smile. His hair was shorter, but still wind-tossed.

He was real. Not a dream. Not a fantasy. Real as the flutter in her stomach. And she still wanted him.

"Come on to the lab," he said.

She made her legs move, willing her heart to stop beating so furiously. She was on the verge of tears. Or hysterical laughter. Why did the moment have to be so fraught? Couldn't they just say a big hello and give each other a hug for old time's sake? Why did he look so serious? After all, he didn't know about Davis. *Oh, God. He didn't know about Davis.*

And then they were at the door to the lab and he halted abruptly to let her go first. She ran into him, her cheek grazing the fine wool of his jacket. "Sorry."

He put a hand out but stopped short of touching her. Meg shrank back. It was too awful. "I don't think we can do this," she blurted before she could stop herself.

"Yes, we can." His dark eyes were the color of shadowed seawater reflecting fir trees. They sucked her into their depths. "You never did tell me why you're finishing your degree only now."

She *wanted* to tell him. The explanation was on the

tip of her tongue. But seeing him made her even more confused than she'd been seven years ago. "Why didn't you say goodbye?"

From inside the lab came a discreet cough.

Spencer pushed open the door. "Lee. This is Meg McKenzie, my…honors student. Meg, this is Lee. Research assistant."

"Hi, Lee."

Lee's lidded glance flashed swiftly between them. "Okay if I leave now?" he said to Spencer. "I have to get to bookstore for my texts. I'll be back tomorrow, bright and early."

Spencer smiled. "Not too early. But yeah, I'll see you tomorrow."

"See you, Dr. Val..i—" He broke off, laughing at himself.

"Please, just call me Spencer."

"Okay, Dr. Spencer." Lee gave him a relieved grin. "See you later," he added to Meg, and moved quickly past her.

"Bye." Meg watched him go out the glass doors and run down the steps. Only when he'd disappeared from sight did she turn back to Spencer. Suddenly the hall seemed emptier, the two of them very much alone.

"You've grown your hair." He reached out again and this time his fingertips touched a few strands of the thick ash-blond hair that hung almost to her waist. Static electricity raced from his fingers right to the roots, sending a shockwave tingling along her scalp.

"It's easier than styling it," she said lightly, backing away from his touch. In other words, cheaper. Her life had changed in so many ways. *She* had changed. Undoubtedly he had, too. She realized she'd been liv-

ing with a fantasy image of him all these years.
Maybe they had nothing left in common.

Except for Davis.

And the killer whales.

And the chemistry that still bubbled and fizzed between them like some apocalyptic experiment in a
mad professor's laboratory. Or was that all in *her*
mind?

Spencer gestured for her to precede him into the
lab. She stepped past him and found herself breathing
deeply for the scent of the ocean that used to linger
in his hair, on his skin. But she wasn't close enough.
And wouldn't get close enough.

She moved farther into the lab, glancing around.
She'd seen most of the equipment when she'd met
with Dr. Campbell over the summer to talk about her
honors thesis, but Spencer had added his possessions.
Gravitating to the glass-fronted case where killer
whale teeth and bones had been laid out on black felt,
she said, "Are you staying out at the cottage?"

"Yes..." He paused as though about to say more.
Then didn't.

She bent to inspect the lower shelf, searching for
the baby killer whale tooth she'd found while diving
off Saltspring Island. It was no longer in his collection. Disappointment kept her gazing at the teeth
longer than she wanted to.

"Would you like a coffee?" he asked, holding up
his cup. "The taste hasn't improved over the years,
but it's hot. Well, lukewarm, actually."

Meg straightened, forced a smile. "No, thanks."

He nodded and moved past her to his office, giving
her a wide berth.

Why was *he* so wary? They'd been friends, after

all. Like odd socks, but still a pair. Or had that night on Saltspring rendered null and void all that preceded it? They'd never had a chance to talk after that. They'd paddled back to Victoria the next morning ahead of a squall, locked in silence. If only she hadn't said what she'd said, maybe his subsequent flight wouldn't have been so swift. And maybe he wouldn't now be acting as if nothing had ever happened between them.

"Have a seat."

Meg sank into the safety of the padded vinyl visitor's chair that nestled in front of the overflowing bookshelf. She just caught sight of one title, *The Tao of Physics,* when from the corner of her eye she saw Spencer's lean denim-clad thigh glide by. And then he was sitting in his own chair, swirling around to face her. He leaned back, looking very casual. Or did that controlled stillness mean he was tense, not just intense, as he'd always been?

Under his dark suit jacket, which looked like Armani, but knowing Spencer was probably Salvation Army, he wore a white T-shirt and faded blue jeans. Then she noticed something new. A thin black leather cord around his sun-browned neck, the ends of which disappeared under the curve of white cotton. She remembered the smooth hard heat of the chest beneath…

"…killer whale communication," he was saying. "I've been working with the transient population for the past five years, first in the Puget Sound area, then down around Monterey."

Meg nodded, relaxing a little. "It's interesting how few calls and whistles they make compared to resident killer whales."

Spencer's eyebrows rose. "You're familiar with my research?"

"When I decided to finish my degree, I caught up on the literature." She could see the unasked questions in his eyes and ignored them.

"Then you must also be aware of Deeke's recent findings on intra-pod communication."

She nodded. "They gave me an idea for my thesis..." She stopped. In spite of reading all the journal articles she could get her hands on, she still felt out of touch. What she'd been about to say might be completely off the wall.

"What is it?" He leaned back a little farther and crossed an ankle over the opposite knee.

"Well, I just wonder...what are they *saying* to each other?" *Please don't laugh at me.*

Spencer gazed at her for a moment in silence. "The repetitive staccato clicks they make are used as a form of echolocation to forage for prey and for navigation—as I'm sure you know," he said. "Pulsed calls and whistles are used for social communication. Keeping tabs on members of the pod when they're out of sight of each other."

He must think she was crazy. Except that she knew him. Knew he must have wondered the same thing. "But don't some calls occur more often in some circumstances, such as resting or socializing?" she said.

"True, but so far no one has established a definitive connection between call type and behavior that would suggest certain calls had a specific meaning."

"Yes, I know," she said heavily. Her idea *was* too far-out.

"However, I don't think it's impossible that we'll eventually be able to decode their communications," he said carefully. "You'd have to listen to their sounds in the context of their daily lives and closely monitor behavior. Given the limited scope of an honors thesis, maybe you should confine your study to one small aspect of killer whale communication. In that context, I would support such a project if that's what you're interested in."

Was she interested! But wait. This was her degree they were talking about. The opportunity for which she'd scrimped and saved for seven years. If she blew her honors thesis because Spencer agreed to what someone else on her supervisory panel would consider crackpot research, she wasn't sure she'd have the heart, or the resources, to try again.

"Have you got funding to do this type of research?" she asked. Spencer, she knew, never hesitated to go out on a limb, but if the Natural Science and Engineering Research Council was willing to believe in him, she supposed *she* could.

"I don't have funding of any kind at the moment, but you'll have access to Doc Campbell's grant money." He grinned, showing white, slightly overlapping front teeth. A smile that had once thrown her heart into palpitations. And still did. "Sometimes you've just got to take a chance, princess."

Princess. She'd almost forgotten that detestable yet somehow endearing nickname. "My name is Meg," she reminded him severely.

"Sorry," he replied, looking totally unrepentant. "Not very politically correct of me."

"It's hard to adjust to us not both being students— to you being a prof and me being under you." Meg immediately blushed at her choice of words.

Spencer swiveled to the window as though he

wanted to leap out. "It feels strange for me, too. Can we just skip the professor-student thing and be two people interested in killer whales? The way we used to be?"

Was *that* what they used to be? "Sure, I guess so."

"Good." He spun back. "Do you still have your kayak?"

"Yes, but I haven't used it in a while." *Like seven years.*

"Get it out, check it for leaks." Spencer got to his feet. "We'll pay a visit to Kitasu and the rest of her maternal group. Are you doing anything tomorrow? We could catch the early ferry to Saltspring, drive up to Southey Point and paddle out from there."

"I—I don't know," she said, rising. She'd have to ask Patrick to take Davis to day care in the morning. She'd accounted for afternoon care but not for early-morning starts.

He gazed at her quizzically. "Mornings bad for you? I suppose you're working."

"No. Yes. It's just that I need time. I have things to…arrange."

"Okay, but we really should get in a preliminary look-see before classes start and things get busy for both of us."

She turned to walk out ahead of him. "What will you be teaching—Marine Mammals?"

"Yes. Plus a unit of first-year biology and a course in the philosophy of science. It's a graduate-level course, but you're welcome to sit in on it."

"I'd like that."

"It's in the evening. Wednesdays."

"Oh. Evenings are hard for me, too."

He paused a beat. "Are you married, Meg? Or living with someone?"

"No!" It was so *not* what she'd been afraid of his asking, she jumped. And probably looked guilty as hell, anyway. "Are…are you?"

He shook his head and laughed. "Me? Not likely."

Of course not. How could she be so foolish? More foolish still that the news he was free made her heart go flip-flop.

"Can we leave the kayaking till Saturday?" she asked. Patrick would be on maneuvers all weekend, but this Saturday was the Uplands Garden Club open house and garden sale. Her mother would be busy from early morning till evening, which meant her father, who avoided the annual event as he would a plague of aphids, could look after Davis. He didn't get many opportunities to spend time with his grandson, but when he did, he jumped at them.

"That should be fine. Give me your address and I'll pick you up at eight o'clock."

Uh-oh, complications already. "My kayak is at my parents' place. You know where that is." She started to back out of the office. "I'd better run. I'll see you Saturday. Bye."

She left without waiting for a farewell from him. She'd learned not to.

WHEN MEG GOT TO the ring road, instead of turning toward Esquimalt and the California-style bungalow she shared with Patrick, she pointed her Toyota toward Cadboro Bay Road. If she hurried, she had just enough time to drop by her parents' house to check out the kayak before picking up Davis.

Stone gates guarded the entrance to the parklike

estates of Uplands. Meg rubbed her temples as she drove through, aware of the tension already starting to mount. She hoped her mother wasn't home. Helen never lost an opportunity to inform Meg that dropping out of university at the age of twenty-one to become a single mother had ruined her life. What Helen really meant was that Meg had ruined *her* life. Oh, the *shame* of having to tell her garden club friends that her daughter lived in *Esquimalt*. God forbid she would ever consider visiting her and Davis there.

Meg had learned to live with her mother's disapproval, but what really hurt was the way Helen couldn't warm to Davis. She was a control freak, and Davis was someone she couldn't control. Rather than learn how to deal with his behavior, Helen shunned his company. It was hard for her little boy to understand. And harder still for Meg to forgive.

She turned into the long curving driveway flanked by a high box hedge. It was all so clichéd it would have been boring except that this was her *family*. She missed the big Sunday dinners with her three brothers and their families and the holiday gatherings she now avoided because she couldn't stand having to constantly defend her life. Or to protect her son from feeling slighted by his grandmother.

Thank goodness for Daddy. He wasn't terribly happy with the way her life had turned out, either, but at least he tried to let her live it her own way. And although he'd never thought Spencer good enough for his only daughter, he loved his grandson and treated him accordingly.

The elegant white three-story house came into view, afternoon sun glinting off the mullioned windows. Meg pulled up in front of the portico and got out. She glanced at the conservatory but couldn't see her mother's slim figure moving among the plants.

Daddy was home, though, practicing his putting on the side lawn, his salt-and-pepper head bent in concentration. Meg waited till he'd made his shot, then called out. Roger McKenzie's handsome face broke into a smile. Dropping his golf club into the bag, he strode across the lawn to envelop her in a hug. "Meggie! How's my little girl?"

"Twenty-eight and all grown up," Meg teased as she hugged him back.

Roger glanced hopefully at the car. "Is Davis with you?"

"No. I just came from the university." Darn, why did she go and open that line of conversation?

"Have they found you a new supervisor yet?"

"Yes. An expert on killer whales from Monterey." Daddy would have to know sometime that Spencer was back, but right now she didn't have the time or the emotional energy to discuss it. The fact that Spencer didn't even know he was a father had never absolved him of guilt in Roger's eyes. "We're going kayaking on the weekend to locate the group of killer whales I'm going to work on," she went on. "I came to see if my kayak still floats."

"Andrew used it a few times over the summer. I said he could. Didn't think you'd mind. He said he replaced the 'spray skirt' because the neoprene rubber had deteriorated in spots."

"That's great. There's nothing worse than getting soaked from the waist down because a leaky spray skirt lets water into the cockpit. Let's go have a look."

They went in through the open section of the four-car garage. In the far slot sat Roger's restored Model-A Ford next to his silver 500 SEL Mercedes. Helen's smaller, cream-colored Mercedes was absent. The rest of the garage was given over to sporting equipment—skis and tennis rackets, snowboards and sailboards, golf clubs and archery sets.

Meg's single-seater Orca kayak had been taken down from the overhead beams and was propped on wooden blocks at the back of the garage. She ran a hand down the shiny red fiberglass hull, then lifted the new spray skirt to inspect it. "Looks okay."

"I'm sure it's fine," Roger said. "You know how finicky your brother is."

"I'll be sure to call and thank him for using my stuff," Meg replied with a grin, and walked to the stern to test the rudder movement. "Where's Mother?"

Roger's voice became deliberately casual. "She's looking after Cassie and Tristan a couple of afternoons a week. Maybe you haven't heard—Anne's gone back to work, part-time."

Cassie and Tristan were Meg's niece and baby nephew. Meg bit her lip, hoping the physical pain would override the inner pain. It wasn't that she wanted to use her mother as a baby-sitting service, but never once had Helen offered to look after Davis. The few times Meg had asked, Helen had always been too busy. Finally Meg had stopped asking. Helen sent expensive and inappropriate gifts for Davis's birthday and at Christmas, but Meg could count on the fingers of one hand the number of times she'd gone out of her way to see her grandson.

"I'd better go," she said. "I've got to pick up Davis at day care. He hates it when I'm late."

"Is he excited about starting school?" Roger asked as he walked her back to her car.

"One minute he can't wait and the next he's not so sure." Meg opened her door. "Oh, I almost forgot. Would you be able to look after him on Saturday while I'm kayaking?"

"Sure! He can caddy for me." Roger put his arm around her. "We don't see enough of him, darling."

Meg gripped her father's hand where it rested on her shoulder. "You know Mother and I can't be in the same room for more than ten minutes without fighting."

"Your mother is just proud and stubborn—like her daughter. She does love you, Meggie."

Funny kind of love. "Bye, Dad," she said, giving him another hug. "I'll see you Saturday morning. Early."

It wasn't until she'd turned her car out of the driveway and onto the road that she remembered Spencer would be picking her up at her parents' house at roughly the same time she'd be dropping Davis off. She had to decide fast what, if anything, she was going to tell Spencer about his son.

CHAPTER THREE

SPENCER SPOTTED the dusty Econoline van in the driveway and grinned. Ray was back.

He parked and ran up the steps, his jacket slung over his shoulder. The afternoon had warmed up and the front door was open to let in the sunshine. Through it came smells of cooking and the brassy sound of a blues band.

Spencer climbed onto the porch steps. He could see his dad moving around in the kitchen dressed in black leather pants and a dark blue shirt. He was singing along with the music, and when he stopped to play a riff on an air guitar, his body vibrated right up to his graying ponytail.

"Ray!" Spencer pushed through the screen door and dropped his jacket on the couch on his way into the kitchen.

"Spence, my man!" Ray came around the counter, arms extended, ebullient as ever. "Is this a coincidence or what?"

Spencer met his dad in a back-slapping embrace. "Sooner or later we had to land here at the same time. Sorry I missed you this morning."

"I ran into an old buddy of mine in Victoria last night. We tied one on and I spent the night on his couch. When I got back to the cottage this afternoon and saw your note, I went right out and got us some grub and a bottle of Kentucky's finest.'' Ray moved back into the kitchen. "Come on, I'll pour you one."

"Great." Spencer walked over to the fridge and took a handful of ice cubes from the freezer. He dropped them into a glass and Ray sloshed in a healthy shot of Jack Daniel's. "How long has it been since 'Frisco? Two years? Three?"

"Four, I think." Ray grinned, his black eyes crinkling, and added more bourbon to his glass. "It's a good thing we meet occasionally by chance."

They raised their drinks, glasses clinking. The bourbon hit Spencer's empty stomach like a fireball. The spreading warmth blended with the gutsy music and his father's positive vibes. *Let the good times roll.*

"So when did you get into town?" Spencer asked, leaning against the counter.

"Coupla weeks ago." Ray set his glass down to wrap a potato in tin foil. He did another one and tossed them in the oven. "What brings you up north? I thought you never stayed in the same place twice."

"Not if I can help it. I'm teaching up at the university."

"Coming back to your old haunts *and* teaching, which I know you don't like as much as research. You're changing, Spence. Here's to it." He lifted his glass.

Spencer shook his head. "Just doing a favor for my old prof is all."

"Adults go through stages same as kids," Ray said. "Some changes are harder than others."

Spencer laughed. "Come off it, Ray, you haven't changed a bit." He opened the fridge door and peered in. The shelves, bare this morning, were now full. "What are you making? I'm starving."

"The finest New York steaks money can buy. Outside New York, that is. I was there, let's see, two years ago. Had a few gigs lined up, so off we went." He brushed his palms together, one hand sweeping off in a curving arc. "What a life."

"I attended a conference in New York last April," Spencer said, grabbing an apple from the bottom rack.

"Crazy town. I love it." Ray unwrapped the steaks from the butcher's paper. "Did you get to any clubs?"

"One or two. Heard a few old tunes by my namesake." He crunched into crisp green skin. "I like their style of bluesy rock and roll, but do you know how hard it is to go through life as Spencer Davis Valiella? People either think it sounds affected or that Davis Valiella should be hyphenated." Grimacing, he recalled his encounter with Ashton-Whyte. "I don't care for hyphenated names."

"It was cool at the time. Hey, I *still* like it."

"Ah, forget it, Ray, I'm just razzing you. I sure appreciate you buying all this food. I'm living on credit till they put me on the payroll here. Or until my money arrives from Monterey." He gestured with the hand holding the apple. "How come banks require weeks to electronically transfer money when it only takes a split second to send an e-mail?"

"You got me, man." Ray's smile wavered. "No money, eh? What a bummer."

"So how's your new band working out?"

"Fantastic!" Ray widened his smile, but something flickered in his eyes. He turned to the counter hesitantly, as though trying to remember what he was looking for.

"Your last CD was great, but it was a while ago,"

Spencer said. "I'm looking forward to the next. When's it coming out?"

"Uh…soon." Ray grabbed the bottle of bourbon. "Here, let me top you up."

"Thanks. Whoa, easy."

Ray splashed some more into his own glass and put the bottle down. "Enough about me. What's going on in your life?"

Spencer took a sip of his drink. Should he tell Ray about Meg? Would he mention her if she meant nothing to him? He decided he would. "Talk about coincidences. My honors student is a girl I knew from before. Meg McKenzie." Her name fell self-consciously off his tongue.

"Hey, I remember meeting her. Blond, sassy smile—right? That's great. You won't want to hang with your old man all the time." Ray slid a cast-iron frying pan onto the stove.

"I doubt I'll be seeing her socially. The university frowns on fraternization between faculty and students." It was a good excuse, anyway.

Ray poured cooking oil into the pan and turned on the heat. "I could see it if you're talking about an old fart like me hittin' on some sweet young thing, but you and Meg are about the same age."

Spencer found he didn't want to talk about Meg, after all. "Do you ever see Mom?"

Ray's ever-present grin faded.

Damn. Surely he could have come up with something better than *that* to change topics.

"I called her to say hello before I came north," Ray said.

"I went through San Clemente around Christmas last year," Spencer said. "She seemed fine then."

Ray rolled the oil around the pan. "She's doing *great*. Big house, rich hubby. Most importantly, she's happy. And *I'm* happy *for* her. You don't have to pussyfoot around my feelings."

Spencer nodded skeptically.

Ray laughed and spread his arms. "Hell, it's been over twenty years. I haven't exactly been alone all that time. How do you like your steak?

"Medium-rare." Spencer eyed his father over the rim of his glass. Ray was always up, but tonight there was something a little manic about him.

Ray threw the steaks in the pan where they sizzled and sputtered in the hot oil. Spencer got plates out of the cupboard and carried them to the small wooden table tucked against the wall. A bentwood chair sat on either side. "How about giving me a preview of your new CD after dinner?"

"Oh, you don't want to hear your old man play. Let's take a run into Victoria. We could hit some clubs, catch up with each other."

"I still haven't caught up with my sleep. I was planning on an early night." Spencer got knives and forks out of the drawer and returned to the table. With his back to Ray, he laid out the cutlery. "What do you say? Just a tune or three right here."

Silence.

Spencer straightened, turned. "Ray?"

The sober expression on his father's face made the bourbon churn in his stomach.

Over the sound of the sizzling steaks, Ray said quietly, "I can't play for you. I pawned my guitar to buy the food."

Spencer felt the world shift on its axis. Ray had

pawned his guitar? It was like the Pope giving up religion. "No way."

"The band went bust," Ray said, suddenly looking years older than fifty-two. "I haven't worked in almost a year. I only came here because I had nowhere else to go."

MEG CAME THROUGH THE DOOR of the bungalow, textbooks piled in her arms. In the kitchen Patrick sang in his hearty baritone, "'I am the ruler of the King's navy,'" then switched to a falsetto for the chorus, "'Yes, he is the ruler of the King's navy.'"

"Can I watch TV, Mom? Thanks." Davis took off for the living room and in less time than it took her to shout, "Keep the volume down," she could hear Daffy Duck lisping his way to destruction, and Davis chuckling like a maniac.

Meg kicked the door shut and shuffled into the dining area of the kitchen to set her pile of books on the table. Patrick had changed out of his uniform and into linen slacks and a matching taupe shirt. He'd donned an apron and was at that moment waving a carrot baton in front of Noel's cage. Noel cocked his head to one side and squawked, *"Na-vy!"*

Meg took in Patrick's grin. "You got the promotion!"

"It's not official...but I'm ninety-nine percent sure."

"Oo-ooh, that's so great," Meg squealed, and ran around to hug him. "What will be your official title?"

"Lieutenant Patrick Warren, at your service," he replied with a snappy salute and clicking heels.

"Very impressive." Containing a smile, she stepped back to study him, one finger laid alongside her cheek. "But don't you think the frilly pink apron rather mars the effect?"

"Oh, don't be a spoilsport." Patrick went back to the kitchen counter and began tearing lettuce into a salad bowl. "There's just one teensy-weensy little thing you should know."

"What's that?" Meg eyed him narrowly. Patrick's teensy-weensy little things generally turned out to be the size of battleships.

"I might have given the selection panel the impression I was married. With a son."

"Patrick! How are you going to pull that off? And why? I thought it was against navy rules to harass people for their sexual orientation."

"That's *official* policy, sweetcheeks. Sure, I could win a case if it came up, but after all the trouble I go to being discreet, I don't want the publicity. Daddy would not be amused."

"He's some high-mucka-muck in the navy, isn't he?"

"My dear, he's practically an admiral."

"How amused is he going to be when he hears you've got a family you haven't bothered to mention?"

"He's based in Ottawa. Gossip doesn't travel that far east. A harassment suit would." Patrick ripped at the lettuce as though storming the beaches.

"Patrick, does your father know?"

"I told him a couple years ago. He hasn't disowned me or anything, but he doesn't like it spread around."

"Oh. Well, okay, I'll be your cover. Those navy types aren't going to come poking around the house, are they?"

Patrick flapped a hand. "I doubt it. But if anyone

calls whose voice you don't recognize, can you throw in a reference to 'my husband, Patrick'?''

"I'll try to remember," Meg said, and reached for a carrot stick.

"Those are for Davis," he said, slapping her hand away. "So how did it go at the university?"

Meg let her shoulders sag. "Emotionally exhausting. Terrifying. *Weird.*"

"And you haven't even started classes yet." He pushed an open bottle of chardonnay across the counter. "Pour yourself a glass of wine and tell me all about it. I've been prostrate with curiosity about your mysterious phone call."

Meg got herself a glass of wine and sat on the bar stool across the counter from Patrick. "That was my new honors supervisor who called."

Patrick stopped tearing lettuce. "Go on. Is he a hunk?"

"You could say that. But mainly, he's Davis's—"

"Mom, when's dinner?"

Meg gave a start. Drops of cool wine spilled over her fingers. "Davis! Don't sneak up on me like that."

"I wasn't sneaking, I was just walking," Davis said with an expression of bewildered hurt. "Is it dinnertime yet?"

"Almost," Patrick said. "How about setting some plates on the table, champ? That way dinner will happen a lot quicker."

"Okay." On his way to the cupboard, Davis paused at the recycling bin to pick up a plastic yogurt lid. Forgetting about the plates, he wandered around the kitchen, swooping the lid through the air. *"Bweep. Bweep. Bweep. Bweep."*

"Davis," Meg said. "The table."

"I'm a UFO. *Bweep. Bweep. Bweep.*"

Meg exchanged a glance with Patrick. Some days were better than others. Unfortunately Davis's bad days often seemed to coincide with hers. She got up and pulled a stack of plates out of the cupboard. "Earth to Davis," she said in her best automaton voice. "Transport circular space stations to planet Table."

"*Bweep. Bweep. Bweep.*" Davis took the plates.

They got through dinner. Then Davis's bath and bedtime story and the ritual arranging of his toys around the edge of his bed. Then the bedtime song. Twice. When he was finally tucked in, Meg remembered they hadn't played catch. Well, she wasn't foolish enough to mention it now.

She returned to the kitchen and gratefully accepted a cup of decaf from Patrick.

"So, where were we?" Patrick sat opposite Meg at the table and added a spoonful of sugar crystals to his coffee.

Meg ran a thumb around the rim of her cup. "My supervisor is Spencer Valiella—Davis's father."

Patrick ceased stirring his coffee. "No!"

"Yes." She didn't need to explain the complications. She'd told Patrick the whole story years ago, ruining his best silk shirt with her tears in the process. But she hadn't cried over Spencer in years. And she refused to start again now.

"So how do you feel about this?" Patrick asked.

Meg sipped her coffee. "Confused. Worried. I don't know what I'm going to do."

"You're going to tell the man," Patrick said firmly. "Right away, before you start lying about it."

"I've been lying by omission for years."

"And feeling guilty about it, right?"

She couldn't deny it. "Spencer's got his own life. How's he going to feel if he suddenly finds out he's got a kid?"

"Good question. Tell him and find out. For all you know, he might be thrilled." Patrick paused. "Do you still love him?"

"I haven't seen him in seven years. In all that time he's never so much as sent me a postcard."

"That doesn't answer my question."

Meg ran a hand down her hair and pulled up a fistful of ends for inspection. The chemistry between her and Spencer had to do with lust, not love. "No, of course I don't love him."

"Hmm." Patrick sounded unconvinced.

She made a face. "He's probably already planning where he'll be going after he leaves here. A son would be an inconvenience."

"You're not giving him credit."

"Okay, I agree Spencer has a right to know. But I have a right to protect my child from hurt. Do you have any idea what it would do to Davis to meet his father only to have him leave again? *As he will.*"

"You can't be sure of that. Anyway, a part-time father is better than none."

"The last thing I need is him popping in and out of my life every six months."

"You're *not* over him."

"I don't know," Meg wailed, and propped her head in her hands. "Everything's finally coming together for me. Davis is about to start school and he's got more than enough to adjust to right now. You know how hard transitions are for him."

Patrick wagged a finger at her. "You're rationalizing. This Spencer character should be paying support, if nothing else.''

Meg gazed wearily at her friend. ''I know he would if I asked. But *I* made the decision to have Davis. Nobody else. I can do it on my own. *And* get my degree.''

''You don't have to prove anything to *me,* darling. *I'm* not your mother.'' Patrick lifted his cup with slender fingers and drank.

''The problem will be keeping the two of them apart,'' Meg went on. ''I'm dropping Davis off at my dad's on Saturday while Spencer and I go kayaking. One look at Davis and Spencer will *know* he's—'' Meg froze, her head tilted toward the hallway. ''Did you hear something?''

Patrick put his cup down quietly. ''No.''

She got up and tiptoed into the hall. Crouched behind the door was Davis. Meg went cold all over. ''What are you doing out of bed?''

''I can't sleep.''

''How long have you been sitting there?''

''I don't know.''

She took him by the hand and tugged him gently to his feet. It was hard to be cross when she knew the medication made him wakeful, but she felt sick thinking about what he might have heard. ''You've got to get used to early nights, honey. When school starts, we'll have to be up early.''

''Can I stay up for a while?''

''No.'' She led him back down the hall to his bedroom. ''Did you hear what Patrick and I were talking about?'' She hoped her interest sounded casual.

''Kayaking. Can I come? Please?'' Davis tugged on her hand. ''I've always wanted to go kayaking.''

Relief made her knees weak. He must not have heard the whole conversation. "This Saturday Grandpa's taking you golfing with him. Remember I told you about it in the car?"

"Oh, yeah," Davis said happily as he climbed back into bed. "I like Grandpa. He lets me keep the tees."

"Good night, honey." Meg placed a kiss on his forehead.

"Can I have my song?"

"You had it already."

"Can I have another one?"

"No. Good night. And stay in bed."

DAVIS WATCHED HIS MOM close the door. His eyes remained open, adjusting to the darkness. Mom had said the guy she was going kayaking with was named Spencer. His dad was named Spencer. But if this man *was* his dad, Mom would have told him. Grown-ups acted real dumb sometimes. And sometimes they lied. But not Mom. She never lied to him. And she wouldn't keep something that big a secret.

Gradually Davis's eyes drifted shut despite his best efforts to keep them open. Images floated through his head. There was water all around, and islands, like when he and Mom went on the ferry. Only he wasn't looking down at the water from above. He was in a kayak. A two-seater. A man sat behind him, paddling. Davis couldn't see the man's face, but somehow he knew it was his dad. Drops flew off the paddle blades as they rose and fell, splashing on Davis's cheeks. His father's strong strokes were taking them toward the tall black fins of the killer whales. Davis drifted deeper toward unconsciousness. Just before he went under, he saw Tommy's face floating mysteriously above the kayak. Davis smiled at him. *See, Tommy, I do too have a dad.*

SPENCER PAUSED outside Doc's room in the cardiac unit. Now that he was here he almost didn't want to go in and see his mentor diminished. One fallen idol was bad enough.

But when he'd come by the other day, Doc had been asleep. So Spencer put on a smile and strode into the room. "Hey, Doc."

Angus Campbell sat propped up in bed with his knees bent, as though his six-four frame was too long for the mattress. Doc had been bald as long as Spencer had known him and his weathered face was deeply lined, but he had the vitality of a man half his age.

"Spencer, m'boy! You came." Despite Doc's enthusiastic greeting, the right side of his face sagged and the faint Scottish burr of his native Glasgow was slurred.

"Of course," Spencer said, taking a seat beside the bed. "How'd you land up here, anyway? Eat too many cheeseburgers? Or was it too many run-ins with Ashton-Whyte?"

"Don't talk to me about Ashton-bloody-Whyte," Doc growled. "The only good thing about this infernal place is his absence. As for the stroke…I was divin' for abalone with my grandson. We were in the water for hours and I got hypothermia, for God's sake. That set off cardiac arrhythmia. A blood clot formed in my heart, traveled to my brain. Next thing I know, I'm in here, providin' free entertainment to the nursing staff who love nothin' better than sticking a thermometer up my bum." His blue eyes twinkled at the pretty young nurse who was currently strapping a blood-pressure cuff around his upper arm.

"You're a disgusting dirty old man," she scolded with a smile. "The sooner you're out of here, the happier we'll all be."

Spencer turned to Doc. "What about it? Will you be back at the university after Christmas? You know I've applied to Bergen, but I don't want to let your students down." *One in particular.*

"I'll be back. Got research to finish." Talking suddenly seemed an effort and Doc paused to take a deep breath. "But I'm glad you're here, lad. First chance you get I want you to check the stationary hydrophone I've got positioned in Trincomali Channel. Lee tells me it stopped broadcasting."

"Sure, no problem."

"Lee is a good lad. I hope you'll keep him on."

"Of course. He's analyzing the data you and he collected over the summer. Good thing you got him on the payroll before you checked into the hospital, though. Randolph isn't giving me a bean more than he has to."

"That bloody…!" Doc's face turned red. "He was nosin' around here the other day, tryin' to read my chart. Just because he's a vertebrate physiologist, he thinks he's a bloody doctor. He works with hamsters, for cryin' out loud—last time he did any real research, that is."

"Now don't go getting yourself worked up, Dr. Campbell," the nurse admonished, letting the pressure off the cuff. "Time for your tablets." She handed him a paper cup containing pills and another cupful of water.

Doc took them with a growl and shot a glance at Spencer. "They're feeding me rat poison!"

"Warfarin is an anticoagulant," the nurse explained with an indulgent smile. "Take your pills like a good boy."

Doc gulped down the tablets and tossed back the water. A little of it dribbled out the paralyzed side of his mouth. The nurse had moved on and Spencer had to stop himself from leaning forward to wipe it away.

"How's Meg?" Doc rasped. "Weren't you two friends years ago?"

Spencer shrugged noncommittally. "She seems fine."

"Has she decided on a thesis topic yet? We only talked in general terms when we met in June." Doc gripped Spencer's hand. "She's keen as mustard. Make sure she's got a project she can get her teeth into."

Spencer squeezed Doc's hand. It was hard to see someone who'd always been full of piss and vinegar brought so low. "Don't worry. I'll take care of everything."

"Good lad." Doc's eyelids flickered. He seemed to tire suddenly and he slumped back against his pillows. "When Lee's finished doing the stats on those recordings, he can start writing up the paper. And for God's sake, keep Ashton-Whyte away from here if you possibly can. He mustn't find out…"

"What?" Spencer leaned closer. "What shouldn't he find out?"

"My age." Doc's eyes closed again. "He'll force me to retire."

"He can't do that…" Spencer began, then realized Doc had fallen asleep.

Gently he replaced Doc's hand on the coverlet and went around the end of the bed to peruse the chart hanging there. He scanned the vital statistics.

Age: seventy-two. Spencer blinked and looked again. Unbelievable but true. He would have sworn Doc wasn't a day over sixty.

"Be a good lad and alter the numbers for me, son."

Doc's sudden request made him drop the chart with a metallic clatter against the bed rails.

"Thought I was asleep, did you?" A feral grin played around one side of Doc's mouth. "Caught Ashton-Whyte that way."

"How come the university doesn't know your correct age?"

The good side of Doc's mouth curved into a smile. "Years ago when I was getting close to retirement age, I cultivated the acquaintance of a verra' obliging lassie over in Records…"

"Doctor Campbell, I'm shocked." Spencer grinned. "But your secret's safe with me."

Spencer didn't know which was more surprising— that Doc looked so young for his age or that he hadn't had a stroke before now, given his temperament and his frequent contact with Ashton-Whyte.

SATURDAY MORNING, Meg was parked in front of her parents' house. It was already later than she would have liked and Davis was in one of his obstinate moods, refusing to get out of the car.

"Come *on*, Davis," she said. "It's time to go inside."

Davis picked at a tear in the fabric seat cover. Meg could feel a pain start to throb in her temple. She glanced at her watch, then down the curving drive-way. Empty—so far.

Straightening, she threw her father an apologetic glance.

Roger frowned. "Doesn't he want to stay with me?"

"He's really excited about it, honestly." She took a bottle from her purse and handed it to him. "Give him one tablet after lunch. No matter *what* he says. He might not be very hungry, but you should try to get something into him."

Roger tucked the bottle in his pocket. "Are you okay, Meggie? You seem nervous. Is your new honors supervisor some kind of ogre or something?"

Meg pulled her father away from the car and lowered her voice. "He's Spencer Valiella."

Roger's eyebrows pulled together in a tight frown and his jaw jutted forward. "Spencer Valiella is *not* welcome on my property."

Meg put a hand to her damp forehead. "We can't talk about it now. He's due to arrive any minute. I want to get Davis inside. They can't meet. Not yet."

"Damn right they can't meet!"

Which only made Meg want to argue on Spencer's behalf. Ridiculous. She went back to the car. The passenger door was open. Davis was on his knees in the gravel, staring intently at a bug crawling through the stones.

"Come on, honey." She bent and took his hand. "I bet Grandpa would like to show you the fish in his aquarium."

Davis jumped up. "Does he have any new ones?"

"I don't know. Why don't you ask him?"

"You ask him." The boy pressed against her side,

darting a glance to Roger. Roger smiled and Davis turned his face into her waist.

"Let's go ask him together." Meg knew trying to hurry him was fatal, but the pace was excruciating. She glanced over her shoulder at the driveway again.

"Hello, Davis." Roger bent and extended his hand. Davis shook his head, and looked at his mom.

"Go on, honey, shake," Meg said. She turned to Roger. "He could hardly sleep last night he was so excited."

"So you said. Don't worry about it." Roger dropped his hand.

Davis touched Roger's pant leg. "Did you get a new fish?"

"No, but I've got a new castle. The Siamese fighting fish like to swim through the archway."

Meg heard the roar of a mufflerless car turn into the driveway. "Why don't you go see, Davis? Quick, before they get tired."

Davis rolled his eyes. "Fish don't get tired of swimming."

The car was still out of sight behind the box hedge but was getting closer by the second. She didn't need to see the driver to know it had to be Spencer. None of her parents' friends, or even their children, would drive something that sounded like that.

She fixed her most powerful stare on Davis. *"Go. Now."*

Roger touched his grandson on the shoulder, turning him toward the house. "Do fish ever sleep, Davis?"

Meg watched them go into the house through the garage and almost broke into tears at the relief. She *would* tell Spencer, but in her own time. If he found out by surprise, it would be too dreadful.

The door had just shut behind Roger and Davis when Spencer's black Camaro, kayak strapped to the roof rack, came to a halt beside her Toyota. Meg remembered suddenly the Matchbox cars Davis carried with him wherever he went. Had he left any lying on the back seat where Spencer might see them? The back door was still wide open.

Spencer got out, and closed his own door, his gaze fixed on her. Without so much as a glance inside her car, he reached over and flicked shut the door on the Toyota. Meg let out her breath, her heart pounding crazily. She wasn't going to survive, she just wasn't.

CHAPTER FOUR

"MORNING," Spencer said. He'd forgotten how great her tanned legs and shapely hips looked in shorts. His body responded to memories of its own, and he jammed his hands into his pockets. "Ready?"

She tugged nervously on her long braid. "My kayak's in the garage. Can you give me a hand?"

He started walking over. "How are your folks?"

"Fine. Mother's got her garden club thing today."

"And your dad doesn't want to breathe the same air as me."

Meg stopped short. "That's not—"

"I saw him high-tail it into the house."

"He—"

"Forget it. It doesn't matter." Spencer moved under the open garage door. "Who's the boy?"

"The boy?" Her voice sounded strangled.

He glanced at her. "Yeah. Is he one of your brother's kids?"

"What? Oh. Yes. That's right." She hurried past him to the far end of the kayak.

"It's Nick who's married, isn't it?" He'd liked her brothers, Nick more than the other two, but maybe that was because Nick was a geologist and not a lawyer or a banker. Her parents were another matter altogether.

"All three are married now." Meg moved to the

far end of the kayak. "You don't have to be married to have a child."

"Ever the nitpicker." Spencer bent to pick up his end. "We'd better move if we're going to catch that ferry."

They loaded the Orca onto his roof rack and tied it down. Spencer lifted the trunk so Meg could put her backpack inside. He glanced up at the house and saw the living room curtain twitch. Some things *never* changed. With a mocking salute at the window, he slid into the driver's seat. Then he gunned the engine and with a roar spun around the circular drive and back out to the road.

Meg shook her head. "What are you, Jimmy Dean?"

Spencer laughed. "Your father would be disappointed if I didn't put on a show." He glanced at her T-shirt. "Are you going to be warm enough? It can get cool on the water, especially if you get wet."

"You mean *when* you get wet. Don't worry, I've got a sweatshirt in my backpack." She glanced around the interior. "From the outside this car looks like it belongs in a Mad Max movie, but inside it's immaculate."

Spencer shrugged. "The inside is what I see. Didn't know you were so easily impressed."

She grinned. "Cleanliness is always impressive where least expected."

"Very funny." He scowled to hide the pleasure he felt at simply being with her. "Put on a CD if you like."

She flipped through the disks. "Hey, this is your dad's band. 'Ray and the Brass Monkeys, Live.' Remember the time you took me backstage at his concert? Gosh, he was good. Where is he these days?''

Spencer frowned. He'd forgotten Meg had heard his dad play. And met him. And liked him. Hopefully he could keep the two apart. He'd hate Meg to see his father in his current state. Hate for her to pity him. Hey, what was he thinking? This was Ray! He was just in a slump. Back up in no time.

''He's, ah, he's at the cottage.''

''Really?'' Meg glanced up. ''Is he in town for a concert?''

''He's...taking a breather. He probably won't be around long. You know him—here today, gone tomorrow.''

''Like father, like son,'' Meg murmured, and put the disk into the state-of-the-art CD player.

The opening bars of Ray's upbeat brassy style of blues-rock fusion drowned out some of the muffler noise. Then the gravelly voice of Ray Valiella came on, and the background noise just seemed to blend in. Spencer began to tap his fingers on the steering wheel.

''Are you going to get your muffler fixed?''

He had it booked into a local garage, but he couldn't resist teasing her. ''It's supposed to sound that way.''

She threw him a look. *When are you going to grow up?*

''I like your hair long,'' he said. Now this was the understatement of the year. Her hair fascinated him. Thick and fine and heavy, like braided corn silk, it hung over her shoulder and down her blue cotton-clad breast. His gaze lingered where it shouldn't. Then met hers.

She turned to look straight ahead. "What happens once I decide on a project?"

Damn. For a few minutes they'd slipped into their old way of talking—but then her cool wariness had brought him back to reality. *He* might not have changed, but the situation sure as hell had. *Get used to it, Valiella.* "You'll need to write up your experimental design using proper scientific method. But you know that."

"I think I do, but it's been so long. I'm afraid I may have forgotten things."

Spencer glanced at her. That straight little nose didn't ride quite as high as it used to. He wondered why. "Then you'll just learn it over again," he said. "Or ask me—I might know."

She smiled at that. He'd forgotten the way her smile could warm him deep down inside. There'd been other women, before and since, though right now he couldn't recall a single one. But who had Meg McKenzie become? One minute she wore her maturity like she used to wear silk blouses, with confidence and style. The next minute she was a mass of nerves, as jumpy as a spooked cat.

They cruised down the highway to Swartz Bay, hitting every green light from Elk Lake on. "It's times like this you've just gotta believe in a supreme being," Spencer said, one hand draped across the top of the wheel.

"Oh?" Meg replied with a sarcastic grin. "You mean, he's turning the lights green so Spencer Valiella won't have to slow down?"

He grinned. "*She* is making sure Meg McKenzie catches her ferry." He paused. "It is still McKenzie, isn't it?"

"Yes." She frowned at him. "I told you I wasn't married."

"Right." Then who was the guy who'd answered her phone this morning when Spencer had called to let her know which ferry he was aiming to catch? He'd sounded sleepy, as though he'd reached over to the bedside table to pick up the receiver. "Got a boyfriend?"

"Is that any of your business?"

"Guess not."

They came over the rise and into the vast paved area comprising row upon row of lanes filling with cars lining up for the ferries. Spencer curved off into the one leading to the ticket booth for Fulford Harbor on Saltspring Island. As the attendant handed over their tickets, she expressed some doubt as to whether they would make this sailing.

"We'll make it," Spencer assured her. He sped down the appropriate lane, careered around a curve and zipped over the ramp even as the warning buzzer was sounding for the seamen to cast off. The Camaro hit the steel deck with a deafening *ka-thunk*. The muffler sounded like thunder in the echo chamber of the car deck until he cut the engine. The ferry gave three short and one long blasts of the horn, and they were under way.

Spencer turned to Meg with a self-satisfied grin.

She rolled her eyes. "I need a coffee."

They went upstairs to the cafeteria and got coffee to go.

"Outside," Spencer said, and led the way to the bow where the wind blew their hair straight back and the green shapes of the Gulf Islands were spread out before them. Blue water, blue sky, glaucous-winged gulls wheeling overhead, and the majestic white prow of the *Queen of Nanaimo* as she came around the point.

Spencer leaned against the rail and drank in the fresh salt air. Being on the water always put him in a more mellow mood. "I'd forgotten how beautiful it is up here."

"You never would have known if you hadn't come back."

He glanced at Meg. She'd spoken lightly, yet he sensed a change in her mood, too, only she'd gotten serious. Still, there was history between them and her words meant something whether he acknowledged them or not. "I shouldn't have left without saying goodbye."

A swift glance, as blue as the sky. And then she was clutching her foam cup so hard it bent. "You hurt me," she said quietly. "I thought we were friends."

"We *were* friends." The sudden tensing of her mouth told him he'd hurt her again, unwittingly. God, he was inadequate when it came to the spoken word. He tried to catch her eye and communicate his caring. But she wouldn't look at him.

"Were you happy *at all* when you lived here before, Spencer?"

He was surprised at the question. Surprised at himself for not knowing the answer. "Sometimes you can't tell if you're happy until you go back to a place and see what feelings it evokes."

"*That* is the statement of someone completely out of touch with their emotions." A loose strand of hair blew across her face and she brushed it away. "So, what feelings does Victoria evoke in you?"

She hadn't asked about Saltspring, although they were nearing the island. That would have been too loaded a question. But the edge to her voice told him she meant what feelings did *she* evoke. He'd repressed those feelings for so long he wasn't sure he could define them. He only knew she shouldn't expect too much from him. "I don't know. Guess I'm still out of touch."

She was silent, watching the timber-and-glass houses perched on the island's steep shoreline slip past.

He didn't want her to want something he couldn't give her. But to say so would be presumptuous. "I've applied to Bergen for a research position."

"Bergen? You mean in Norway?"

"Yes, at the marine research institute there. The position may come up before the year is over."

She nodded. "I thought it would be something like that."

When the announcement telling passengers to return to their vehicles came on, Spencer was relieved. He tossed his empty cup into a bin and held the door open for Meg. Her hair whipped around his bare elbow, anchoring her to him for a moment. Their eyes met as she pulled it away. There was sadness in her gaze.

Spencer hated himself for putting it there.

THE DEEP BLUE WATER off the north end of Saltspring Island sparkled invitingly. Meg stood on the edge of the cobble beach while her kayak rocked gently in the shallows at her feet. In spite of the warmth of the sun, a cool breeze blew over the water and she was glad of her fleece pullover.

"Ready?" Spencer asked.

"Yes." *No.*

Spencer had stripped off his track pants to a pair of gray surfer-style shorts, and his feet were bare. He waded into the icy water as though he didn't even feel it, pushing his kayak, a well-used blue Sea Otter. Inside the forward compartment, he'd put the hydrophone equipment, as well as a waterproof camera and a pair of binoculars.

"Do you really think we'll find them?" she asked.

"Locating killer whales is always a long shot without a directional array," he replied. "But Doc and I consistently found Kitasu's matrilineal group in this area at this time of year. There's a good possibility we'll get to eavesdrop on them today."

When Spencer was up to his knees in the water, he braced his hands and the paddle across the rim of the cockpit and swung his feet inside, barely rocking the boat. With a deft dip and turn of the double-headed paddle, he spun the kayak around to face Meg and looked at her expectantly.

She fumbled with her paddle, bracing it across the cockpit as he had done. Saltwater leaked in through the seams and lace holes of her tennis shoes. She smiled self-consciously. "It's been a long time for me."

He darted forward and held the side of the tippy craft for her. "It's like riding a bicycle."

Meg held her breath. She got one foot in, braced her arms, then the other foot. The kayak rocked wildly. The muscles on Spencer's tanned arm bunched and held. She sat with a little thump, grazing her knee against the fiberglass rim as she slid her legs into the hollow bow. She was tense. The kayak seemed to know it and vibrated with jerky sideways movements that threatened to spill her into the sea.

"Relax," said Spencer. As his hand held her kayak, his eyes held hers. "Be fluid like the water and you won't tip."

Meg breathed in. Breathed out. Better. Another breath and the jerking settled down. When she felt herself relax and her body become low and centered, she knew her kayaking skills would return. She'd forgotten how great it was, the sensation of sitting in the water. Then she remembered a killer whale could flip a kayak with a casual wave of a flipper or fluke—not that that was likely. But the thought quickened her pulse and made her muscles tense; the kayak started to wobble again. Spencer held on, calm and patient. She made herself relax again, then tightened the spray skirt around her middle.

"I'm okay," she said at last. "Let's go."

Spencer moved away with a brisk practiced stroke. Meg dipped her paddle, tentatively at first. Within a few minutes she was paddling smoothly and efficiently. Her hands would be blistered and sore before the day was over.

To their right was Galiano Island, to their left, Vancouver Island, and in the distance, the overlapping silhouettes of other islands and inlets rose blue-green above the misty water. Meg glanced back at the beach. A bald eagle lifted out of a pine tree and flapped lazily across the shore. Her chest swelled as she breathed in the crisp salt air. It felt good to be alive and on the water.

They traveled north for about an hour at a pace slow enough for Meg to sustain but which made Spencer look as though he were paddling in his sleep.

She focused on the rhythmic flex and thrust of his shoulder blades. He had a great back. A little more filled out but still lean and muscular. He slowed so she could catch up, and lifted a dripping paddle to point out a sleek brown head just before it ducked under the surface. Harbor seal. Food for the transient killer whales Spencer used to study. Meg wondered if he saw the seal in those terms or whether—

Suddenly, a hundred feet away, a tall black fin broke the surface, water sheeting from its bent tip. Meg caught her breath. Excitement tingled down her arms. She hadn't been this close to a killer whale since she and Davis had gone whale-watching the previous year. But standing on the deck of a cabin cruiser was nothing compared to being in a kayak, right among the animals. She dragged her gaze away to glance at Spencer. He was looking through the binoculars, his back and shoulders straight and tall, his hair ruffling in the breeze. For a moment she forgot about the killer whales.

Then she heard a splash and glanced back to see another black dorsal fin break the surface. A spray of water erupted from the blowhole. Spencer lowered the binoculars and maneuvered his kayak closer to hers. "It's Kitasu," he said, an undertone of excitement in his voice. He pulled the binoculars over his head and handed them to her. "Look at the dorsal fin. There's a nick in the posterior edge, right at the base."

"And the other one?" Meg said, focusing the binoculars on the killer whales.

"It's a male. I'm not sure if it's Geetla or Joker. I need to see the saddle patch behind the fin more clearly." Spencer reached under his spray skirt and pulled out a pencil and a pocket-size plastic ring binder filled with waterproof paper.

"What are you doing?" she asked, lowering the binoculars.

"Making a note of the sighting for Doc's records. Date, time, place. Can you see the saddle on the first? Is there a scar across the front half?"

"I can't see it," Meg said. "But...oh, my goodness. There's another one."

"Let me see."

Meg handed back the binoculars.

"That's Joker. His dorsal fin always drooped more than Geetla's. But where's Takush?"

"Takush?"

"Kitasu's daughter." He looped the binoculars over his head and let them dangle against his chest. "Let's get closer."

The killer whales were only moving at one or two knots, but it was fast enough for Meg to feel the strain in her arms as she paddled to keep up. Slowly the gap between the whales and the kayaks closed. When they got near, Spencer lowered the hydrophone over the side of the kayak.

He wove in and out between the whales, making notes and frowning a lot. Meg knew he was worried about Takush. Killer whales had no natural predators, but sometimes they died of disease or beached themselves for unknown reasons.

The silence was broken suddenly by an eerie high-pitched whine that vibrated over the water and raised the hairs on the back of Meg's neck. Another whale returned the call, then another, and soon the air was filled with overlapping calls and piercing whistles that seemed to be coming from everywhere at once. Spencer turned to her, his demeanor charged with excitement. Meg grinned. It was hopeless trying to talk. The killer whales fanned out, picking up speed. Spencer's kayak sliced through the water after them, skimming the tops of the low waves. Meg worked hard, not wanting to be left behind.

And then, just as suddenly as they'd started, the calls died down. The whales slowed, converged, and Meg saw a fourth dorsal fin and a spout of water from a blowhole. Panting hard, she paddled over to Spencer, who had the binoculars out again.

"Takush?"

"Yes. And look!" He handed her the binoculars.

Meg raised the binoculars to her eyes. Swimming alongside the newcomer was a baby killer whale. The calf nudged its mother's flank, then ducked right under to pop up on the opposite side. "Oh, isn't it cute!"

"Is that your scientific assessment, Dr. Mc-Kenzie?"

Laughing from sheer exhilaration, Meg flicked a paddleful of water at him, dampening his hair and the front of his shirt.

Spencer shook the water out of his eyes and started to paddle toward her. "You're in trouble now."

"Behave yourself," she shrieked, backpaddling as fast as she could. "Remember the killer whales."

"These whales are on *my* side."

Just then a black-and-white shape burst through the surface behind him. The water tilted, Spencer's kayak tipped sideways, and Meg glimpsed the surprise on his face as he went under.

Through the water she saw his paddle moving to roll him back to the surface—just in time for the wall of water caused by the breaching whale to flow over him.

His laughing curse rang out across the water.

Meg steadied her own kayak against the backwash. "Whose side did you say the killer whales were on?"

"That's why Doc and I nicknamed him Joker," Spencer said, slicking back his wet hair. "This isn't the first time he's done something like that."

Meg's attention was diverted by the sound of Kitasu blowing. The whales started to swim away from the area, too fast for her and Spencer to follow even if she wasn't already exhausted. "Oh, no. They're leaving."

"Never mind. We'll book the biology department's research boat and come back another time to do some real work." Spencer pulled his wet T-shirt over his head and began to wring it out.

"Good, because I want a better look at that calf—" Meg broke off and stared.

On the end of the thin leather thong around Spencer's neck was a baby killer whale tooth set in silver. Just like the one she'd found on Saltspring seven years ago. She'd laid it in the palm of his hand, a gift, because giving herself hadn't seemed enough, or what he wanted.

He noticed the direction of her gaze and shrugged. He didn't make any dumb macho comments about his chest even though it would have been worth a stare for its own sake. He just said. "I kept it."

Stating the obvious was so unlike Spencer she knew it had to be a cover for what he *wasn't* saying. In spite of the years, in spite of the heartbreak, she took that small sign that he wasn't indifferent and turned it into hope.

CHAPTER FIVE

CLASSES STARTED just two weeks later. Spencer arrived at the lab that Monday morning to find Meg and Lee engaged in an excessively polite argument over the student desk located behind a partition that separated it from the rest of the lab. Like the one in his office, it faced the window and the biology pond.

Spencer nodded to them and walked into his office. Ah, good, the electronics technician had checked over and returned the spare preamplifier and hydrophone with which Spencer would replace the broken one in Trincomali Channel. Setting it aside, he booted up the computer to read his e-mail. Through the open door he could hear Lee and Meg still going at it. What a pair of pussycats.

"You have the desk," Lee was saying earnestly. "You are honors student."

"All I need is a corner to drop my things when I come in," Meg replied. "I can do my homework at home—where it's meant to be done."

Spencer's hands stilled on the computer keyboard as he listened to the sound of her laughter. She didn't laugh nearly as much as she used to. And some of the sparkle had gone from her eyes. She'd changed; become more mature, more thoughtful. Sometimes a little strained. Well, life held strains for everyone and they usually increased as time went on. There was no reason Meg should be an exception. But she used to chatter on about anything that popped into her mind—her family, her friends, a book she was reading, a place she wanted to travel to. Not anymore. What had happened during the years he'd been gone?

"I not need the desk excessively," he heard Lee argue. "I am here only between 4:00 and 6:00 p.m. and early in morning before class. Then mostly I work on the computer."

"Are you sure you won't want to use it during the day?" Meg asked. "Between classes? At lunch?"

"No, no, I am very sure."

That was when it struck Spencer that Lee was something of a mystery, too. He *wasn't* around during the day. Not between classes and not at lunch. Spencer had never seen him in the student coffee area or the study carrels, at the noticeboard outside the office or wandering the halls with his boxy aluminum briefcase.

Spencer rose from his chair and moved to his doorway, where he leaned on the jamb, listening openly. How could they say so much toward the same end, yet still not reach a conclusion?

"Okay, here's the deal," he broke in. "Lee, you use the desk before class and while you're working. Meg can use it the rest of the time. Fair enough?"

"Very fair, Dr. Spencer."

"Brilliant," Meg said with a grin.

"Don't be a brat." He turned to his assistant, keeping his tone casual. "By the way, Lee, what courses are you taking besides Marine Mammals?"

Lee fiddled with his tie. His grin flickered on and off. "I take Fish Ecology."

Spencer nodded. Fish were a major food source for

dolphins and killer whales. Why was he so nervous?
"And?"

Lee glanced suddenly at his watch and clapped a
hand to his forehead. "Oh, wow! Excuse me, please.
Time to pick up photos of killer whales from photog-
raphy lab."

Spencer glanced at Meg as Lee hurried out and
they both burst out laughing. "It's a pretty strange
biology major who only takes two courses in the department," Spencer said.

"Sure is. What do you suppose he does the rest of
the time?"

"Not a clue." Spencer ran a hand through his hair.
"By the way, I went to visit Doc last week. He asked
about you."

"I wish you'd told me—I would have come, too.
How much longer will he be in the hospital?"

"Could be another month, it's hard to say. Once
he's out, he'll have to attend the outpatient clinic for
physiotherapy, but there's a good chance he'll have
recovered enough to come back to work in January."

"I'm glad. I've been worried."

"Me, too," he admitted. And for more reasons than
pure concern over his old friend and teacher. Unless
Doc returned, he couldn't, in good conscience, leave
for Norway.

Spencer sat on a stool, hooking his boot heels on
the rungs. "Have you thought more about your project?"

"Yes!" Meg's eyes lit from within, recapturing
some of her sparkle. "I want to study mother-calf
communication with Takush and her baby. There are
so many questions. Does the young one have the same
vocabulary as older killer whales? Does Takush share

specific calls with her calf that she doesn't use with the others? Does the mother-calf pattern of communication change as the calf grows older?''

''Whoa,'' Spencer said, laughing and holding up his hands to stem the flow. ''You've got enough there for a Ph.D. But it's good. I like it. Write it up.'' God, he loved her enthusiasm. He leaned forward. ''So, what are we going to call our baby?''

Meg's glowing cheeks turned pale as alabaster.

The smile froze on his face. ''I meant the *killer whale* baby, obviously.''

''I know that.'' Pink flooded back into her skin. She flipped her hair back over her shoulders and paced across the lab away from him. ''What does Takush mean?''

Spencer focused on Meg's slim hips encased in snug blue jeans and the rocking hemline of her black sweater that was almost obscured by her long pale hair. ''She's named after Takush Harbor. All local killer whales have a letter and number assigned to them according to their pod, but I prefer calling the ones I know by name. The names usually come from places on the British Columbia coast.''

''How about 'Southey,' since we set out from Southey Point?'' Meg suggested. ''I wonder if it's a girl or a boy.''

''With luck we'll find out. I booked the *Cape Beale* for two weeks from now. That's the first weekend in October—the only time I could get two days in a row. Can you make it?''

''Uh, yes, I think so. I mean, of course, I'll make it. I know how hard it is to get time on the research vessel.''

Her nervousness communicated itself to him, making him uneasy, too, though he didn't know why. Slipping off the stool, he walked over to a filing cabinet. "In here are reprints of every paper written on killer whale communication going back twenty years. If you find anything new, make an extra copy for the file. I've talked to Stores, the biology supplies room in the basement, and told them you'll be putting whatever you need on Doc's account—which is still under Doc's name. He also has an account at the campus computer store. Let's see, what else? Oh, yeah. It's five o'clock. How about a beer over at the faculty club?"

He hadn't actually meant to say that. After she'd seen the killer whale tooth around his neck, he'd decided to keep his distance. Now he wondered how much of his invitation had to do with not wanting to go home to his old man.

"Thanks, but...I can't. I'm late now. And, Spencer?" Her blue eyes were clear and devastating, her cheeks tinged pink. "I don't think we should see each other socially. I mean, we could lose our... objectivity."

"You're not a science experiment I'm conducting."

"You know what I mean."

He searched her eyes, looking for...what? A sign that she wanted him to argue? He didn't find it. "You're right. It was a bad idea." He backed into the doorway of his office, hands propped on either side. "You'd better run."

TWO DAYS LATER Meg hurried into the biology building and down the corridor to the lab, glancing at her watch and groaning. She was really late. This morn-

ing Davis had woken up with a slight headache that
made him grumpy and slow. He was into his third
week of school and, apart from a reluctance to get
moving in the morning, seemed to have settled in.
Against his protests, she hustled him off to school and
then hurried on to the university where Spencer was
waiting to demonstrate the computer program with
which he analyzed killer whale calls.

He was already seated at the computer when she
ran into the lab. ''Hi,'' she said, and dumped her
books on the desk behind the partition.

'''A dillar, a dollar, a ten o'clock scholar…'''
Spencer quoted mildly, punching keys on the keyboard.

''Sorry, I'm late. I, uh…never mind, it doesn't matter.'' Meg scooted a chair up next to Spencer's.
''What are you doing?''

''Just getting ready to enter the recordings we made
the other day into the computer. We plug in the digital
audiotape recorder here.'' He connected the tape recorder, only a little bigger than a Walkman, to the
back of the computer. ''The recording is made in digital format—in other words, CD quality. Bioacoustic
analysis software is then used to digitize the data,
analyze it and format it into spectrograms, or voice
pictures. We should see some come up on the screen
in a few minutes.''

''Spectrograms record the energy and frequency of
the call over time, right?'' She knew the theory from
the journal articles she'd read, but it was exciting to
be working on the actual data.

He nodded. ''Each call type is assigned a number.
We can then measure the length and height of the
various spectrogram components and compare them

statistically to one another to distinguish between discrete call types."

She groaned. "So that's why I need the biostatistics course."

Spencer chuckled. "Still hate statistics, eh, princess? Don't worry, the computer does most of the work."

She shot him a glance. He was smiling at her, inviting her to remember the old days. Her mind flashed to Davis. She hoped his headache hadn't gotten worse.

"Can we hear the sounds as they're entered?" she said.

"Sure." Spencer punched a few keys and the killer whale vocalizations came through the speakers connected to the computer. "It's a good idea to become familiar with the calls so you can relate sound to the visual record of the spectrogram."

Meg listened hard, trying to pick out the separate whale sounds. *Weeeow, weeeow.* Amid the louder calls and whistles, she thought she heard a softer shorter set of calls that might be the killer whale calf, but she couldn't be sure. The spectrograms, layers of wavy lines, started to appear on the screen. They might as well have been Martian heart rhythms.

Spencer caught the look on her face. "Don't worry, by Christmas you'll be able to read these as easily as you read English. And with this whizz-bang new program I worked up in Monterey, the computer can distinguish between the calls of individuals."

Her gaze shifted from the monitor to Spencer. They were sitting so close their arms were almost touching where they rested on the computer desk. Beneath his dark green, open-neck shirt she could see the leather cord attached to the killer whale tooth. The hope it had given her so unexpectedly that day on the water had dissipated quickly when she applied a little rational thought. So he had a sentimental streak. So he asked her out for a drink. It didn't mean he'd changed.

"Can you tell which is the calf?" she asked, focusing on the spectrogram again.

"We'll have to run the stats program to be sure." Spencer rose and reached over Meg's head for a box of computer CDs on the shelf above the desk. "I've got an earlier set of recordings for Takush's group. Whatever spectrograms turn out to be different should be the new arrival."

"Do you have written instructions for using this program?"

"It's pretty easy. But if you need help and I'm not here, Lee knows."

"If Lee is around."

Spencer glanced at her sharply. "He doesn't spend much time in the department, does he?"

Meg shrugged. "Doesn't seem to. But every morning when I come in, I see evidence he's been here." She glanced at her watch. Davis should be coming in from recess now. She hoped he'd remembered to wear his jacket outside. Or his teacher remembered for him.

There was a knock at the door. "Hello," a female voice called. "Anybody home?"

Spencer's and Meg's attention was diverted to the doorway and a tall woman with lustrous auburn hair and cheekbones you could hang a hat on. She wore a lab coat over her slim short skirt and looked to be in her late thirties, maybe even early forties. Meg hoped she'd look half that good when she got to that age.

Spencer rose to his feet. "Hi."

Meg smiled, but the woman didn't seem to see her.

"Rachel Walsh, resident algologist," she said, extending a hand to Spencer. "Welcome to the department." Her green-blue eyes swept his lazy hip-cocked stance from head to toe. Meg felt like throttling her. And him.

"'Walsh, 1998,'" he quoted, still hanging on to her hand. "'Productivity of the giant kelp, *Macrocystis integrifolia* in relation to nutrient concentrations in Howe Sound.'"

One of Rachel Walsh's finely arched brows slid upward. "Clever boy."

Spencer shrugged modestly. "Salmon feed on organisms living in kelp forests, and killer whales feed on salmon. I'm Spencer Valiella, taking over for—"

"Oh, I know all about *you*." Rachel's gaze flicked to Meg, then back to Spencer. "I can see you're busy. I just wanted to invite you to join me and a few others for a drink at the faculty club on Friday."

"Excuse me," Meg murmured, "I've got to make a phone call. Humming to herself to block out Spencer's answer to Rachel, she went to her desk. Rachel Ward had to be eight years older than Spencer, minimum. Hussy. Cradle-snatcher.

She dialed her girlfriend Gina's number, even though she knew Gina was working, and had a little chat with her answering machine. Then she dialed the weather forecast. When she couldn't think who else to call, she hung up and stared out at the pond, trying not to listen to the murmur of voices on the other side of the partition. Were they still talking about kelp? Or had they gone on to Friday's coming attractions?

She had no right to be bitchy about Rachel Walsh after she'd turned down Spencer herself, but now she regretted leaving Spencer alone with the woman.

She emerged from behind the partition to hear Rachel say, "See you soon," and give Spencer one last brilliant smile.

Spencer turned around, saw Meg and shrugged. "Women find me irresistible. What can I say?"

Meg laughed, though she felt like bopping him one. Then she realized his smile had faded and his gaze had turned intense, as though he was trying to tell her he wasn't really interested in Rachel but couldn't get the words out. *Say it, goddamn it. Just say it.*

The phone rang.

"I'll get it," Spencer said, and went past her into his office to answer it. "Hello?" He listened a moment, then his jaw went slack and he turned to stare at Meg.

"For you," he said, holding out the receiver. "Esquimalt Primary School. Your *son* is ill and wants you to pick him up."

Oh, hell.

She reached for the phone, avoiding Spencer's eyes, and had a brief conversation with the school secretary, promising to be there as soon as possible. Davis had a fever and a sore ear and the nurse suspected an ear infection.

Meg hung up. "I have to go."

Spencer grabbed her by the arm. "*A son?* You never told me you had a son. When did this happen?"

"Six years ago." She saw the anger and hurt in his

eyes and dropped her gaze. She jerked her arm away. "I've got to go."

Flabbergasted, Spencer watched Meg grab her jacket and purse and run out of the lab with nary a backward glance.

A son? Six years old? That would mean he'd been conceived sometime back in... *No way.* The boy couldn't be his child. They'd only made love twice. Okay, three times, but the third time...well, suffice it to say, she couldn't have gotten pregnant *that* way. And both other times they'd used condoms, for heaven's sake. Besides, Meg would have told him if he'd fathered a child.

Fathered a child. The thought gave him a cold shiver that had to be fear, because it sure as hell couldn't be excitement.

But if the child wasn't his, then whose was it?

And where was the bastard now?

Spencer paced across the lab. If Meg got pregnant seven years ago, whoever the father was, he must have come hot on Spencer's heels. Unless she'd been seeing someone else all along? No, that couldn't be right. Long before they'd become lovers they'd been friends. She would have told him if there'd been someone else. Meg was so honest she wouldn't filch a grape from the produce section of a grocery store.

Meg was so honest she'd told him she loved him.

Spencer found himself whistling to cover the sound of her words echoing through his memory.

He shut down the computer, then locked the door to his inner office and pulled shut the outer door. He had to get away. Had to get in his car and drive.

He took the steps outside two at a time, striding down the path to the parking lot, brushing past students, barely noticing their tentative smiles and quick waves. When he got to his car, he stopped dead. And took his bearings. Back row, third spot from the end.

He'd parked in this exact spot yesterday. Probably the day before, too. The fact that he didn't remember freaked him out even more. He'd only been here a few weeks and already he'd fallen into a routine.

Spencer roared out of the city, his pulse thumping along to the music blasting from the Camaro's speakers. Had she loved that other guy—the father? That was her right. *He didn't care.* But man, she hadn't wasted any time taking up with someone new. Maybe she'd been hurt, on the rebound... He cranked the music louder.

Ray's van was parked in the driveway when Spencer pulled up at the cottage. Good. Yesterday Ray had left the cottage early and gotten home just as Spencer was going to bed. He'd been surly and uncommunicative, not like himself at all. Spencer was getting worried about him. Then he patted his breast pocket and smiled. When Ray got a load of what Spencer had for him, he'd cheer up.

"Hey, Ray! Guess what I..." His voice trailed away as he came through the front door. Ray was lying on the couch in his dressing gown, unshaven and uncombed, reading a detective novel.

Seeing him, Ray tossed the book on the pine side table. "Lousy book. Figured out who did it before I was half through."

Spencer sat in the rocker opposite the couch and gripped the arms, telling himself not to panic. Ray was entitled to relax the way he wanted to; that was why he'd come north. He pulled the wad of bills from his pocket and tossed them onto the coffee table.

"Got a cash advance on my credit card. Two thousand smackers. You can get your guitar out of hock, and…hell, do anything you want with the rest. Pay me back whenever."

Ray scratched his bare chest beneath the plaid dressing gown. "Put away your money, son. You don't want to lose your hard-earned bucks on a bad bet."

"So you've had a little setback. You'll bounce back, get another band together."

"I'm too old to be getting a band together." Ray settled a patchwork cushion behind his head and shut his eyes.

Spencer forced a laugh. "You're younger than Mick Jagger."

One eye opened and Ray glared at him balefully. "That ain't young, son. And comparisons like that just ain't funny."

Spencer stared at him, incredulous. The world was a scary place when Ray Valiella lay down and wouldn't get up.

THE NEXT MORNING Spencer found the money on his dresser next to his wallet and keys. *Damn*. He had to get his father out of the cottage and interested in something—anything. If all Ray was going to do was lie about and put away a mickey of Jack Daniel's every day, well, something had to give.

When Spencer arrived at the lab that morning, Lee had his briefcase open on the lab bench and was packing his calculator next to a large textbook with dollar signs on the cover. When he saw Spencer, he snapped his briefcase shut.

"Morning, Lee," Spencer said wondering briefly about that textbook. "How's it going?"

"Just great. I am almost finished statistical analysis of Pod C28 and Pod C12. I think we find they have close matrilineal ties, as Dr. Campbell suspected." From the glow in Lee's eyes, an outsider might think he'd just won the lottery.

"Good. Doc says when you're done analyzing the data, you can start writing the results up for publication."

Lee's eyes widened and he laughed with excitement. "I hope my English is good enough."

"Doc will go over it and he'll be first author, of course, but you'll have your name on the paper. If I can be of any help, just ask."

Lee picked up his briefcase, still grinning. "Thank you very, very—"

"Don't worry about it," Spencer said, and laughed simply because Lee's good humor was contagious. Then he added casually, "Where are you off to now?"

Lee's round face became instantly blank. "I attend class."

"Let's see, Marine Mammals isn't till this afternoon, and Fish Ecology is on Friday, right?"

"That is correct. You have a very good memory." Lee backed out the door. "Goodbye for now, Dr. Spencer."

From Spencer's office window he could see Lee exit the building and head across campus. Spencer glanced at his watch. His first-year biology class wasn't until ten, so... Pausing only to snatch Lee's silver pen off the computer table, he strode out the door. Lee was well ahead, almost lost in the throng of students hurrying to class. Spencer lengthened his stride, his long legs eating up the distance across the quadrangle. He came to a crossing of footpaths in time to see Lee's black head, white shirt and aluminum briefcase disappear into the McCallum building. *Business and Commerce?* Had Spencer's initial assessment been correct? He ran forward and slipped through the closing door.

"Lee!"

Lee whirled around, his narrow black tie flying out. His eyes widened, his mouth opened, but he couldn't seem to speak.

"You forgot your pen," Spencer said, holding it out to him as students swirled around them. "What are you doing here? Are you taking a business class?"

Lee took the pen. His wide grin came and went. He swallowed hard and ran a finger around the inside of his collar. He laughed nervously. But still he didn't speak.

"Come clean," Spencer said, smiling. "Or are you up to your ears in white-collar crime?"

Lee laughed, a little hysterically, then hung his head so low Spencer could see the black hairs against the white of his neck. "I am a business major," he said in a dramatically woeful voice. "My father is big Hong Kong businessman. He sent me here to get a degree in commerce."

"Wow, you're kidding. Why the secrecy?"

Slowly, Lee raised his head. "My father does not know I take biology classes. He would be most upset to learn I waste credits on courses other than business."

"Why didn't you tell Doc? Or me?"

"I worry you would think I am not a serious student. Not let me work in the lab.'' He put his hands together in a gesture of prayer. ''Please, don't send me away.''

''No one's going to send you away. You've got a job to do.'' Spencer scratched his head. ''But…your interest in killer whales—what's that all about?''

Lee's face lit up. ''I saw *Free Willy* thirteen times in high school. Also *Free Willy II* and *Free Willy III*—many times each. I am so excited about killer whales I learn everything I can—in the library, on the Internet… There I saw Dr. Campbell's name. I read his book, his journal articles. I adopted a whale through the Vancouver Aquarium. I decide, more than anything else, I want to be a marine biologist and study killer whales.''

''And?''

''And so I convince Father to send me to Victoria for business school. I knew he would not agree to biology, but he think it great idea to get Canadian education. And finally I see killer whales in the wild.''

''Let me get this straight,'' Spencer said, scratching his head. ''You're majoring in business and doing biology courses on the side. How close are you to getting a bachelor of science?''

Lee flung out the hand that wasn't holding his briefcase. ''I need *fifteen* more credits. Since I can do only two or three credits per year I will have to do a Ph.D. in business just to get my biology degree.''

Spencer bit back the urge to smile. ''Why don't you just tell your father you'd rather be a biologist than a businessman?''

Lee shook his head. ''Oh, no. I am an only son. Only *child*. My father would be dishonored.''

"How do you plan to be a biologist and run your father's business at the same time?"

Lee shrugged unhappily. "I will worry about that bridge when I cross it."

"Well, maybe we can think of a way for you to speed up your degree. One thing you could do is take summer courses at Bamfield Marine Station. But for now, you'd better get going or you'll miss your class."

Lee smiled gratefully. "Yes, *sir,* Dr. Spencer."

Spencer rolled his eyes. "Get outta here."

SPENCER GLANCED SIDEWAYS at Meg. They were at the computer again, going over spectrograms of Takush and the others. Meg's profile was obscured by her long hair, but he could just see the tip of her nose. He remembered kissing that nose. It was *his* nose, dammit. Who was the father of her child?

He told himself her nose did *not* belong to him. He had no right to feel proprietorial about it. About *anything* of hers. Because of the killer whale tooth, he'd already been caught caring. He had to keep his distance, because eventually distance would be the only thing between them.

A moment later he was amazed to hear himself say, "Meg, I'd really like to go out with you."

Blue eyes stared into his, wide and wary. "Pardon?"

"If getting a baby-sitter is difficult, you could bring your...your—"

"The thought of children is pretty terrifying all right." She spoke lightly, but he noticed her lips tremble.

Someone had made her pregnant and then left her.

How could anyone do that to *Meg?* Protective instincts surged through him. "What's his name?"

She went pale. "Whose?"

"The father of your son."

"He's... What do you care? You left without saying—"

"I know, I know—without saying goodbye. Meg, I'm sorry." He turned her chair so she could see his face straight-on. Took her hands in his. "The research boat left early. When I got back from Saltspring that last morning, there was a message to go straight down to the harbor with my things. I tried to call, but you weren't home. At least that's what your father said."

"If that's what he said, then it's the truth. But you could have called me when you got back. Why didn't you?"

"I was off to Seattle within a day of my return. I'm not a good correspondent. I barely keep in contact with my family. I didn't intend to hurt you, whatever you may think. Anyway, you must have found yourself a new boyfriend by then. What did you say his name was?"

"I didn't." She pulled her hands from his and dropped her head, hiding her face from him.

With his fingertips he lifted the curtain of light blond hair. "Was it someone I knew?"

"I don't want to talk about it."

"Is he still on the scene?"

Her head came up as she laughed, short and bitter. *"No."*

"I've missed you, Meg. Do you think we could be friends? Because I would really like that."

"Friends?" The beginnings of a real smile faded.

"Yes. We used to be friends, remember?" Maybe

it wasn't right getting personal when he should be keeping his distance, but Meg was important. "I've always considered you one of the best friends I've ever had. If not *the* best."

Moisture glazed her eyes. "I'm not sure what it means to be friends with you, Spencer. Will you come when I've got a flat tire? Give me a shoulder to cry on if I'm down? No, don't answer. I know you would. You'd do anything for a friend—if you happened to be in the country."

"If you don't want to be friends, just say so."

She gazed at him in silence, her eyes sending messages he couldn't decipher. The silence expanded until he wanted to twine his fingers around the thick strands of her hair and pull her into a kiss just to break the tension.

"I'll go out with you," she said at last. "And I'll be your friend because I can't do otherwise. *If,*" she added, her voice low but firm, "you promise not to hurt me again."

He thought of the letter he'd received today from Dr. Henrik Jorgensen acknowledging his application to Bergen. Whether Spencer was accepted there or not, sooner or later he would leave Victoria. But you didn't hurt a friend if you could help it.

"I should have called you from Seattle." He touched her hair, willing her to believe how sorry he was. "Next time, I promise I'll say goodbye."

Suddenly she was laughing through the tears that burst forth to course down her cheeks. "You *bastard.*" Shaking her head, she wrote her address on a scrap of paper and handed it to him.

"Saturday evening, seven o'clock," he said, elation setting in despite his misgivings. "Dress warmly."

CHAPTER SIX

"*DRESS WARMLY.* What does that mean?" Meg demanded of Patrick. Her housemate lounged across her bed while she stood at her open closet in a black bra and panties and leafed through the clutter of expensive dresses her mother kept pressing on her though Meg had begged her to stop. Even if the clothes had been her style, she had no place to wear them.

"Call him up and ask," Patrick suggested.

"That would be too unspontaneous of me," she said, holding a conservatively tailored wool dress against herself.

Patrick flapped a hand in disgust. "That won't suit you for at least fifty years."

Meg hung the dress back in the closet. "Maybe we're going night diving. But surely he would have told me to bring a wet suit. And the time—seven o'clock. Is that dinner or what?"

"Maybe it's a picnic on the beach."

"He *would* do something like that." Finally she sighed and took down blue jeans and her favorite black cashmere sweater from the top shelf. Spencer never went anywhere you had to dress up. "Shouldn't you and Davis be leaving for the movies soon?"

Patrick glanced at his watch. "Relax, it's only six-thirty. Davis is getting his socks and shoes on."

"I really appreciate this, Patrick," she said, pulling

on her jeans. "You won't let him stay up too late, will you? His ear infection is better, but he might have a relapse if—"

"Don't worry." He watched her suck in her stomach to pull up the zipper. "Are we gaining a little weight?"

"They shrink in the wash," she said, sticking out her tongue at him. "How's it going at the base? Any word on your promotion?"

Patrick groaned. "Today I got an anonymous note from someone who apparently applied for the same job I did. He's threatening to blow my cover."

Meg pulled her sweater over her head then lifted her hair from the scooped neckline. "You're kidding. What did the note say?"

"Something like, 'I know what you are' and he wants to 'discuss the matter.' I think he knows who my father is and he's trying to blackmail me."

"He can't harass you like that. I hope you threw it straight into the garbage," she said, tilting her head to brush out her hair.

"Better than that. I'm going to take the wind out of his sails. I'm going to go to the selection panel and tell them *everything*." He shrugged. "Lying doesn't feel right, anyway."

"Good for you. I'm sure it's the right thing—"

"Shh!" Patrick held up a hand and cocked his ear toward the door.

"What is it?"

"I thought I heard a car pull up."

Meg laughed. "When Spencer arrives, you won't just *think* you hear a car. His muffler sounds like a 747 taking off. You know he's coming before he's halfway down the block."

"Maybe so, but I think I'll go see where the champ has got to." Patrick paused in the doorway. "For goodness' sake, Meg, put on a little lipstick."

Meg set down the brush and hesitated over a tube of cranberry lip gloss. Spencer had told her once he hated the feel of lipstick when he kissed a woman. Defiantly she whipped off the lid and brushed it lightly over her lips. If he was going to kiss her, it wouldn't be until later and the lipstick would have worn off by then.

She pursed her lips at her reflection in the mirror. "I can't believe you just thought that."

The doorbell rang.

Omigod. Her watch said ten to seven. Why hadn't she heard the car? Where was Patrick? Where was *Davis?*

She rushed out of her bedroom to meet a wild-eyed Patrick, baseball mitt in hand, pushing Davis toward the kitchen and the back door.

"I thought we were going to the movies," Davis said.

"In a few minutes. First we're going to play catch."

"It's almost dark," Davis complained. "And you throw like a girl."

"Do you want to learn baseball or not? Say goodbye to Mom."

Davis planted his feet and craned his head around to speak to Meg. "Where are you going?"

"Out with my professor. I told you at dinner." She'd also told him at breakfast, as well as last night when she'd tucked him into bed. Davis only remembered things he wanted to remember.

"Is this a date?" Davis demanded.

"What do you know about dates?" She whisked past Patrick and opened the back door for them.

"His name is Spencer, isn't it?"

The doorbell rang again.

Meg's heart leaped into triple-time. "A lot of people are named Spencer." She bent to give Davis a hug. "See you later, sweetheart. Be good for Patrick. And no getting out of bed."

She shut the door behind them and leaned against it for a moment to catch her breath. What she was doing was stupid. She strode back through the house to the front door. *Stupid, stupid, stupid.* She opened the door. *Stup—*

God, he looked good. Tall and lean in a thick cream sweater that looked as if it had been knitted by someone's grandmother in Ireland. His hair was windblown and he had a slight beard growth, which reminded her he didn't shave on the weekends. But though his jaw appeared bristly, she knew his beard was soft. It framed his mouth, leading her gaze across the sharply defined upper lip and the soft sensuality of the lower.

He peered over her shoulder into the house. "Are you going to introduce me to your son?"

"My son?" she squeaked. "No. The baby-sitter took him…out. They won't be back for a while." She grabbed her blue wool jacket off the hook beside the door, stepped onto the porch and shut the door behind her. "Shall we go?"

He drove across the bridge into Victoria. Soon the Camaro was purring up Dallas Road beside the row of expensive homes that faced the Strait of Juan de Fuca.

"When did you get the muffler fixed?" Meg asked accusingly.

Spencer shrugged. "I don't know. Thursday, maybe. I thought it bothered you."

"Is that why you got it fixed?"

He grinned sideways at her. "No. But I didn't think you'd complain."

She sighed. "I'm not. Where are we going?"

"You'll see." A few minutes later he pulled off the road at Gonzales Point and parked in a spot with a view. It overlooked the strait to the Olympic Mountains, where the last rays of pink reflected off their snowy peaks.

"Hungry?" he asked as he shut off the car.

"A little." Actually, she was starving. The savory smells emanating from the covered cardboard box on the back seat had been driving her crazy all the way here.

They got out and Meg went around to the back to help carry things. She was surprised when he loaded a rolled-up sleeping bag in her outstretched arms. "You didn't tell me we were camping."

"Just keeping warm," Spencer said, and handed her a second sleeping bag. He tucked a bottle of wine under one arm, grabbed a thermos and put the box of food under his other arm. But instead of leading the way down the cliff to the beach, he crossed the road and scrambled up the bank to the Victoria Golf Course.

"We can't go up here," Meg said, glancing anxiously around for stray golfers. Her father had a membership here. He would not be amused if his daughter was caught picnicking on the green.

"Come on, Meg, where's your sense of adventure?

Golf is finished for the day. The view is better up here.''

The view was indeed spectacular when Spencer finally allowed that they were in the best place. They were far enough in from the road that cars wouldn't catch them in their headlights, and far enough away from the clubhouse to be invisible to lingering players or people going to the restaurant.

"Just think, my mother and father could be having dinner over there right now," Meg said.

Spencer gave her a pained look. *"Please."*

They rolled out the sleeping bags and sat on top with the box of food between them. Spencer opened the bottle of Chablis while Meg removed containers of takeout and lifted the foil lids. Greek food—a favorite of their student days. Chunky salad, deep-fried calamari, spinach pie and stuffed grapevine leaves. Even Metaxa, the Greek brandy that had warmed the night on Saltspring Island. Her heart turned over. Just for a moment she was transported back to a time before the heartache and loneliness.

She smiled at Spencer. "This is great."

He poured her a glass of wine. "I had a craving for Greek food."

Okay, message received; she wasn't to accuse him of sentiment. Or read anything into this evening. *Then why did you ask me out, Spencer?* "It's a beautiful night. The warmest for days." She stabbed up a plastic forkful of feta and tomato. "What's your dad doing tonight?"

Spencer bit down on a calamari ring, his eyebrows pulling together. "Nothing much."

"Spencer, what's going on with your father?"

"Nothing. Why do you ask?"

"Because every time I mention his name, you frown. You never used to do that." She picked up a spinach pie and bit into the flaky filo pastry.

Spencer stared out to sea. When he spoke at last she thought he was going to talk about Ray. Instead he said, "It's too bad you never got a chance to finish university."

"I *never* regretted having my son. Not for an instant."

He glanced around in surprise. "I didn't mean to suggest you did."

"Sorry. I'm so used to defending myself against my mother." And the wine was already going to her head.

"What did you do for money? Did your parents help?"

"Some. But...I wasn't a child anymore, you know? I chose the path I took, so after a while I said thanks but no thanks. I went to work as a waitress, salesclerk, whatever I could get. It was good for me." She could admit that now.

"So you moved out of home."

She nodded. "I shared an apartment with another single mother I met in the hospital. We helped each other out with baby-sitting." That had been Gina, the first of the few good friends who'd helped her create a new life for herself. Her Uplands friends had waved goodbye without a second thought when she'd moved across town.

"Must have been rough."

It had been incredibly rough for someone used to having all the money and material comforts she needed just handed to her. "I got by. About a year later my friend reconciled with her child's father and they got married. Then I answered an ad for a roommate and got Patrick.''

"Patrick?'' Spencer repeated, frowning slightly.

Her smile stretched wide. "He's in the navy. Fantastic guy. Funny and sweet. I don't know what I'd do without him.''

Spencer's frown deepened to a scowl. "Is he the guy who answered the phone the morning we went kayaking?''

Meg sipped her wine. "Must have been. And no, he's not my boyfriend.''

"What's your son like?''

It was a question guaranteed to elicit a rush of words from any loving mother. Especially when wine had loosened her tongue. "He loves animals. And Lego toys. He's smart. Mechanically minded but able to think in the abstract. He likes to do his own thing— a bit of a loner, really. He's—''

Meg broke off abruptly. Except for the Lego toys, she could be describing Spencer. Luckily he didn't seem to recognize himself.

"He sounds pretty amazing for a six-year-old,'' Spencer said. "Is he easygoing like you?''

Nothing was easy about Davis. But her protective instincts stopped her from saying anything negative about him to Spencer. "He's a great kid.''

And now it was time she stopped talking about him altogether. She stacked one empty container into another. "Do you want that last *dolmathes?*''

He popped the stuffed grapevine leaf into his mouth. Then with the aid of a flashlight, they tidied up the box of food and set it to one side, leaving out the thermos, cups and the bottle of Metaxa.

"Should we have our coffee in the car?" Meg suggested. "It's getting chilly."

"Didn't I mention the meteorite shower?" He gazed up at the clear night sky. "We should be seeing something any minute."

Meg gaped at him. "*Now* you tell me we're here for the evening? After I've consumed half a bottle of wine and was ready to start on coffee and brandy? Already I have to—"

"You could go to the clubhouse…or there's a convenient clump of bushes behind us."

Meg shook her head at the grin in his voice. She snatched up the flashlight and headed toward the clubhouse, hoping she wouldn't meet anyone she knew.

When she got back, Spencer had pulled the sleeping bags closer together and gotten into his bag. He lay on his back with his hands behind his head. Meg wriggled into her sleeping bag. It was warm and thick and bore his scent. Memories of Saltspring and lying next to Spencer rushed into her mind. She searched for stars in the darkening sky and tried not to feel so intimately aware of him stretched out beside her now.

Pinpricks of light began to dot the blackness as the stars winked on and the Milky Way slowly thickened to a band of light across the firmament. So far, no meteorites.

"Well?" she said.

"Be patient. The height of the meteorite shower is supposed to occur around ten o'clock." He held his watch up to his face and the phosphorescent numerals could be dimly seen. "Another hour or so." He paused. "Warm enough?"

"Yes. Thank you. Is…is this your sleeping bag?"

"Yeah. I'm using Ray's."

"What *is* going on with your dad, Spencer? I can tell something's not right."

She heard his sigh, followed by a long silence. Finally he said, "The band folded. He's broke."

"Oh, no!"

"Yes. Apparently the band members started to go different ways musically, plus they were sick of touring. Two dropped out completely and the new guys Ray got to replace them didn't work out. He had to cancel a few gigs, and then it became harder to get engagements. Over the space of a couple of years it all just fell apart. It wasn't Ray's fault, but he blames himself."

"That's awful. But how could he be broke? I thought he was doing really well."

"He made some bad investments. Plus, he frittered away a lot of money on his jet-setting life-style."

"Was that hard for you as a kid?" she asked. "Him being on the road so much?"

"I liked it when I could go, too. But when I was five, my parents went on tour and left me with some people I didn't know."

"That's awfully young to be left. How long were they gone?"

"Seemed like forever—for a while I wasn't sure they were even coming back—but I think it was about eighteen months."

"Oh, Spencer, you poor thing."

He was silent a moment. When he spoke, his voice was cool and neutral. "It was no big deal."

Then he turned on his side, facing her. "The worst part about Ray is that he's completely lost interest in life. He sits around all day in his bathrobe playing solitaire or just staring out to sea. He's taken to drinking, too, something he never did that much of before. I offered him money to get his guitar out of hock, but he won't take it. It's not natural for him not to be playing. I'm really worried.''

''I don't blame you.'' Meg lay back and pondered the problem. ''My dad went through something similar a while back.…''

''You can't compare your father to mine,'' Spencer said. ''Roger was born with a silver spoon in his hand. He never had to struggle for anything.''

''Let me finish! Roger and Ray *are* very different, but they're similar in age. Maybe your dad's going through a midlife crisis. Loss of youth, fear of dying, that is-this-all-there-is feeling.''

''Okay, but Ray is fifty-two. Isn't that a little old for a midlife crisis?''

''Maybe it's been delayed because until recently he's lived the life-style of a younger man. Or maybe it's been going on longer than you think. You don't see him that often, do you?''

''No,'' Spencer admitted. ''And he's damn good at covering up with his good-time-Charlie act.''

''The crunch came for Daddy when his hair started to get seriously gray. Suddenly he couldn't pretend even to himself that he was young any longer.''

''What did he do—buy a bottle of hair dye?''

Meg chuckled. ''He tried it, but it looked awful, so he learned to live with a revised image of himself. Now he takes pride in looking 'distinguished.' At least he says he does.''

''Yeah, well, Ray's main obstacle at the moment is lack of money. He's never going to get a band together without it. And until he does, he's not going to feel good about himself or get on with his life.''

"Yet he won't take a loan. Could you make it look as if he's doing you a favor? Like, I don't know...buy the cottage off him?"

Spencer propped himself up on one elbow to stare down at her. "And what reason would I give for wanting to do that?"

"Put down roots?"

He rolled on his back again. "Ray would never believe that."

"Can't you pretend? Even a little bit?" she demanded, raising herself to peer through the darkness at his face.

"No, I couldn't. Forget it, Meg. It wouldn't work."

"You're telling me you can't compromise your integrity long enough to help your father?" She was starting to get annoyed at him for his stubbornness, maybe more than the situation warranted, but she couldn't seem to help herself.

"I'd do anything to help him. But what happens when I leave? How much worse is he going to feel knowing I lied? Is that what *you* want to hear, Meg? Lies?"

"We're talking about your father, not me." She flopped onto her back and pulled the sleeping bag up to her chin.

Spencer fell silent. Meg tried to look at the stars, but they kept blurring into shiny tear-washed streaks. She and Spencer had been so close for a little while, almost like the old days when they'd talked until they were so tired they couldn't keep their eyes open. Talked to keep from touching each other. And now...

"Okay, let's talk about me—no, I don't want lies," she said at last. Her voice sounded more quavery than she would have wished; she was afraid it was the wine doing the talking, but she'd imagined this conversation too many times to stop now. "I want the truth. I just don't happen to believe that your resounding silence on the subject of our relationship *was* the truth.

"Seven years ago on Saltspring, I told you I loved you. We were right in the middle of making love. Do you remember? I no sooner said the words than you stopped touching me and turned away. I laid my heart open for you and you *turned away*. Can you even begin to imagine how crushing that was? Is that the kind of friend you are, Spencer?"

He didn't answer. His eyes were closed, shutting her out. She pounded a fist on the thick padding of his sleeping bag. "*Do you hear me?* You say you won't lie, but when your body says one thing and your actions say another, isn't that a lie? What about the tenderness before that? The way we laughed and talked and knew what each other was thinking before we said it. You loved me. Why couldn't you have said it? Just once."

She broke off, swallowing her tears, and gulped air past the tightness and pain in her chest. She hadn't meant to beg, and now she felt ashamed and sick at heart.

"What did you expect from me, Meg?" His voice was an anguished whisper. "Saying…you know, *love,* and all that. It's like a promise. You were special to me—it's true, I don't deny it. You're special to me *now*. But making promises I can't keep is worse than any lie."

"Can't, or won't?" she asked bitterly.

"I don't want to stay in one place. I don't want a mortgage. I don't want a house in the suburbs. It's all too safe. Too much sameness. The monotony, the boredom, scares me.''

"It doesn't have to be that way."

"Too many times it is. I couldn't stick it. You would end up hurt and I couldn't bear that."

"Don't be so damned noble." She was hurting *now*.

"Meg." He reached for her, and in the darkness his fingers lost their way and landed on her nose. They moved on to caress her cheek before tangling in the hair at her temple.

"Don't," she pleaded, trying to quell the shudder of longing sweeping through her.

His hand moved to the back of her neck, pulling her closer. "I've never forgotten you, Meg, not for a second. I dream about you. When I was in California I'd look up at the night sky and think, These same stars are shining down on Meg. When I was on the water, I felt the ocean currents connecting us even though we were apart. When we're together, I want to be *with* you. I want to make love to you. That night on Saltspring was the best night of my life because it was with you. Do you remember, Meg, how good it felt?"

His low rough voice was like a siren's song, immobilizing her. His fingers poured liquid fire into her blood as they moved across her skin. She turned her face into his palm and, on a sigh, planted a kiss. She felt the shudder go through him. Then the stars blacked out as his head and shoulders descended to hers.

His mouth tasted of coffee and Metaxa. The scent of the ocean was in her nostrils. She was falling through fathoms of dark water. Spencer's arms were around her, saving her or dragging her down, she didn't know which, didn't care. Desire came in on a wave and left its wet imprint between her legs. A moan escaped and was lost in the mingling of their breaths.

Spencer's sleeping bag rustled as he shifted closer and put his leg across her thigh, the familiar weight of her fantasies. Touching, but still so far apart. "Meg." He spoke her name in a voice as dark as midnight, "I want you."

She couldn't think. If she had, she might not have twined her arm around his neck to pull him into another kiss. As their tongues joined, her eyes flickered open to glimpse a golden fireball streak across the blackness. Then they shut again and all sensation focused on Spencer, whom she'd loved and lost.

And found again. The ache inside her was part physical need, part emotional connection that defied time and logic. Only Spencer could cure the ache and the longing. But could she handle a relationship on his terms? Put aside her dreams of a family? He felt so good, so warm and inviting. Yes, she could sacrifice everything for the moment. She could, she would, yes, yes....

Davis. The thought of her son thrust through the wash of emotion like a rocky outcropping, and she slammed into it head-on. She'd forgotten for a moment what her involvement with Spencer could do to Davis. He was so young, so trusting, so defenceless against hurt.

Her blood cooled. Her eyes opened. She pushed on Spencer's shoulders, clumsily trying to move him off her.

"Meg?" Spencer sounded bewildered, confused.

"I can't do this, Spencer." Another meteorite blazed across the sky and was gone. Tears threatened to spill, but she blinked them back as she struggled to a sitting position. She would not cry over Spencer. Never again. "I can't make love to you one month and wave goodbye to you the next."

"I guess I got carried away," he said quietly. "It's too easy to do with you. I should have known—I *did* know—a physical relationship wouldn't be enough for you."

"Is it enough for you?" she asked resentfully. "Is sex all you want out of a relationship?"

"No." He sat up and pushed his hands through his hair. "I want all the things *you* want—warmth, companionship, tenderness. I just can't give them in return. At least, not for long term."

Her heart bruised and aching, Meg struggled out of the sleeping bag. "I've had enough. Please take me home."

WHEN SPENCER DROPPED Meg off, he walked her to the door but didn't ask if he could come in. Nor did she invite him. They were numb, like people whose emotions have taken such a beating they can't feel any more. And because they couldn't feel, they couldn't talk.

Heading back to Sooke, he rolled down the windows and let the cool night air flow through the Camaro. Soft jazz drifted from the speakers and disappeared into the blackness outside as he followed the curves of the road, his headlights alternately illuminating dense stands of trees or the pale sides of cottages, ghostlike in the night.

Make it look as if he's doing you a favor. The image of Meg's face, compassionate and understanding, appeared in the blackness before him. He'd forgotten what it was like to have someone to talk to. Someone close. He'd locked those memories away when he'd left Victoria as surely as he'd locked the door to the cottage.

The cottage. Ray was no dummy, but what did it hurt to try?

The light was still on in the living room, and when Spencer pushed through the front door, Ray was sitting on the couch, hunched over the coffee table, playing solitaire. Spencer tried to imagine Ray dyeing his hair, and failed.

"Hey, Spence," Ray said, looking up from his handful of cards. His words were slurred. "Howya doin'? How's Meg?"

"She's fine. Sends her regards." Spencer sank into the rocker opposite the couch and gazed at his father with a sick feeling in his stomach. A grimy highball glass stood at Ray's elbow next to a half-empty bottle of Jack Daniel's. His father wasn't a serious drinker. Whatever he was going through must be bad. "Winning?"

"Nah, I never win at this game." Ray took a swig of his drink then scooped up the cards and began to reshuffle them.

Spencer cleared his throat. "I've got a favor to ask…Dad."

"'Dad,' eh? You buttering me up for somethin' big?" Ray began to lay out the cards in long uneven rows.

"You've got an ace there," Spencer pointed out. "Yes, it's pretty big. I hope you'll help me out."

"Yeah, yeah, enough foreplay, cut to the chase."
Ray moved the ace of diamonds to the top.

"You know I'll be working at the university for a
while."

"I thought you were finished at Christmas." Ray
rearranged cards, stacking red on black and vice
versa.

"If Doc were to take early retirement, I might be
offered the position on a permanent basis. So I could
use a permanent address." It was totally unlikely Doc
would give up research, but Ray didn't know that.

"The cottage," Ray suggested, scanning the rows
of cards.

"Now there's an idea!" Spencer exclaimed, deliberately misinterpreting. "If I could buy the cottage
off you, I'd always have a place to go."

Ray's bleary eyes suddenly focused sharply.
"You've always been able to come here whenever
you want. Nothin's changed."

"I'd like it in my own name."

"You tryin' to kick me out of my own house?"

"Hell, no, Ray. This would still be your home
whenever you like, for as long as you like. In fact, if
I end up in Norway for a year or so, you could caretake the place for me. I'd even pay you to do it."

Too late Spencer realized his mistake. He saw com-
prehension dawn in Ray's eyes and kicked himself
for trying to be too clever.

Ray shook his head and went back to flipping
cards. "You almost had me going there. How are you
gonna go to Norway if you've got this permanent
position here, eh? This house has sat empty on and
off for years. It doesn't need a caretaker. It needs a
demolition crew."

"Let me buy half, at least. Get a toehold in the real estate market."

Ray leaned against the back of the couch and spread his hands. "You blew it, Spence, admit it. What would you want with half of an old dump like this? If you *were* going to buy a house—which I don't believe for a second—you'd be better off buying something on the outskirts of Victoria, maybe out on Saanich Peninsula, with a bit of land attached."

"I don't want a house—" Spencer broke off at his father's cackle of laughter. He jumped to his feet in frustration. "Goddamn it, Ray. Why won't you let me help you?"

"Because I don't know what the hell I'm doing with my life besides pissing it down the toilet. When I figure it out, I'll take your money. Maybe. But definitely not before."

Spencer gave up and stalked into the kitchen to tackle the pile of dirty dishes in the sink. How could he fix Ray's problems when he couldn't fix his own? He hadn't been prepared for all the relationship issues he'd had to face since coming back to Victoria. His father. Meg.

His feelings for Meg were surfacing, gathering intensity and force, like a wave building as it approached shore. He was afraid of hurting her again. Afraid, too, of his own pain and loss when he left. He contemplated confiding in Ray and immediately dismissed the idea. Their roles had reversed as Ray became more childlike in his irresponsibility and dependence.

Dispirited and heartsore, Spencer plunged his hands into the hot soapy water. Where was his free-and-easy life-style now?

CHAPTER SEVEN

MEG SILENTLY TAPPED the arms of the guest chair in Spencer's office as she waited, nervous and impatient, while he read through her project design. Her professional future was riding on this project, and although she almost hated to admit it, she admired Spencer so much as a scientist she wanted his approval.

Finally he finished scanning the last page and glanced up. "Looks good, Meg. The background is well-researched, your statistical tests are sound and your overall hypothesis is both realistic and adventurous. Doc would be very impressed."

The warmth in his dark green eyes told her *he* was impressed, and somehow that meant even more than Doc's opinion. Their personal relationship aside, working with Spencer would be rewarding and exciting. "Thanks. And thanks for your help."

The phone rang and Spencer picked it up. Meg started to leave, but he motioned to her to stay.

"Damn," he said after a moment on the phone. "When will she be ready to sail again?" The answer he received brought another mild curse to his lips. "Okay," he said, resigned, "put us down for the next available two-day slot."

"Bad news," he said, hanging up and swiveling around to face her. "The *Cape Beale* ran aground on her last trip out. She has a hole in her hull that's going to take some weeks to repair.''

"Oh, no!" Meg sank back into the guest chair. "There goes our field trip this weekend.''

"It is a setback," Spencer admitted. "You need to get at least two trips in before the killer whales disappear for the winter.''

They gazed at each other, knowing without saying, that the killer whales' behavior was not the only factor. The New Year would see the departure of Spencer and the return of Doc, who might not have the physical stamina to do fieldwork.

Meg slapped the arm of her chair in frustration. "What am I going to do? Kayaks are no good. We can't keep up with the whales or take along the directional hydrophone I'll need to isolate Takush and her calf's calls.... Wait a minute. I'll ask my father to take us in his boat.''

Spencer's face shut down. "I guess that could work. I'll go over the operation of the hydrophones with you again before your trip.''

"Oh, no, you don't," Meg said. "You can't bail out on me. I've never used this equipment.''

"Lee has. I'm sure he'd welcome the chance to go along.''

"Lee can come if he wants, but *you're* the expert. *And* you're my supervisor. You *have* to come.''

"Roger would not welcome me on board, and frankly, I don't need the kind of crap he dishes out. You'll be fine on your own.''

"You said yourself my opportunities to get this data are limited," she argued. "Besides, the only way to overcome my father's antipathy is for him to get to know you. So he can see what kind of a person you really are.''

''Your father already knows what kind of person I am. In what matters to him, at any rate. I'll never be rich. I'll never be stable—''

Meg's fists clenched in her lap. Sometimes men could be so damn stupid. ''We're not discussing *marriage*. This is my thesis we're talking about. Daddy will understand he has to set aside personal prejudices. I don't see why you can't do the same.''

Bristling at the challenge, Spencer spun away to the window. ''You're right,'' he said, turning back after a minute. ''I apologize. I was letting personal factors influence my behavior. You've got a thesis to research and it's my job to help you.''

''Damn right it is.'' Then she smiled. ''But thanks.''

''I'VE TOLD YOU before, Meggie, Spencer Valiella is not welcome on my property and that includes my boat!'' Roger stood with his back to the fireplace. One hand was tucked into the pocket of his gray cardigan, the other swirled his crystal highball glass, setting the ice to an angry tinkling.

Meg leaned forward in her favorite wing chair, her glass of sherry forgotten on the antique mahogany side table. ''Please, Daddy, be reasonable. Spencer doesn't like you any more than you like him, but at least he's willing to give it a try.''

Outrage lifted her father's eyebrows. ''*He* doesn't like *me*? How dare that—''

''Roger, dear, I think you should reconsider,'' Helen said, much to Meg's surprise. Helen had been standing to one side, cool and aloof as an orchid in pale green linen, every hair in her golden chignon in place. Now she stepped between them. "Margaret's waited a long time to go back to school. Look how she's had to live for the past seven years. Do you want that to go on indefinitely? I think we should support her efforts to regain an acceptable life-style."

Meg sighed. Even when her mother was supposedly on her side, Helen still managed to make her feel like a failure. And both of them were treating her as if she was twenty-eight going on twelve.

"I'm sorry I asked," she said. Rising to her feet, she grabbed her jacket from the back of the chair. "I'd better go."

"Roger!" Helen commanded action from her husband.

Roger glared at Helen. Meg started for the door.

"Oh, all right, Meggie," he said, resigned and resentful. "I'll take you and Spencer out on the boat."

She paused. "Promise you'll try to get along with him?"

"I'll try. But when are you going to tell him about Davis?"

"What? You agreed I shouldn't tell him."

"I've thought about it and changed my mind," Roger said, setting his glass on the mantelpiece. "He's making good money as a university professor. There's no reason he can't support his family. He should take responsibility for his son. Maybe pay a few bills."

"She doesn't need his money," Helen interjected sharply. "If she and Davis need cash, she can always take what *we've* offered. If she needs a place to stay, she can always come home."

The long, windowed room suddenly felt stifling in

the afternoon heat of the Indian summer. Her mother meant well. Meg *had* to believe that. Maybe it was time to put her to the test.

"I appreciate your concern, Mother, but we're doing okay, honestly." She paused. "I do need a favor from you, though."

"Anything, darling."

"Could you look after Davis for the weekend while I'm on the boat? Patrick can take him on Saturday, but Sunday he's busy."

A panoply of emotions struggled for dominance on her mother's patrician features. Reluctance to caretake the unmanageable Davis conflicted with her repugnance at letting her grandson fall into the clutches of someone she viewed as an immoral freak. If Helen's extreme prejudices weren't so hurtful, they'd almost be funny, Meg thought.

"You can't let him stay with Patrick overnight," Helen said at last. "He'll have to come here for the whole weekend."

Meg didn't waste time telling her mother there was as much chance of Patrick doing anything inappropriate with Davis as there was of Roger abusing little girls; in other words, zero. She'd tried educating Helen in the past and gotten nowhere. Besides, she was too grateful for her mother's offer to question the motivation behind it.

"Thanks, Mother," she said, crossing to the unyielding Helen to give her a hug. "Davis will be so excited."

"Before he comes you've got to tell him not to run in the house. He won't listen to a word *I* say. The last time he stayed here overnight he broke a very expensive antique vase in the dining room."

"That was three years ago," Meg protested. It was also the last time Davis had been allowed anywhere in the house but the family room and the kitchen. And if Davis didn't listen to Helen, it was because everything she said to him was an order. Davis didn't take kindly to orders from strangers. Meg sighed and hoped the weekend wouldn't be a total disaster.

She went over to hug her father. "Thank you, Daddy."

"Anything for you, sweetheart. But Valiella had better watch his step." His face set in grim lines, Roger left the room.

Helen touched Meg's arm in an uncharacteristically sympathetic gesture. "He doesn't want to be mad at *you,* Meggie, for not legitimizing his grandson. But he has to blame someone."

AT DAWN the following Saturday, Meg pushed a wheelbarrow loaded with supplies onto the wharf at the Oak Bay marina. The cool air was tangy with salt, and the coming day beckoned her the way a summer morning calls to a child. Her barrow rumbled over wooden planks to the faint clang of stays on masts as sailboats bobbed in the gentle breeze.

At the end of the wharf, *Helen of Troy,* her father's fifty-foot cabin cruiser—a 1930's fishing boat converted to luxury—gleamed in the first shafts of sunlight. Roger waved to her from the deck, then disappeared below. A second later she heard the low thrum of the big diesel engine.

Meg increased her pace, weaving between buckets and coiled ropes littering the wharf. She worried about Davis, who'd clung to her when she'd left him with Helen. His shyness could quickly turn to defiance unless handled with a sensitivity she feared her mother lacked. *He'll be all right,* she assured herself. Davis was in one of his "good" phases. If Helen gave him half a chance, his engaging personality would win her over.

Meg set the wheelbarrow down beside the boat as Roger stepped out of the cabin. The wire guardrails were down and a wooden step allowed access to the deck. Meg passed her things up to her father—a backpack with a couple of changes of clothes, a duffel bag containing her diving gear and a box of food. She'd stayed up last night baking chocolate-chip cookies—both Spencer's and her father's favorite. It was not bribery, simply a preemptive peace-keeping measure.

"Has Spencer arrived yet?" she asked, handing up the box.

Roger's thick eyebrows pulled together. "No. But he'd better show up soon or we'll leave without him. I said seven o'clock on the dot. We have to cast off before the tide turns."

"He'll be here," Meg said, climbing aboard. They couldn't leave without Spencer; he had the hydrophone equipment. She put her backpack in one of the berths, stowed the food in the galley, then went back up to the gate to wait for Spencer.

At five minutes past seven, his black Camaro swung into the parking lot and pulled up beside her Toyota. He emerged from the car and stretched his arms over his head, glancing around at the marina before flashing her a wide grin. His hair was unkempt, his jaw unshaven, and he looked gorgeous. She realized then how much she'd been looking forward to this weekend and spending time with him. She must have a self-destructive streak in her somewhere.

"You're late," she said as she wheeled the barrow over.

"Morning, princess." He lifted her long braid and tickled her under the chin with it.

"Daddy's champing at the bit," she said, ignoring the teasing gleam in his eye. "This weekend is going to be difficult enough without deliberately flaunting orders."

"I've been a bad boy already, have I?"

She stopped beside the closed trunk of his car and waited silently for him to come and open it.

His grin faded as he stepped to the rear of the car. "There was an accident on the highway."

"Oh, dear." She should have known it was something unavoidable. Spencer might give the impression he was above mundane things such as being on time, but he wouldn't be late without a good reason. "Was anybody hurt?"

"Don't know. The ambulances had just arrived." Spencer unlocked the trunk and loaded her barrow with his gear. "Lee isn't coming—he's got a bad cold and wouldn't be able to dive, anyway." He slammed the trunk shut. "Come on. We'd better get moving before the tide changes."

Spencer slung his duffel bag over his shoulder and picked up the poles that would support the directional hydrophone. Meg trundled the barrow back down the wharf. Spencer and her father *should* get along; they both loved boating and the sea. Unfortunately they both liked to be captains of their own ship.

"Morning, Roger," Spencer said, his voice stiff but respectful. "Good of you to help us out."

On the deck above, Roger stood with arms akimbo and issued a thinly veiled warning. "I'll do what-

ever's necessary to ensure my daughter's welfare—
academic or otherwise.''

Spencer nodded curtly and began loading the electronic equipment on board. Meg glared at her father.
This was going to be a long two days.

With Roger at the wheel on the flying bridge, they
motored out of the harbor. During the journey toward
Saltspring Island, Spencer and Meg assembled the directional hydrophone inside its parabolic dish, which
would concentrate the sound of the killer whales. Using it and the attached headphones, they'd be able to
locate the whales from many miles away.

Meg noticed an extra hydrophone encased in sili-
cone. ''What's that for?''

''Doc asked me to check the unit he set up in Trincomali Channel this summer. It's stopped broadcasting and needs to be replaced. That's why I asked you
to bring your diving gear.''

''And here I thought you just wanted to collect
abalone for dinner.'' She grinned and ducked his
playful cuff of her shoulder. ''I wish we could dive
with the killer whales.''

''It would be great, wouldn't it? But they get irri-
tated by the noise of the bubbles escaping from reg-
ulators. I'm sure you wouldn't want to drive them
away from the area.''

''Definitely not.'' Meg rose to her feet and scanned
the water. They were between Saltspring and Pender
islands, just about to turn up Trincomali Channel. ''I
hope we find them soon.''

Around noon she made sandwiches and coffee,
then left the plate with Spencer and ran up the gangway to the flying bridge. Roger stood with his legs
wide, bracing himself against the rocking motion of

the boat on the light chop. Behind his sunglasses, beneath the bill of his fishing cap, Roger was frowning and his jaw was set. Oh, dear. Daddy had a tendency to brood and he'd been up here on his own for hours.

"Do you want me to take the wheel while you eat?" she yelled over the roar of the engine and the whistle of the wind.

"Have you told Spencer about Davis yet?" he shouted back.

Meg pulled a long strand of blond hair off her face. "We're working—this isn't the time or place. Ham and Swiss cheese, or chicken and avocado?"

"Ham and cheese—you know avocado gives me hives." He took one hand off the wheel to jab a finger in her direction. "Because if you won't tell him, I will."

"Daddy, you can't! I agree he has a right to know and I plan on telling him, but—"

"I don't give a damn about his rights," Roger countered forcefully. "The man's got to live up to his obligations. You and Davis are struggling to make ends meet while Valiella's jaunting around the world doing whatever the hell he wants."

Meg glanced over her shoulder and her heart leaped into her throat. Sandwich plate in hand, Spencer was leaning against the stern railing, gazing up at them. Had he heard what her father had said? But no, eyebrows raised, he was holding up the plate. Breathing out, she smiled and held up a finger. Just a minute.

"We can't talk about this now," she said to Roger, speaking firmly. "And *you* are not going to tell Spencer *anything!* When the time is right, *I'll* do it. In the meantime I'd appreciate it if you'd try to be civil."

"I can't help it. Every time I look at him I see Davis."

"Don't think about it." Easier said than done, as she well knew. "Why don't I take the wheel? You go get something to eat."

Roger glanced down at the deck where Spencer was still eating, and a calculating look came into his eyes.

"On second thought," Meg said, "why don't I send Spencer up and you and I can go over the charts while we have lunch?" This weekend was going to be a logistical nightmare if she couldn't leave the two of them alone together.

Roger agreed and she skimmed back down the gangway to find Spencer finishing off the last ham-and-cheese sandwich.

"Everything okay?" he asked.

She smiled wearily and took the plate. "Just peachy-keen."

Spencer grabbed his cup of coffee and a handful of cookies and headed up to the flying bridge. He paused, one step up the ladder. "You don't have to run interference for Roger and me. We're big boys—we'll work it out."

"Yeah, sure."

Stepping back, she watched the interaction between her father and Spencer. Roger was pointing to the gimbaled compass installed next to the wheel, and Meg knew he was explaining in excruciating detail what course they were on and what would happen if Spencer deviated from it. Spencer stood at a distance, nodding stiffly.

Shaking her head, she ducked through the sliding doors to make her father a fresh sandwich.

Roger came in a minute later and took the plate she held out to him. "So what's your plan of attack?" he asked around a bite of ham-and-Swiss-cheese-on-rye.

Meg poured two cups of coffee and explained to Roger what she and Spencer had discussed. "Once we locate the pod, we'll need you to cruise parallel to the whales while we lower the hydrophone."

"How far away?"

"That's the tricky part. The killer whales don't like motor noise, plus the sound can interfere with the recordings. We need to stay as far away as possible while still being able to observe their behavior. If possible I'd like to get Takush and her calf on their own so I can distinguish their calls from those of the other whales. The computer can do that in the lab, but I'd like to hear it with my own ears."

Roger swallowed, took a sip of coffee. "What are you going to do with this information?"

"If I can prove a correlation between specific call types and killer whale behavior, it will allow me to speculate on the meaning of their communications. Simple, really."

Roger nodded seriously.

"*Not,*" she exclaimed, laughing. "It would be fantastic to know what they were saying, but actually doing so is a pretty tall order."

"Well, Meggie, if anyone can do it, you can."

Meg smiled at her father's faith in her. Unrealistic but heartwarming, nevertheless. "If nothing else, I'll be able to report on mother-calf interactions. I think that alone is pretty significant."

She set down her coffee. "I'd better get out there with the headphones and listen for the whales."

Out on deck Roger squinted at the sky. A freshening breeze had blown thin clouds into long corrugated streaks. "'Fish scales and mare's tails,'" he quoted. "A storm's coming. But it's not supposed to blow hard till tomorrow afternoon. Let's hope the weather holds till you can collect your data."

Meg shifted uneasily, taking note of the swell beneath the boat. "Yeah."

"I'd better get back to the bridge," Roger said. "Navigating the currents at the entrance to Trincomali can be tricky."

And you can't trust Spencer to do it right. She would *not* react to the unspoken criticism. If she took offense at every slight, real or imagined, on Spencer's behalf—and on her father's—she'd spend the next two days in a state of anxiety. She'd looked forward to this trip too long to ruin it.

She went to the bow of the boat where the directional hydrophone was set up while Roger went back to the flying bridge to relieve Spencer. A few minutes later Spencer appeared beside her, a well-worn chart in his hand. "See that rocky point?" he said, directing her gaze to the coast of Galiano Island. "That's where we'll be diving tomorrow."

Meg took off the headphones to squint along Spencer's arm. His other hand rested gently on her lower back, his thigh brushed the back of her leg. She could feel the warmth of his body in contrast to the chill where the wind blew. "That's something else I haven't done for seven years."

"Diving? Are you worried? I can go down alone."

"Of course I'm not worried. I can't wait. Besides, you know it's not safe to dive alone." She slipped the headphones back over her ears. "I'd better keep listening."

Five hours later and there was still no sight or sound of the whales. Meg was tired and discouraged and beginning to think the whole effort was a waste of time. They'd circumnavigated Galiano Island and were heading back up the channel. The afternoon was turning to evening and before long they'd have to head for port.

"It can take up to twenty hours to locate a pod," Spencer said, resting a hand lightly on her slumped shoulder. "We were really lucky that day in the kayaks."

"Sure." She smiled wanly. "There's always tomorrow."

"I'll go make some coffee," he said.

He was squeezing down the narrow bit of deck beside the cabin when Meg heard the sound.

"Wait!" she shouted. A whale call, faint but clear, sounded in her ears. *Weeeoaw.* It sent a chill down her spine. Excitedly she motioned to Spencer to come back, and pulled off the headphones to let him listen.

"That's Kitasu's pod," he said after a minute.

"Are you sure?"

"I've listened to hundreds of hours of tapes of these whales. I'm sure." He handed the headphones back to Meg and loosened the lashings on the pole supporting the directional hydrophone. Slowly he moved the parabolic disk in a circle, scanning the horizon, his eyes watching for Meg's reaction.

"Stop!" she exclaimed, pointing to a spot in the distance to the right of the boat. "The calls are coming from over there."

"Roger," Spencer shouted up to the bridge.

"Killer whales off the port bow. Change heading to nor-northeast."

Roger scowled. Clearly he disliked being directed by Spencer. But a second later the boat began to change course and pick up speed.

They soon caught up with the pod, a breathtaking row of tall black fins rising from the waves. Now their calls and whistles could be heard without the aid of the directional hydrophone.

Roger motored alongside the pod and slowed to match their pace, staying a discreet distance away. Meg lowered the hydrophone into the water from the port side. Then she went to the bow and trained her binoculars on the black-and-white shapes. The whales had spread out across half the channel and were moving north at about eight knots.

"Spencer, look," she called. "Isn't that Takush and her calf near the back?" She'd studied Spencer's and Doc's photos until she could pick out the individual whales.

Spencer looked through his own binoculars. "You're right. They're lagging behind. Maybe the calf can't keep up."

"Poor thing—but that's great for us. Turn the dish toward them so we can pick up their calls."

"Aye, aye, Cap'n."

They stayed with the whales for well over an hour. Meg's fatigue vanished. She wrote down her observations and took dozens of photos, thrilled to be getting useful data for her thesis.

"Did you see?" she said to Spencer as she changed the tape in the recorder. "I got that whole exchange between Takush and her calf. It was just like they were talking."

"How could I miss it?" Spencer asked, grinning. "You homed in on them like a reporter at a political rally."

"I did not!" She jabbed him good-naturedly with her elbow.

Spencer responded by pulling her close, a gleam in his eyes. "I'm not going to get heavy, I promise. Just a kiss."

Meg's gaze darted to the flying bridge—her father was gazing dead ahead—then dropped to Spencer's mouth. The stubbled jaw, his sensual lips were coming closer—

"Hey, you two," Roger shouted from above. "What's going on?"

Meg jerked back guiltily. Then realized he was talking about the killer whales. They were moving quickly away from the area, and their long whistles and pulsed calls had given way to a series of rapid clicks.

"Looks like they're chasing something, possibly a school of salmon," Spencer said.

"I'll tell Dad." Meg ran up the gangway to the flying bridge. "We think they're after salmon," she said to Roger, shading her eyes from the salt spray as she gazed ahead. The killer whales' dark torpedo-like shapes could be seen speeding through the water below the surface.

Roger pushed on the throttle to increase their speed, then stepped away from the wheel. "Here, Meg, you steer for a minute."

Meg slid in beside him and took the wheel. Roger disappeared below. A few minutes later she glanced sternward and grinned. He was rigging a fishing line off the back of the boat.

The killer whales' high-speed chase took the *Helen of Troy* out of the channel and zigzagging northward across Georgia Strait. As the lights of West Vancouver were winking on to starboard, Meg and Spencer pulled in the hydrophone gear and went up to the flying bridge.

"Look!" Meg shouted, pointing.

They were on a collision course with a B.C. ferry. The huge white ship with the blue-and-red stripes on its hull bore down on their port bow as it made for dock at Horseshoe Bay.

Roger pulled back on the throttle and slowed to a rocking halt in the four-foot waves. The ferry slowed, too, to allow the killer whales to pass. Passengers crowded the outer decks, pointing and shouting as the pod raced past the bow. Then slowly the ship gathered speed again and moved on.

Roger cut across the ferry's wake, but he could only go so fast through the lines of choppy waves. Dead ahead through the falling dusk was the mist-shrouded tip of the Sechelt Peninsula; to starboard lay Howe Sound; to port, Georgia Strait stretched northward. The whales could no longer be seen, even through binoculars.

"Which way?" Meg wondered aloud.

"We've lost them," Roger declared.

"Damn," Spencer said.

Roger handed the wheel to Meg again and went below to check his fishing line. Spencer put an arm around Meg in a quick hug. "Don't worry. We'll find them again tomorrow."

She shrugged and gave him a half smile. They both knew that by morning the killer whales could be many miles away, out of range of their tracking device. It could take all day to locate the pod again. If they ever did.

"Hoo-wee, boy! Look at this baby!" Roger's shout rose above the keening wind as he pulled a huge silver fish, flopping and twisting, over the transom.

"WHAT WOULD BE really interesting to know," Spencer mused over his third piece of grilled salmon, "is who the father of Takush's calf is and what pod he belongs to. No one knows exactly where and when killer whales get together to mate, only that when it's over, the males return to their maternal groups rather than staying with the female."

Roger directed a dark glance across the table to Spencer. "Seems a funny system, all right, when the father doesn't take responsibility for his offspring."

They were docked at the government wharf in Horseshoe Bay, sheltered from the worst of the weather. Even so, waves rocked the boat, and the rubber fenders protecting the hull from the pilings squealed in protest.

Meg glanced nervously from her father to Spencer, recalling that Roger hadn't actually promised not to say anything about Davis. As dinner progressed, his hints had become broader and more hostile.

"Killer whales are highly intelligent creatures, but it's not fair to impose human values on their behavior," Spencer replied, seemingly oblivious to Roger's innuendo.

Or *was* he oblivious? Meg wondered. Spencer had a talent for knowing exactly what buttons to push. Roger had been ordering him around ever since he'd come aboard this morning, and she knew Spencer must be chafing under such a blatant assumption of authority. He'd restrained himself so far, but the two men were pushing each other toward a showdown.

"Want some more salmon, Daddy?" she asked passing the plate across to him. "It sure is good."

Roger leaned back in his chair, holding his stomach. "Couldn't eat another bite. Though I might find room for one of your cookies." He turned to glare at Spencer. "If killer whales are so smart, how come the males don't stay with the pod to protect them?"

"Killer whales' only enemy is man," Spencer replied. "What could a male do to protect his pod from a shotgun? Or a tranquilizer gun?"

"They could try to do *some*thing," Roger maintained stubbornly, taking a cookie from the plate Meg held out.

"Daddy, don't you think you're being a little unreasonable?"

Spencer leaned forward. "Yes, Roger. Why does this bother you so much?"

Meg thrust the cookies under Spencer's nose, smiled sweetly at him and kicked him under the table.

"Ow," he protested, and gave her a bewildered look. To Roger he said, "It's an interesting topic, certainly. When I go to Norway my research will focus on interpod mating behavior."

"You mean *if* you go, don't you?" Meg cut in. "You haven't actually been accepted yet, have you?"

"As a matter of fact, I have," Spencer said, avoiding her eyes. "I got the letter yesterday and didn't have a chance to tell you." He took a sip of his beer and began to talk enthusiastically. "I'll be looking at some of the questions I raised earlier like, how long do the males spend with their mates? Where do they go afterward? Do they mate with the same female the next year, or do they choose another, from another pod?''

Meg felt the sinking feeling she'd known seven years ago when she'd called him in Seattle and he'd talked so eagerly of Stanford. She couldn't blame him for his plans; it's what she'd want to do herself if she could. But seeing his face in the soft light of the wall lamp, she realized she'd been hoping against hope he would decide to stay, whether or not he was accepted in Norway.

As Spencer wound down his discourse, Roger emitted a low growl. His face was flushed and veins stood out in his temples. ''It's perfectly obvious what the males do,'' he ground out. ''They get the female knocked up, then bugger off to *wherever*, to do *whatever* takes their fancy. Never giving *her*, or the baby, another thought.''

Spencer sat up straighter and pushed a hand through his untidy hair. ''I think I see where you're coming from. It's natural to feel anger at the jerk who left your daughter to bring up their child alone. If I knew who he was, I'd give him a piece of my mind, as well. But frankly, Roger, I don't think it's fair to project your feelings about him onto the killer whales.''

Roger rose with a strangled cry. ''I'm going to project *you* right into outer space!''

''Daddy!'' Meg jumped to her feet and clutched his arm.

He shook her off and took a step toward Spencer. ''You—''

''*Daddy!*'' Her cry was half plea, half threat as she moved between the two men.

Roger shut his mouth. With a final hate-filled

glance at Spencer, whose eyes were wide with stunned disbelief, he strode across the cabin and disappeared into his berth.

Dizzy with relief and sick with anxiety, Meg sank into her chair and put her head in her hands. She couldn't look at Spencer.

A moment later she felt his hand on her shoulder.

"Meg," he said in a low voice, gently tugging her hand away from her face, exposing her to his piercing gaze. "Does your father know something I don't know?"

She had to tell him. But she couldn't. He was going away. He hadn't stuck around on her account the last time. Why would he do so now? Besides, she didn't want to use Davis to hold him. And she was so confused she wasn't sure what was best for her son anymore.

"No, of course not," she said, dashing the moisture from her eyes. "He's just on edge."

"You'd tell me if there was something I should know, wouldn't you?" he persisted, still gripping her wrist.

Meg gazed at him in misery. The thought of being a father frightened him so badly he couldn't even speak the words.

"Honestly," she lied in a hoarse whisper. "There's nothing you need to know."

CHAPTER EIGHT

RED SKY AT NIGHT, sailor's delight. Red in morning, sailor take warning.

Protected against the wind by his wetsuit, Spencer studied the thick dark clouds obscuring the sky. A sky that this morning had dawned blood-red. A storm was brewing and it wasn't far off.

All morning they'd searched for the pod without success. Now, with time running out, they'd returned to Trincomali Channel to replace the faulty hydrophone before making the trip back to Victoria. It was too deep to anchor, so Roger was forced to motor slowly in tight circles while Spencer and Meg donned wetsuits and prepared to dive.

"You can't go down there. It's too rough," Roger yelled, his words spun into ragged wisps and blown overboard by the wind. Salt spray beaded his face.

Spencer ignored him and helped Meg ready the scuba tanks. Conditions were marginal, he had to admit. The swell tossed the boat as if it were a child's toy, and the wind, which had backed around to the north, ripped at the red-and-white dive flag on the stern of the boat. He'd dived in worse and so had Meg, but for her that was seven years ago. And this morning she looked in no condition to dive. The dark circles beneath her eyes spoke of a sleepless night. As she struggled on with her wetsuit, she met his gaze, then quickly turned away. Something gnawed at her, something very upsetting. Was it about Norway?

Or was it...

He let the thought fly away on the gusting wind. Vague guilt pressed on him. Clasping Meg's shoulder to get her attention, he said, "I'll go down by myself."

She flashed him a grim glance and added a five-pound chunk of lead to her weight belt. "Like hell you will."

"It's my responsibility, not yours."

"Never dive alone. *You* drilled that into me."

"How much weight have you got there?"

"Enough, I hope. I have a hard time staying down at shallow depths, especially with the surge tossing me around. If I have to work to maintain depth, I'll use up a lot more air."

He frowned as she added another two-pound weight. "Don't overdo it. You get too deep, and the weight of the water and all that lead will pull you straight to the bottom."

"*Yes,* Dr. Valiella. That's why I wear a buoyancy compensator." She twisted the weight-belt strap on itself to secure it before threading it through the slot on the last weight. Then with a grunt, she hoisted thirty pounds of lead around her waist.

"Meg..." He gripped her arms, willing her to look at him, though he hardly knew what he wanted to say, only that it wasn't about the dive. As she raised her eyes to his, Spencer felt Roger's hand reach from behind and tighten around his shoulder.

Roger's face was a black scowling mask. "You can

break your fool neck for all I care, Valiella. But if anything happens to Meg, so help me, I'll—''

''For God's sake,'' Meg said, glaring at her father as she twisted out of Spencer's grip. ''There's enough testosterone here to fill a Spanish bull ring. Back off, both of you.''

She perched on the edge of the cockpit to shrug the straps of her scuba tank over her shoulders. Then she rose to her feet, staggering on the listing deck to cinch the straps tight and clasp the waistband.

Spencer hoisted his own scuba tank over his shoulders. The sooner they got this over with, the sooner he could get back to Victoria and off this boat.

Meg was already sitting on the edge of the boat, hand holding her mask and regulator in place, ready to enter the water. Suddenly she took the reg out of her mouth and pointed across the cockpit. ''Look! Killer whales!''

Spencer turned. About half a mile distant a great black shape leaped from the white-tipped waves and fell back down with an almighty splash. It could be Kitasu's pod, but he wasn't sure; only three dorsal fins were visible. From this distance it wouldn't be surprising if they didn't see the calf. But where was the fourth adult whale?

He glanced at Meg and motioned her to lift her hood away from her ear so she could hear. ''If we don't do the dive, we could probably get more recordings,'' he shouted over the wind. ''But if we do the dive, we'll almost certainly lose the opportunity.''

''But Doc's hydrophone...''

''It's important, but so is your thesis. Your research is the main purpose of this trip. It's your call.'' She looked so weary at the thought of having to make a decision he almost wished he hadn't felt obliged to give her the option.

"Let's dive," she said at last. "We're pretty far away from the whales. Maybe they won't leave, or if they do, we might be able to find them again."

"Okay. When we get down, stick close. Visibility will be poor, and the hydrophone is located on an underwater cliff face."

He reached for the net bag containing the replacement hydrophone assembly and clipped it to his belt, then attached the hose connecting the air tank to his buoyancy compensator and checked that it was working. Depth control on this dive was going to be tricky for him, as well.

Feeling vaguely uneasy, he swung on his weight belt and sat to ease his fins over his diving boots. Roger watched and his angry frown seemed an extension of the brewing storm. Spencer could understand his concern for Meg; he was worried about her, too, though he had more faith in Meg's ability than her father apparently did.

Spencer pulled on his hood and mask and took his place beside Meg. Just before he inserted the regulator into his mouth, he shouted to Roger, "I'll watch out for her."

Roger didn't appear to be reassured, if the purple hue his face was turning was anything to go by.

"Why should I trust you with my daughter? You don't even take care of your own son!"

Spencer watched Roger's lips move and wondered what he was shouting now. But with a quarter inch of neoprene over his ears and the wind whistling around his head, he couldn't hear a thing. With a careless shrug, he waved farewell. Then he nodded at

Meg and over they went, somersaulting backward into the trough of a wave.

The swell rolled them around in a circle as the wave passed through the water column. Cold seeped down the neck of Spencer's wetsuit. Bubbles swarmed around his head. His breath, given a mechanical sound by the regulator, rasped in his ears.

He twisted in the water to face Meg. Holding her gaze, he made the ''Okay?'' signal with thumb and forefinger. She nodded and returned the signal. Spencer took her hand and kicked hard, pulling them down, down below the clutches of the surge.

At thirty feet they leveled out and battled through the turbulent water toward the shore. Spencer glanced at his compass every few seconds. The eerie calls of the distant killer whales seemed to surround them, disorienting him. Visibility was limited to fifteen feet, and below them the dark water stretched fathoms deep. At his side, Meg was working hard to stay level. Too much weight, he thought as she injected another burst of air into her buoyancy compensator. His sense of unease intensified.

Suddenly the rock face and the hydrophone station loomed out of the murk. His relief at finding it quickly was overshadowed by a sudden burst of intense staccato clicking. The killer whales were hunting.

Spencer took off his wetsuit mits and stuffed them into his net bag. Working as quickly as he could, he detached the broken hydrophone from the cable that led to the relay station on shore. His breath rasped louder. The clicks increased in volume, coming closer. The water roiled around him, pushing him this way and that. He lost his grip on the wrench and it slipped out of his hand. He lunged downward and snagged it before it dropped into oblivion.

Meg clung to the rocks, her weights dragging at her. Behind her mask her face was white, her brows pinched into a frown. Spencer worked feverishly, his only thought, *Get Meg back to the boat.* At last he freed the damaged hydrophone and handed it to her to hold while he installed the new one. Above the whales' clicks he could hear the putt-putt of the motor. He hoped Roger would follow their bubbles and be close by when they came up.

There, he was finished. He put his tools back in the net bag and held out his hand to Meg for the damaged hydrophone.

Without warning a wave surged over them, smashing him against the rocks and tossing Meg aside like a leaf. Spencer saw the hydrophone drop from her hand and tumble down the vertical rock face.

Silver shapes flashed by. Salmon.

He sensed the momentous rush of water even before he saw the huge black-and-white shape approaching at great speed. In the split second before the surrounding water erupted in a froth of bubbles and he was knocked sideways, he saw Meg kick away from the path of the oncoming killer whale. She seemed to be swimming through molasses. Too late. Too slow. Too deep.

Joker's flipper caught her head and shoulder as he streaked past after the salmon. The blow knocked her mask off and the regulator out of her mouth and sent her tumbling backward, downward, through the water.

Spencer gave a strangled cry around his regulator and dove, his fins flaying the water in his effort to get to Meg. She was obviously disoriented, blindly reaching for her mask, she retrieved it and put it on, instead of grasping her regulator and restoring her air supply. Bubbles rose from the sides of her mouth. She was already fifty feet down. And sinking.

Meg. Meg. Ditch the weight belt!

Instead, her legs lashed the water as she tried to halt her descent. It was futile without an injection of air into her buoyancy compensator. She seemed to have forgotten about that, too. Spencer kicked harder, his lungs straining, heart pounding. He focused his entire being on reaching her because any other thought was untenable.

She remembered her regulator at last and tried to grasp hold of the thin black tube that floated above her scuba tank. And all the time she was still sinking.

Her face tilted up. Behind her mask a wide band of white surrounded the blue of her desperate eyes.

She was suffocating. Falling and suffocating.

With every ounce of power he possessed, he churned his legs, surging down. His fingertips stretched, strained, and finally grasped the mouthpiece of her regulator.

He hauled on it, yanking Meg to him. His arm circled her waist below the tank and he started to fall with her. The skin around her eyes was white and tight. Her nostrils were pinched. Her mouth opened. No bubbles escaped. She was out of air.

He pushed the regulator into her mouth. She sucked like a starving baby taking the teat. His eyes closed. Safe. Meg was safe.

His eyes snapped open. Not safe. They were still falling, their combined weight and the weight of the water pulling them down. He reached for his depth gauge. Eighty feet, eighty-five… And no bottom in sight.

Meg was pulling on her reg as if breathing was soon to be outlawed. Spencer flicked the clasp of her weight belt and it dropped away. With a dizzying sense of relief he felt their descent slow. He pressed the valve that controlled the intake into his own buoyancy compensator and heard a hissing as air inflated the bladder. They hung in the water, going neither up nor down.

He released his grip on Meg to inflate her buoyancy compensator. Her panicked eyes darted to his and she grabbed his arm with the hand that wasn't clutching the reg to her mouth.

Air filled her buoyancy vest. Slowly they began to rise. Meg was rigid inside his encircling arm, sucking in deep breaths and holding them as long as she could. If she didn't breathe out, she was going to burst her lungs.

Spencer tapped her stomach with his knuckles. She stared at him, clearly still too spooked to release oxygen without a fight. He tapped again. No response. She was holding her breath. *Damn.* He'd almost lost her once, he wasn't taking any chances. He punched her hard in the gut.

It knocked the wind out of her. And the regulator.

Quickly he grabbed the mouthpiece and gave it back to her. She glared at him but breathed out in a cloud of bubbles that told him she'd realized her error.

He smiled around his regulator. He would have taken it out and kissed her if he hadn't been quite certain she'd sock him in the jaw if he tried to take away her air supply again.

They broke through the surface. A hard rain was falling, bouncing off the water, pelting their heads and shoulders. Spencer pushed his mask onto his forehead and pulled her into a fierce hug. "Don't scare me like that."

Her face was almost as gray as the water, but she summoned up a shaky grin. "Do we have adventures or what?"

Spencer just looked at her and shook his head. Then lifted a hand to signal Roger to come and pick them up.

MEG CLAMBERED UP the ladder attached to the stern, ahead of Spencer. Roger was waiting, the boat bobbing in neutral. "What happened down there?" he asked her anxiously. "Did you see that killer whale go by?"

Spencer hung back so Meg could tell the story her way. No doubt this would be the last time he'd be allowed on Roger's boat regardless of how the situation had unfolded. Surprisingly, Roger hadn't seemed to notice Meg's missing weight belt.

"My mask got knocked off when Joker went by," she said, blandly understating the truth. "He was chasing salmon."

Roger's searching gaze darted from Meg to Spencer and back again. "So there were no problems?"

Spencer waited. Meg glanced at him. She seemed to reach a silent decision and made a pact with him with her eyes. *It's over,* she seemed to say. *We won't rehash a disaster that didn't happen.*

"No," she said, turning back to her father. "No problems."

Spencer shed his scuba tank, then his weight belt,

feeling lighter with every pound dumped. He felt ir-
rationally, irrelevantly, victorious. Meg had aligned
herself with *him,* not her father.

But later, when Meg was dressed warmly in a fish-
erman-knit sweater and wool pants, she huddled alone
in a corner of the settee in the main cabin, sipping a
mug of steaming coffee and evading all Spencer's at-
tempts at conversation.

Outside the wind whistled relentlessly and the rain
beat against the wide, sliding-glass doors. Frustrated,
Spencer dropped his empty mug in the sink, reached
for a raincoat and went out onto the deck.

Gripping the bow rail, he stared into the driving
rain, heedless of the water sheeting off his face. The
currents that flowed between him and Meg were deep
and strong, sometimes invisible from the surface. But
currents could be treacherous to the unwary traveler;
they could take a person off course.

I'm here for a good time, not a long time. Weren't
those some of the first words he'd spoken to Meg?
Right from the beginning he'd recognized a kindred
spirit in her and it had scared him. He'd realized that
the feelings they shared would bind him despite the
differences in their backgrounds. *If* they were allowed
to grow. If, if, if.

If only they hadn't gone to Saltspring. After wanting her all year and holding himself back, he'd
walked into that weekend knowing he'd make love to
her if she let him. It had been crazy to succumb, days
within leaving. But he'd been crazy about her. She
was soft and warm and giving. Bright and smiling
and loving. He hadn't been able to resist any longer.

Those days were long ago. She'd changed. He'd
changed. What he was imagining now couldn't be

true. She would have told him. *Surely she would have told him.*

Spencer's head lifted as the boat slowed to approach the marina. On the hill above sat the Tudor-style Oak Bay Hotel, warm yellow lights glowing in the windows of the Snug.

Spencer jumped onto the wharf as Roger threw the boat into reverse and brought the stern in close. Meg tossed him the lines and he tied them securely to the bollards. Roger cut the engine and leaped off the boat, stalking past him in hostile silence. Oh, well, he was getting used to it. The irony was, he respected Roger's knowledge of boating and might have liked him under other circumstances.

Meg climbed down from the boat as Spencer wound off the last line and straightened. He thought at first she was going to walk straight past him, as well. But she stopped, her eyes bright and lips tremulous. She put her arms around his neck, laid her head on his chest and heaved a deep sigh.

His arms went around her, pulling her close. *Oh, Meg.* "It's okay. We're both okay," he murmured into her hair.

What if it was true? All these years...

Meg was *still* warm and soft and giving. But needful, too. *It's okay to need,* he wanted to say, but couldn't. Because it wasn't okay for her to need *him.* A strand of her hair fell like a whisper across the back of his hand.

She was stirring, lifting her head, when he heard voices in the distance. Her eyes were so blue. "Meg?"

"Sorry. It's been a long two days." She started to

ease away from him. "I want to thank you. You saved
my—"

"Don't say it," he broke in, tightening his embrace. "You can't know that."

With her defences stripped away he could see she
was keeping something from him. He had a sick-to-
the-stomach feeling he knew what it was. He didn't
believe she'd lie if he asked her outright.

So why don't I?

"Spencer, there's something I should—" She
broke off, anguish twisting her face.

"What, Meg? What is it?"

The wire gate at the top of the wharf clanged
against the fence, startling them. Roger had found a
wheelbarrow and was bumping down the ramp over
the strips of wood nailed across as rudimentary steps.

Meg jerked away as if she were guilty of something. Spencer let her go.

"You can start bringing out your things, Meg,"
Roger said, depositing the wheelbarrow beside the
boat. "Go on," he added when she hesitated, his stern
gaze never leaving Spencer's face.

"Go on, Meg," Spencer repeated softly. So this
was it. The showdown between the father and the
undesirable. If it wasn't so hurtful to Meg, it would
be laughable. If he wasn't halfway to agreeing with
Roger that he was wrong for her, he'd stay and fight
for the woman he loved.

When Meg had disappeared inside the boat, Roger
took a step closer to Spencer. His gray eyes looked
cold and the skin around them was strained. "I'm
going to tell you this just once, Valiella. *Stay away
from my daughter.*"

Spencer thrust his hands into his pockets and tilted

his head in an expression of bored insolence calculated to drive Roger into a frenzy of irritation. "Pretty hard to do, *sir,* when I'm supervising her honors project."

"You know what I mean. No contact outside university unless absolutely necessary."

"Meg is an adult. I wouldn't presume to tell her what she can and can't do. Or whom she can and can't see." He straightened, tired of the phony man-to-boy skit. "Look, Roger, I know you don't like me. But believe it or not, we have one thing in common— we both care about Meg."

"How dare you claim to care about Meg, you piece of sh—"

"Daddy!"

Spencer turned to see Meg standing on the boat deck, her arms full, her expression one of hurt and surprise. She dropped the duffel bag and sleeping bag in the wheelbarrow and jumped to the wharf. Stepping between Roger and Spencer, she spoke to her father in a lowered voice. "You're being ridiculous and you know it. You're going to be very embarrassed later."

"Don't bet on it. But if making a fool of myself is all it takes to keep that creep out of your life, I'll turn cartwheels on the steps of the parliament buildings."

"Stop it." She turned to Spencer and it hurt him to see her eyes awash with tears. How many times and in how many different circumstances had he been the cause of her tears?

"Never mind, Meg. I'll just get my things and go."

"But…I was going to help you take the hydrophones and the rest of the equipment back to the university."

"Don't worry about it. Stay and help your father."
Spencer started toward the boat. His gear was packed.
Just a matter of picking it up and he'd be out of here
so fast—

"Yes, Meg, you come back to the house with me,"
Roger said, his voice thick with satisfaction. "Your
mother will be worn out, and Davis will be anxious
to see you."

Spencer halted in midstride. *Davis?*

He turned back to Meg and stared at her. "Davis?"
he repeated. "Who is Davis?"

She swallowed hard, her fingers busy twisting her
braid into knots. "Davis is the name of my son." Her
voice fell to a whisper. "*Our* son."

Since last night he'd been half expecting it. But
hearing the actual words hit him like a fist to the solar
plexus. He didn't think he was breathing, and only
force of will kept him from doubling over with shock.

Him, a *father?*

He couldn't deal with the notion of having a child,
couldn't comprehend. He needed time to think....

No, he needed to talk to Meg. *Oh, God, Meg.* Her
beautiful eyes met his. Her sweet smile quivered in a
bid for control. She was gazing at him expectantly,
hopefully, trustfully.

What did he have to offer her? Nothing.

He couldn't be a father. He was only just discov-
ering what it was to be a son.

He glanced from Meg to Roger, who stood behind
her like the Wrath of God. No wonder Roger hated
him, running out on his pregnant daughter. *I didn't
know!* he wanted to shout. But that didn't alter the
fact that, child or no child, he had run out on Meg.

They'd been friends, they'd made love, then he'd dropped her cold.

He and Meg needed to talk—but not with Roger around.

Spencer stepped past Meg and picked his duffel bag off the deck. Her pleading look intensified the pain in his heart.

"Spencer…" Her voice, liquid with tears, cracked.

He loaded everything that was his into the barrow, knowing that when he unloaded it, he was going to get into his car and get the hell out of there as fast as he could.

He paused in front of Meg. "I'll call you," he said, his voice rough. He tried to convey love and regret with his eyes, but hers were blurry with unshed tears. He'd failed. Again.

"HE JUST CUT AND RAN," Roger said for the third time with grim satisfaction. "Just what you'd expect of that son of a bitch."

"*All right,* dear." Helen pressed her fingers to her temples. "Meg, can you *please* ask Davis to stop making that noise? He's been doing it *all* weekend."

"Sorry, Mother." Meg bent to take the toy fire engine out of Davis's hand, cutting his siren sound off midwail. "Go get your bag from the spare bedroom, honey. We have to go now."

Davis's dark green eyes were alert and curious. "Who's Grandpa talking about? What's a son of a bi—"

"Nobody and nothing. Please go." She'd exhausted her emotional energy defending Spencer to her father on the drive back from the marina, although she didn't know why she bothered. Spencer had confirmed her worst fears—he didn't want to know his son.

"Wait a minute, Davis," she said as the boy was about to run off. "Let me give you a big hug. I missed you." She pressed his small body close. They didn't need Spencer. *They didn't.* She had enough love to give her son and more.

"Dad," she said when Davis had left the room, "you simply must watch what you say around Davis. It's bad enough you let the cat out of the bag today with Spencer. I was going to tell him, but now he probably thinks I planned to withhold the information forever."

"I don't care what he thinks." Roger circled her shoulders with one arm. "I'm just worried he's going to hurt you again."

"Look, you're not even being consistent. You say you want Spencer to know about Davis, and then you warn him to stay away from me. He's not the evil person you think he is. And I'm not going to get hurt because I don't expect anything from him. I never did."

This was technically true; she'd *hoped* for love and warmth for her and Davis, but she'd never *expected* it. "What's the worst-case scenario?" she went on. "He leaves at Christmas as he said he would from the beginning. As long as Davis doesn't find out who he is, nobody will be worse off than before."

Roger threw up his hands. "I suppose you think you know what you're doing. But don't come running to me when you're down and brokenhearted again."

"Oh, Roger, of course she can come to us," Helen surprised Meg by saying. "She's our daughter. Davis is our grandson. We're not going to turn our backs on them.''

Well, that was news to Meg. Helen had turned her back on her and Davis for the past seven years. ''Thank you, Mother,'' she said cautiously. ''I hope Davis wasn't too much trouble. Next time I'll arrange my field trip so Patrick can look after him.''

''You most certainly will not!''

Meg took a deep breath. ''I know you mean well,'' she said through her teeth, ''but Patrick is perfectly trustworthy.''

''That's not what I meant, darling.'' Helen's voice softened. ''It's just that…I wouldn't mind looking after Davis again. If you want me to, that is.''

Meg stared. ''Are you serious?''

Helen laughed self-consciously. ''He *is* a handful. I had to tell him twenty times to brush his teeth. And he's constantly wriggling and jiggling, tapping and banging. Then there was the hole he… Well, never mind about that. He surprised me. I never knew he was such an affectionate little thing.'' Her expression turned quizzical, as though she still couldn't understand Davis's appeal. ''He comes up with the most extraordinary ideas. He's really quite an intelligent child…''

What had Meg been telling her for the last six years?

''…in spite of his handicap,'' Helen continued dampeningly. ''I guess he got that from Spencer.''

''Yes, didn't you say Attention Deficit Hyperactive Disorder usually comes from the male side?'' Roger said. ''Probably explains why Valiella can't settle down. He's hyperactive.''

Meg had to laugh. "Davis could have got it from *my* side of the family," she said.

"Nonsense!"

It was unlikely, she had to admit. Then she had an awful thought. If Spencer found it hard to cope with the idea of being a father, how much worse would it be for him knowing his son had a learning disability? Not that Meg saw it as such. True, Davis found it harder than other kids his age to learn to read, but she was working with him on that. And there was no doubt his intelligence was above average. He just couldn't always express himself clearly. Kind of like his father.

ON THE OTHER SIDE of the dining room door, Davis clutched the backpack containing his pajamas and change of clothes. He was glad Grandma hadn't told Mom about the great big hole he'd dug in the garden. She wasn't so bad when she wasn't telling him what to do. She smelled really nice and her clothes felt soft and smooth.

They were talking about that Spencer again. He *had* to be his father. The thought made his insides feel funny, like the time Patrick had taken him on the front seat of the roller coaster in Vancouver. Excited but scared, too, and a little sick. Grandpa and Grandmother didn't sound as though they liked Spencer very much. And they talked like they thought his dad, if it *was* his dad, wouldn't like *him* very much, either.

Tears burned the backs of Davis's eyes. They were wrong. His dad would *so* love him. Mom said he would.

CHAPTER NINE

SPENCER LEFT THE MARINA and hit the highway, his mind in neutral and his car in overdrive. *She'd lied to him.* She'd lied by omission and she'd lied outright. He'd thought Meg the most honest, most caring person he'd ever known. He'd imagined himself falling in love with her again. How could he love a woman who lied about something so important? How could he trust her?

He would leave tomorrow. Go directly to Bergen. Do not pass Meg's house. Do not collect hugs from son. *Son.* He had a son. He had a son and she hadn't told him.

His thoughts went around in circles, blurred but not obliterated by the music blasting from the CD player. He was halfway to Nanaimo before he decided running was not an option. It was too late for that. He had a responsibility to Meg and their son. *Their son.* And Ray. Not to mention the commitment he'd made to Doc and the university. But what of the future? Could he really go to Norway and leave his son behind? Spencer rubbed his eyes. He couldn't think about that now.

Slowing, he made a U-turn across the deserted highway and retraced his journey south to Victoria, west to the cottage.

The lights were still on when he climbed the steps,

even though it was nearly eleven at night. Wearily he pushed open the door and walked into a pigsty. Empty beer cans crowded the coffee table. Newspapers were strewn over the floor.

Spencer kicked the front page of the newspaper out of his way in disgust. This wasn't like Ray. Years of living on the road in the limited confines of a bus had given him a sailor's appreciation for tidiness.

But Ray had ceased acting like Ray for weeks now.

His father lolled on the couch in his bathrobe, a can of beer at his elbow. Out of bourbon, on to Spencer's beer. Ray's uncombed hair hung lankly around his shoulders as he dealt himself a hand of cards. "Hey, Spence, how ya doin'?"

Spencer couldn't find the words to express how he was doing.

Ray glanced up, bleary-eyed. "Wassa matta? Don' I even get a hello anymore?"

"Hello." If he said more, if he let his feelings show, he just might explode. He walked past Ray into the kitchen. He sat at the table and laid his throbbing head in his hands.

Ray shuffled into the room to toss his empty can into the overflowing garbage pail. "He shoots, he scores! Aw, shit." The can bounced out and rolled across the floor spilling drops of beer onto the linoleum. "Sorry." He bent to pick it up and had to support himself on the edge of the counter. "Sorry, Spence. I was gonna clean up 'fore ya got home. Wha're ya doin' back so early?"

"It's after eleven." Spencer got up from the table, angrily crashing the crusted plates together and piling dirty cutlery on top. "Look at this mess. What's happening to you, Dad? You're turning into a bum!"

"I'm already a bum," Ray said dolefully, and sank into a chair. "I wouldn't blame ya if you threw me out on my ass."

He was tempted. Lord, he was tempted. "It's your house." Under his breath he muttered, "Jerk."

"Huh? Din' catch that last bit."

Spencer looked into his father's red-rimmed eyes and was ashamed. "Nothing. It's just…you've got to pick yourself up, Dad. How are you going to get a band together when you sit around all day drinking and playing cards?"

"I got irons in the fire, don't you worry. First thing tomorra' mornin' I'm callin' my old friend Johnny— he's the big kahuna over at Mega records in L.A. He'll get somethin' lined up for me, you'll see."

If Ray had said this a month ago Spencer would have believed him without question. Now he just nodded wearily. "Sure, Ray."

"You don't believe me! My own son don't believe me." Ray stalked back and forth in the tiny kitchen, working himself into a state of righteous indignation. "Think your old man don't have what it takes anymore, eh? Well, we'll just see about that." He reached for the phone on the wall and began to jab in numbers. "I'm callin' Johnny right now—"

"Ray. Ray. *Dad.*" Spencer rose and took the phone from his father's hand. "It's late on a Sunday night. He won't be at his office."

"Then I'll call him at home. Jus' lemme find my address book." Ray pulled away and stumbled, knocking himself against the counter.

Spencer pulled his father into his arms, supporting him, embracing him. Words tumbled out. "Don't, Dad. It's okay. You don't need to prove you're a big-shot musician to me. I'm your son. Your *son*." His throat choked up and a sob, a release of repressed emotion, shook his shoulders.

Ray staggered backward, still clutching Spencer's arms. "What is it, Spence? What's the matter?"

"I have a son." Tears were rolling out of his eyes and he had no idea how to stop them. "I have a six-year-old son. *And she didn't even tell me.*"

"Who? Who didn't tell you?" Ray straightened. He pushed his hair out of his eyes and peered into Spencer's. He didn't seem quite so drunk anymore.

"Meg. Just after I graduated, before I left Victoria, we spent the weekend together. She got pregnant."

"Son of a—" Ray spun away. "Didn't I tell you to use condoms? From the time you were fifteen, didn't I tell you to *always use condoms?*"

"Yes. And I did." Spencer went to the sink. He ran the water till it was cold, then splashed some on his face. Splashed some more into a glass and drank it. "Seems they're not foolproof."

Ray threw his hands up. "So what are you going to do?"

Spencer slumped against the counter. "I don't know. She obviously doesn't want me to see him."

"You've got to. You're the father." Ray retied his sagging bathrobe and used both hands to smooth back his hair. "Hell, that makes *me* a grandfather."

"I'm leaving in a few months," Spencer said gloomily. "What use would I be to that kid?"

Ray scowled. "You gonna leave Meg in the lurch?"

"She managed just fine without me for seven years." Spencer wallowed in the memory of his loneliness without her. Self-imposed loneliness maybe, but painful nonetheless.

"How do you know she was fine?" Ray demanded. "Did she say so?"

"She didn't say anything. We never talked then and we haven't had a chance to talk about it now. No, that's not true," he said angrily. "She's had plenty of opportunity to tell me in the last few weeks and she chose not to. The only reason I found out is because Roger made a slip of the tongue."

He pushed away from the counter. "Why didn't she tell me when it happened?" Suddenly he remembered her phone call to the group house he'd lived in in Seattle. "Hang on, she called the first year I was away. Let's see, it must have been late November because all the stores were gearing up for Thanksgiving. She'd have been—" he was silent, counting backward "—seven or eight months along. She let me rattle on and on about my acceptance at Stanford. Why didn't she tell me she was pregnant?"

Ray's glance was pointed. "I think you just answered your own question."

Spencer stared at him. Did Meg really think he was so selfish he'd put his university education above their baby? *Was* he that selfish? If she'd said, "I'm pregnant," would he have dropped everything and come back? He honestly didn't know.

Ray moved unsteadily to the sink. He halfheartedly shifted a stack of dirty dishes out of the basin, looked at them a moment, then, as if deciding it was just too much to tackle, turned his back on the mess and went to sit down. "Are you gonna marry her?"

"Marry?" It was an alien concept.

"That's how your mother and I got together."

"You lost me. What do you mean?"

"Lorrie joined the band as a singer. We took to each other right away. Weren't figurin' on a family but…" Ray shrugged. "You know how it is."

"You mean you only got married because Mom was pregnant?" Spencer was a little stunned. He'd never heard this before.

"Hey, we were in love," Ray said a little too heartily. "Okay, maybe we got married too soon. The moving around got to your mom in the end, especially when your sister came along. Lorrie put her foot down then, insisted I stop touring." He rubbed moodily at his calloused fingertips.

"That was when you bought this cottage, wasn't it?"

"Yeah. I tried to stick it, I really did. I got a job playing with a local band, weddings, dances, crap like that. You don't remember, eh? Well, I guess you'd have only been about two. The guys in the Brass Monkey were plenty cheesed off."

"I'll bet. What happened?"

"I lasted six months." Ray got up and paced the room as though still plagued by itchy feet. "Then my agent called. He'd got us a chance to front for some really big bands. Lorrie, she was crying, and I felt like a shit, but I just walked out that door. I still had hopes of being really big myself back then. And bein' a solid citizen just wasn't my gig." He stopped pacing and rubbed his hand along his jaw. "She stuck it out for a few more years, but eventually she went back to California and took you and Janis with her."

Spencer'd already known most of this, but it seemed to take on new significance in light of his own situation. Was he doomed to fail his son the way Ray had failed him?

The thought shocked him. He hadn't realized until this moment that he felt his father had let him down. The eighteen months he'd been left with strangers was the worst, but Ray hadn't been around for a lot of his childhood and all of his teen years—except that summer Spencer was thirteen and he went on the road with Ray and the band.

Anger rose in him. Anger for this pathetic old man he'd hero-worshiped all his life. Well, it looked as if that was a lie, too. He didn't know what was the truth anymore. He wondered if, in spite of his failed marriage, Ray was glad he'd fathered a son. It wasn't something you could ask a person. It wasn't something he'd want anyone to ask him.

He rubbed his temples in confusion. What was he going to do about Meg? Until now, each step in his life had been obvious. This university, that research project. Life had been simple because he'd never allowed himself any deep emotional ties. No commitment. If a girl got too close, he just left. Or sent nonverbal messages that were so clear she'd either get demoralized or pissed off and that would be the end of the relationship. He couldn't do that now. Sure, he could leave, but he'd always know what he left behind. Suddenly he was angry at Meg, too. Not only for betraying him with her silence but for binding him with a child.

"I'm going to bed," he said, and started from the room.

"Sleep doesn't work for long," Ray called after him. "Tomorrow morning you'll be the same person with the same problems. Take it from me—I know."

WHEN SPENCER AWOKE the next day, he quickly found Ray was right. The whole damn mess hung over his head like a black cloud. He didn't want to go into work. He didn't want to see Meg. Didn't want to deal with this new element in their relationship.

But he dragged himself out of bed, pulled on a pair of jeans and threw a pullover over his white T-shirt. He picked up a brush off the dresser and ran it through his hair as he stood in front of the mirror. His hair immediately flopped back into its usual rumpled tangle.

In the kitchen doorway he paused, blinking in surprise. Ray was at the sink, a navy apron tied around clean black denim pants and his damp hair held back in a ponytail. He was washing the dishes but not rinsing them, piling them, foaming with soapsuds, haphazardly in the dish rack.

"Morning," Spencer said. "So you're up already."

Ray glanced over his shoulder. "Been up for hours, walking the beach, doin' some thinking. How about we invite Meg and the boy for dinner? What did you say he's called?"

"I didn't."

"Well?"

"Davis. She called him Davis."

Ray's hands left the sink, dripping with water and suds. He hooted with laughter. "*Davis!* I can't believe it. I told you it was a good name."

His father's laughter dragged a reluctant smile from Spencer. "It's not that funny."

"It's poetic justice." Still laughing, Ray pulled the plug and dried his hands on a towel. "So what do you say? I'd like to meet the boy."

Spencer reached into the fridge for the milk. Supplies were dwindling again. "I don't know, Dad. I'm going to need time to figure out what this means to me. Don't count on meeting Da—my so—the boy right away."

By the time he'd finished stumbling over his words, a sweat had broken out on his forehead. He poured himself a glass of milk and drank it down, backhanding the droplets of white from his upper lip. He couldn't be a father; he wasn't grown up yet himself.

He opened his wallet and tossed a couple of twenties on the counter. "If you get a chance, could you pick up some groceries? I've got to run."

"Sure thing. Right after I give Johnny a call."

Spencer gave Ray a wry half smile but restrained himself from being sarcastic. He wasn't anyone to tell other people how they should run their lives. "Thanks, Dad."

WHEN SPENCER ARRIVED at the biology building, he could hear the high-pitched, haunting calls of Kitasu's pod all the way down the corridor. He entered the lab to find Lee practicing Tai Chi kicks at the lab bench while the printer ran off sheets of data.

"Hey, there, Dr. Spencer." Lee gave him a huge grin and effortlessly raised his leg at right angles to his body. "Hydrophone station on Galiano coming in loud and clear."

"So I hear." Spencer deposited the wooden box containing the electronic gear he'd taken on the field trip on the floor outside his office. "Is Meg in?"

Lee turned down the speaker. "Not yet. She has an eight-thirty class in the chemistry building."

"Right. I'd forgotten." Relief flooded through him

and he realized how much he'd dreaded seeing her. Anger mixed with guilt was a nasty combination, especially when you threw in resentment. For she'd surely want to hash it all out, discover exactly how he felt about having a son and exactly what he was going to do about it. He hardly knew *what* he felt, much less feel able to articulate it.

"How come you do Tai Chi, Lee? You're so speedy I would have thought karate or kick-boxing would have been more your style."

"Tai Chi is my father's idea. He started me on it to slow me down," Lee said as he brought his arm around in a graceful arc. "I am almost ready to start writing the journal article. Maybe you have time to discuss it, yes?"

"Sure." Spencer glanced at his watch. "But don't you have hotel management or something this morning?"

Lee brought his arm in abruptly and his perpetual smile faded. "Economics. But I am not in that class anymore. Did so badly on the first exam I dropped the course." Then his face lit up again. "Now I have more time to work on killer whale research."

"Are you sure that's wise? Maybe you could get your prof to give you a make-up exam."

"It's no problem. I got lots of credits." Lee grinned.

"If you say so. I'm going to get some coffee. Be back in a minute."

In the staff room, Ashton-Whyte sidled up to him, stirring cream into his man-size mug. "Ah, Valiella. A little birdy tells me your research assistant's major isn't biology but business."

"You can't believe everything you hear in trees,

Randolph,'' Spencer said, pouring himself a coffee. ''Lee is only fifteen credits short of graduating with a Bachelor of Science.''

Ashton-Whyte narrowed his eyes. ''That may be, but I suggest you counsel him to choose either business or biology.''

Spencer shrugged, bewildered. ''What's it to you?''

''Just keeping tabs on my department, that's all. How is Angus doing, by the way?''

Spencer added cream to his cup. ''Just fine. He's out of the hospital and recovering at home with the help of some physiotherapy.''

''Good, good. Happy here, are you?''

''Yes,'' Spencer said cautiously. ''Why do you ask?''

''No reason. It just occurred to me that if Angus decides to retire, you would be well qualified to take over his position.''

''Doc has no plans to retire.''

Ashton-Whyte tilted his head to one side and smiled. ''He might not have a choice, dear boy.''

''You can't get rid of Doc. He's the best in his field. He's got years of good research left. He's—''

''He's had a stroke that left him partially paralyzed. Perhaps that fact has escaped you?''

''He's recovering. He'll be back in the lab in no time.''

''We'll see.'' Ashton-Whyte's phony smile turned to a frown. But it was a concerned frown, calculated to let Spencer know he wanted the best for his faculty and that he felt keenly the onerous burden of responsibility he bore as head of the department. ''I'm reviewing his years of service. He's had a very impressive career, although there seems to be a slight discrepancy in the chronology of his curriculum vitae. But that's not your concern.'' He glanced at his watch. ''Oops. Must be off.''

Spencer left the coffee room only to see Rachel Walsh approaching at the head of a group of students carrying buckets and dip nets. Her lab coat hung open over a short skirt and tight sweater. An algologist and a babe. He should be panting for her.

''Spencer,'' she said as she sauntered past, her voice low and husky. Her eyes slid sideways to meet his and she smiled, a mixture of bold and coy that left him cold.

He nodded an acknowledgment. ''Rachel.''

She turned to her students. ''You people go ahead. I'll meet you outside.''

The students moved past to clatter down the stairs, their buckets banging against the concrete wall. Spencer had little choice but to fall into step beside Rachel.

''We still haven't had that drink together,'' she murmured.

''It would be a farewell drink, I'm afraid. I'm leaving for Norway after Christmas.'' He flashed her a smile with no humor or substance. ''I'm here for a good time, not a long time.''

''What a shame,'' she murmured, placing a hand on his arm as though she needed help negotiating the bottom step. ''We'll just have to do our best to make sure it *is* a good time.''

He should have ditched that crummy line long ago. He needed this complication like a hole in his buoyancy compensator.

Rachel lingered by the exit, waiting for his answer.

''I appreciate the offer,'' he said, trying to sound

tempted but regretful. "But I've got a few loose ends I need to tie up before I leave." He felt ill describing his son as a "loose end," but he had to do something to put her off. *How the hell was he going to go to Norway and leave behind Meg and their son?* It was a question that had no answer.

Rachel put on a pouty smile and ran a finger down his lapel. "If you change your mind, just knock on my door. Anytime."

"Sure." His smile was genuine now, one of relief.

He carried on back to the lab. If he went to Norway he ought to at least provide for them. He had savings, but until now hadn't made any conscious effort to maximize his income or increase his assets. Jeez, he couldn't believe he was thinking this way.

He slipped through the lab door and pushed it shut behind him. Lee was working at the computer.

"Hey, Lee. Got any hot tips for the stock market?"

Lee glanced up and grinned. "Buy futures."

"What kind?"

"Any kind look pretty good right now."

Not from where Spencer was standing. "Never mind. Let's go over your results for the journal article."

AFTER HER CHEMISTRY CLASS Meg walked over to the Student Union Building cafeteria. With a coffee and a blueberry muffin on the table in front of her, she pretended to study her notes. Then she pretended to read over the lab book in preparation for this afternoon's physiology lab. She couldn't avoid Spencer forever, but she'd hoped to do so at least until he'd left for lunch. He'd said he would call her and he hadn't. It could only mean he didn't want anything to do with their son.

A couple of hours later she drained the last of her coffee and glanced at her watch. By the time she walked across campus, he should have left the biology building and be halfway to the car park. If she went in the front entrance, she'd miss him entirely.

She wended her way through the crowded tables, smiling at some girls she recognized from her biostatistics class. She knew they'd welcome her if she chose to sit with them, but they seemed so young. Completely devoid of responsibilities beyond homework and maybe a part-time job. It was hard to relate to them.

Between the fountain and the library, students sprawled on the grass or the stone steps, soaking up the feeble rays of precious October sunlight while they ate lunch. Meg checked the time again and slowed her pace. She had no reason to feel nervous. Spencer was the one who should feel nervous. Maybe he did. Maybe he felt guilty. She hoped so. No, that wasn't fair. What she wanted was for him to feel immediate and unconditional love for their son. Ha. Not likely.

Meg went through the heavy glass doors of the biology building and down the long corridor, past the student lounge, around the corner, and paused outside the lab. She had her key out, but the door was ajar. Cautiously she pushed it open and quietly walked in.

And stopped short. Spencer's office door was open. He sat sideways to his desk, facing the door, one long leg crossed over the other as his chair tilted backward at a dangerous angle. He held no book, no journal, no papers, no piece of electronic equipment. Nothing.

He was waiting for her.

Meg swallowed and gripped the shoulder strap of her bag with both hands. She took a step toward her desk behind the partition.

Spencer rocked forward so that his feet fell to the floor. "Meg, I've been waiting to talk."

"I waited for your call last night." Till one in the morning.

"I had to think things through." He beckoned her to a seat. "At least now I know why your father hates me."

She sat. "Daddy doesn't hate you."

"Please. I don't think there's room for doubt. I can't say I blame him."

"I'm sorry you had to find out that way. I was going to tell you about Davis."

"When?"

"I don't know."

They fell into a tense silence. Meg struggled to find a way to ease into the discussion they had to have about their son. She and Spencer had never lacked things to talk about; their words had always poured out in an excited exchange of ideas and opinions. But they'd never before had to deal with anything so deeply emotional, so fraught with consequences.

"I don't expect anything from you," she began, anxious he not think her needy or desperate.

"Why *don't* you?" he cut in harshly. "I'm partly responsible, after all. Am I so goddamn useless I can't be a father to my son?"

She saw the fine film of perspiration on his forehead and knew he'd spoken aloud his secret fear. He was angry with her for not thinking him trustworthy—and at the same time certain that she was right.

"Of course you can be a father to Davis," she said quietly. "If you want to be. Do you have any idea what that entails?"

He stared at her so long she became conscious of the faint ticking of her watch and the murmur of students in the hall. She started to rise.

"I'd like to meet him."

She remained poised on the edge of her seat. "I'm not so sure that's a good idea. He's vulnerable. You see, he—" how could she put this? "—he hero-worships you."

The skin around Spencer's eyes tightened as if he was in pain. "He doesn't even know me. What have you told him about me?"

"Just that you're a biologist and you study killer whales. You have to travel for your work—that's why you don't live with us. I don't know how long he'll accept that explanation if he meets you."

"Why didn't you tell me sooner? Years ago."

"You know why."

He swiveled away from her to gaze out the window. Meg felt weary. It always came back to the same thing—he couldn't be relied on to stick around. It hurt that he didn't deny it.

Finally he swung back to her. "I want to meet him. I...*need* to meet him." His long fingers braided together, knuckles white.

Fear for Davis stopped her voice in her throat.

"Meg, he's my son. Don't make me beg."

She took a breath. "You can meet him. But I won't tell him who you are. Then, when you leave, he won't miss you."

Spencer squeezed his eyes shut. He nodded, then waved a hand, motioning for her to go. Her heart ached for him. For herself and for Davis. She couldn't get out of there fast enough.

CHAPTER TEN

"I GOT IT!" Patrick shouted as he breezed into the kitchen and twirled Meg around. "I got my promotion."

"Congratulations!" She hugged him. "I'm so happy for you."

"Isn't it bliss? We're going to celebrate. Want to join us?"

"I can't. Spencer is coming to dinner to meet Davis."

Patrick brought his hands to his face. "Oh, my goodness. Maybe I'd better stay and give you moral support."

"I'll be fine." She got the white linen napkins out of the drawer. "By the way, who's *we?*"

"Well," Patrick said, taking the napkins from her to arrange them beside the plates on the table, "remember I told you I was going to spill my guts for the selection committee?"

"Yes, what happened? I've been so busy studying for midterm exams and going on field trips it's been an age since we've talked."

"I told them everything and they were *great* about it. They as good as said right then I had the position, but I didn't want to tell you until it was confirmed. Anyway, as I was leaving the sergeant's office, the Human Resources officer *winked* at me."

"No! Isn't he the cute one you told me about months ago?"

"The very same. I had *no* idea he was gay."

"So what did you do?" Meg went to the cupboard for the salt-and-pepper shakers, two white porcelain pigs curled around each other.

"I waited till everyone else had gone, then I popped back into his office and asked him out to dinner." Patrick set the cutlery in a precise line half an inch from the edge of the table. "He said yes and the rest is history."

"That's wonderful. What's his name?"

"Douglas." Patrick picked up a carved wooden bowl full of fruit. "How about this as a centerpiece?"

"Too big." Meg moved the bowl back to the counter.

"So, we both have dates tonight. Fabulous top, by the way."

"Thanks." The clinging stretchy black top shot with gold threads was the first new piece of clothing she'd bought since the beginning of the summer. And the first item in a much longer time that wasn't strictly utilitarian. "I hope he doesn't think I'm trying to be alluring."

"He should be flattered." Patrick tilted his head. "Are you?"

She ignored the question and went to the stove to check the rice. "Or worse, trying to compete with the nineteen-year-old coeds on campus."

"Honey, you'd blow them out of the water. And your hair is absolutely wonderful au naturel. Like a golden waterfall." He gave her a stern look. "If you're going to get serious about this Spencer fellow again, I'm going to have to meet him."

Meg shook her head. "This is a once-off."

"Sure it is. What did you tell you-know-who?" Patrick whispered even though Davis was in the back-yard playing with his new baby lop-eared rabbit.

"Just that he's my professor. Davis thought I was weird for inviting my teacher to dinner." Meg brought a jug of water to the table.

"How is he doing at school?" Patrick asked. "Is that bully still bothering him?"

"Sometimes. He's made one friend, though, I think."

"That's good." Patrick glanced at his watch. "I'd better go get ready."

A short time later Meg walked with him to the door. They'd just stepped out onto the porch when Spencer's Camaro pulled up out front. The knot that had been growing in her stomach all day twisted tighter.

"Have a good time," she said to Patrick, edging him toward the steps as Spencer climbed out of the car. He wore a brown tweed jacket over a black T-shirt and was carrying a bottle of wine by the neck.

Patrick planted his feet. "I'm not going anywhere till I get a good look at Lover Boy."

"Stop it," Meg hissed, jabbing him in the ribs. "And quit ogling him. He's not your type."

"Ooh, but I just love that bad boy-college professor look. My, my, my. What he does for a pair of blue jeans."

"I'll tell Douglas on you."

Patrick raised an eyebrow. "Okay, okay. I'm just kidding."

"Hi, Spencer," Meg said as he approached the porch. "This is my housemate, Patrick."

Spencer extended his hand. "Hi."

"I believe we spoke on the phone once," Patrick gushed. "It's *so* nice to meet you. Meg's told me *all* about you."

Spencer glanced at Meg. "Hope it wasn't all bad."

"Not *all* of it," Patrick said, laughing. He turned to Meg and kissed her on the cheek. "If you need anything at all, you call me on my cell phone, you hear?"

Meg gave him a little shove. "*Goodbye.* Have a nice evening." When he was out of earshot, she said to Spencer, "He's a little protective."

"He's gay." Spencer sounded relieved.

"Do you have a problem with that?"

He shook his head. "Not at all."

"Come in." Meg led the way into the house. "Davis is in the backyard."

Spencer nodded. "What did you tell him about me?"

"Only that you're my professor." She frowned. "I'm a little worried. He knows his father's name is Spencer and that he—*you*—study killer whales."

"Does he know my last name? I mean, his father's name?"

Meg thought for a moment. "It may have come up at some time in the past, but I doubt he'd remember."

"Then introduce me as Dr. Valiella. I don't normally like being so formal, but under the circumstances..."

"One other thing," Meg said, touching the rough cloth of his jacket sleeve. "He looks like you."

Spencer's face went blank as he absorbed the information. His hands gripped the bottle, twisting the brown paper into pleated folds around the neck. "Will he notice?"

"I don't know. Do you still want to see him?" She waited anxiously for his response. If he dared back out now…

"Yes, of course. But if he asks, we'll tell him."

Meg pulled on the ends of her hair. "Okay." She paused. "Spencer?"

"What?"

"I'm sorry I didn't tell you about Davis earlier."

She waited for him to say, "It's okay," but he didn't, and the anger and hurt in his eyes made it hard for her to breathe.

She turned and led the way through the dining room into the kitchen. Noel bobbed his head at the sight of her and gave her a wolf whistle. "Pretty lady!"

Smiling and embarrassed, she took the wine bottle from Spencer and placed it on the counter. He gazed back, unblinking, deep in his own thoughts. With a shrug, she took him through the laundry room and out the back door. So much for being alluring.

Davis squatted in the middle of the small grassed yard, his knees meeting his chin as he watched his pet bunny nibble grass beneath a wire-mesh grazing arc. He wore a bright blue jacket, and his brown hair lifted with the breeze.

Spencer moved onto the top step beside her and gripped the wooden railing. Meg wondered, as she often did when it came to Davis, if she was doing the right thing. Nothing else in her son's short life had ever had such potential for good or ill as introducing him to his father. Either way, she wouldn't know until it was too late.

"Shall we?" she said, and walked down the short set of steps to the yard. Spencer followed.

"Davis," she called as they approached. Davis didn't look up. *Oh, no,* she thought. *Please let this not be a bad day.*

A bad day was one where Davis answered in monosyllables if he answered at all. A day where his focus was so intense and narrow she couldn't get him to do anything that wasn't his idea. A day where, when the tablets wore off, as they inevitably did because she couldn't keep him on them twenty-four hours a day, Davis went into a major blow-out of erratic behavior.

She knew she should tell Spencer about the A.D.H.D., but every time she thought about doing so she felt a rush of maternal protectiveness that closed off her powers of speech. More than anything, Meg wanted Spencer to accept Davis as he was. For Spencer to love Davis seemed almost more than she could hope for. But if he *liked* him, that was a start.

"Davis," she repeated more insistently. Then caught herself. She was sensitized to his moods, too ready to overreact.

"Mom!" He looked up suddenly. "Patch eats and poops at the same time."

"Charming." She laughed nervously and glanced at Spencer.

His face was a mask, his muscles so tense he seemed not to be breathing.

"Eats and poops. Eats and poops," Davis chanted, oblivious once more to their presence. "Eats and poo—"

"Davis!" Her voice betrayed her anxiety, rising in pitch and volume. Meg took a deep breath. He'd done nothing. Nothing to get upset about. "This is Dr. Valiella, my professor. He's come to have dinner with us.''

Davis glanced at Spencer without interest.

"Say hello, Davis," Meg prompted.

"Hello," Davis said, and returned his attention to the wonders of rabbit digestion. The gray-and-white bunny's mouth moved with almost unbelievable rapidity, chomping through stalk after stalk of grass.

"Hi," Spencer said. He hunkered down beside the grazing arc. "Patch is a regular munching machine."

Davis smiled. "Yeah."

"I had a rabbit when I was a boy, for a little while, anyway. His name was Benjamin. He liked to eat tomatoes."

"Yuck." Davis poked a long grass stem through a hole in the mesh and tickled the rabbit's ear. The rabbit hopped away. Davis moved to the other side of the grazing arc and did it again.

Meg bit her lip to stop herself from telling Davis to cut it out, not wanting to interrupt the interaction between Spencer and her son. His son. *Their* son. Saying it, even to herself, invested it with too much meaning.

"What do you suppose that means when he hops away from being tickled?" Spencer asked, his tone neutral.

"He doesn't like it," Davis replied matter-of-factly. He pushed the stem of grass all the way through the mesh into the grazing arc. The bunny hopped over to eat it.

Wow, Meg thought. Spencer handled that really well. Maybe he's a natural father. Fantasies formed unbidden.

"I think his nose is really cute when he eats," Davis said, cutting into her thoughts. He plucked another handful of grass. "Are you a marine biologist?"

Spencer hesitated a fraction of a second. "Yes."

"My dad's a marine biologist. Do you know him?"

Spencer got to his feet, his hand clenching at his side. "I...uh... There are a lot of marine biologists around." His glance at Meg was a blatant plea for rescue.

"Would you like a glass of wine, Dr. Valiella?"

"Oh, yes."

She almost laughed at the fervor of his reply. *Almost*. The situation would be hysterical if it wasn't so tragic.

SPENCER WATCHED the small boy across the table from him pick at his food. So this was his son. He still couldn't quite believe it. But when he looked into eyes the same dark sea-green hue as his, topped by brows the same straight-across shape, saw the finely etched upper lip in miniature and the softly rounded cheeks that would sharpen into angles similar to his...he had to believe it.

What he couldn't come to grips with was his reaction—a mixture of overweening pride, which he had no right to feel, and pure terror.

He was overwhelmed with fear of a sort he'd never experienced before. A fear so profound he was barely able to speak all throughout the dinner he ate but didn't taste. He was terrified of everything to do with Davis. Terrified of saying the wrong thing. Terrified of not saying anything and losing the one chance Meg would allow him to get to know his son. Terrified of loving him. Terrified of *not* loving him. Terrified of leaving him. Terrified of staying.

Thank God, Davis didn't know who he was. The added pressure and expectations would be intolerable. He didn't know how Meg was carrying the largely one-sided conversation, but, boy, was he glad she was there.

"Do you like music?" he managed to ask Davis when she took a break to eat some of her chicken. The boy might show an aptitude if he was nurtured. Goodness knows, Spencer hadn't inherited his father's musical ability.

Davis shrugged. Wriggled in his chair. "It's pretty good."

Spencer realized he couldn't suggest Davis have piano lessons or something. He had no rights. Only responsibilities.

"When he was a baby," Meg said, "he used to bang his head against the wall with rhythm."

"Did I?" Davis exclaimed, fascinated. "What's rhythm?"

Spencer laughed, and some of the tension in his chest eased. "So you're a head-banger already. I'll have to tell your gr—" He choked off the sentence. Coughed. Picked up his knife and put it down again. His gaze flashed to Meg. *I almost slipped up.*

Her expression changed as she read his. Strange how they could still do something as intimate as read messages in each other's faces after so long apart. Did that mean, once you knew someone, you'd always know them? Or was that just her?

Don't worry, her small reassuring smile told him.

He wanted to believe it. And he might have, if he couldn't see that she was worried, too. It was as though the reality of the situation had only just hit them both. They should have met at a park or gone walking on the beach. Anything but sitting together around the family dinner table.

"He likes to listen to records," Meg said. "Don't you, Davis?"

Davis shrugged. He stared at Spencer with the intense curiosity of the very young. "I like the song Patrick always sings about the navy."

Spencer glanced at Meg. "The Village People?"

"Gilbert and Sullivan. Patrick *adores* Gilbert and Sullivan."

He laid his knife and fork across his empty plate. If Davis was never told who Ray was, what Spencer said about him wouldn't matter. "My father plays the guitar."

"Cool. Does he play in a band?"

"Ah, not anymore, but he used to."

Davis turned to his mother. "What's for dessert?"

"Nothing until you eat your dinner."

"Aw, Mom." Davis picked up a forkful of chicken, brought it to his mouth, then put it down uneaten. He squirmed on his chair, pulling his knees up to his chin and dropping them again. Up and down. "Can I have an orange?"

Meg pursed her lips.

What's to decide? Spencer wondered. *An orange is healthy.*

"Okay," she said at last. "Spencer, could you pass him an orange from the bowl behind you?"

Spencer reached behind him to the counter and brought back an orange. "I'll peel it for you."

"Have you lived here long?" Spencer asked Meg

as he dug his thumbnail into the spongy peel near the stem.

"About five years. Davis went to preschool at the recreation center down the road. He took swimming lessons there, too."

Spencer turned the orange, keeping the peel going in one continuous strip. "Do you like swimming, Davis?"

Davis nodded, his gaze on the orange peel. His foot began to beat continuously and monotonously against the leg of his chair.

"Davis…" Meg said in a low, warning voice.

"Maybe you'll be a marine biologist like your mom," Spencer said.

Davis picked up a spoon and tapped it on the table in a contrapuntal beat to the foot on the chair. "I want to drive a dump truck."

Spencer was halfway down the orange now. The peel dangled from his fingertips in an unbroken spiral. Davis's wide-eyed gaze was glued to it. His spoon went tap-tap-tap.

"Enough," Meg said, and laid her hand on Davis's arm.

With the silence Spencer felt an immediate reduction in the tension created by the repetitive noise. The frown disappeared from his face.

Meg took her hand off Davis's arm.

The tapping started again.

Spencer heard a tiny sigh escape from Meg. Man, it must be hard bringing up a kid all by herself. Guilt harpooned his conscience and took it for a ride. Teething, nightmares, illness. He speeded up his peeling of the orange. Davis's lips were pressed tightly together, his eyes unblinking.

Spencer dropped the strand of peel on his plate. Breaking the orange into segments, he handed them across the table. "There you go."

"What do you say, Davis?" Meg prompted when Davis accepted the orange without a word.

"Thank you," Davis said around a mouthful, but his gaze had taken on a strangely watchful quality, as though he didn't dare take his eyes off Spencer. Juice dripped between his fingers where he squeezed the orange too tightly.

Unnerved, Spencer said the first thing that came to his mind. "Do you know what you want for Christmas?"

Davis squeezed tighter. Juice flowed down his upraised arm. "My father to come home."

Spencer felt the prickly heat of adrenaline rushing through his veins. He opened his mouth to say something, he didn't know what. Suddenly Davis dropped the orange pieces among the rest of the discarded food on his plate and scrambled off his chair.

"Davis!" Meg called.

He ran out of the room. *"Whoop, whoop, whoop."*

"You've got sticky hands. Don't touch anything!" She turned to Spencer with a harried apologetic smile. "I'm sorry. He's… I don't know what's got into him. Excuse me."

Stunned, Spencer watched the scenario unfold. Meg, speaking sternly; Davis, ignoring every word, a manic grin on his face as he tore around the house, dodging her outstretched arms. Davis's eyes held a crazed expression Spencer found unnerving. Should he help her? What could he do? He'd never seen a child act this way before. His sister's kids were docile little lambs by comparison.

"Whoop. Whoop. Whoop."

The situation demanded action, but he couldn't act. Courtesy demanded he avert his eyes from Meg's difficulties, but it was *his son* behaving like a brat. He rose and began stacking dishes together, glancing over his shoulder every few seconds to see if Meg wanted him to help. She didn't appear to.

Finally, Meg caught the boy as he rounded a corner, grunting as he slammed into her stomach. She clamped her arms around him and he could only squirm, his eyes wild and brimming with mischief, his grin an exaggeration of his mother's impish smile.

She wasn't smiling now. Exasperation pushed her lips into a straight line. Her long, tangled hair moved around her shoulders as Davis struggled in her arms. She spoke in a low controlled voice. "Quiet, Davis. Calm down." Still holding him, she sank to the floor. "Calm. That's right, breathe slowly."

Gradually, Davis quieted in her arms. Bit by bit she relaxed her grip, still talking to him softly. Spencer moved around the kitchen, tidying things, staying out of their way. If he'd felt too much part of the domestic unit before, now he felt like a total outsider.

Meg sent Davis down the hall. His feet dragged as though they were pulling dead weights, in direct contrast to the frenzied behavior he'd exhibited only minutes before. All Spencer could do was feel vaguely guilty and wonder why such a neat kid should behave so abominably for no apparent reason.

Meg came into the kitchen, her arms wrapped around herself, her face drained of energy. "Sorry about that," she said. "He gets wired sometimes. Too much excitement, I guess."

"I guess." Spencer put down the salt-and-pepper

shakers he'd removed from the table. "Maybe I should go."

Two sharp lines appeared between Meg's light brown eyebrows. She nodded, as though she'd been expecting him to say that.

"I won't run out if you want me to stay," he tried to explain. "But if I'm the cause of the excitement…"

"He's going to have a bath. That usually calms him down." She moved around him to reach for the kettle. "Do you want some coffee?"

What he wanted was to pull her into his arms and kiss the tension from her brow. Not a good idea under the circumstances. Anyway, there was something he had to get off his chest, and it was hard enough to say without the added complication of being too close to Meg.

"Is…is it because he doesn't have a fath— I mean, because I'm…not around?"

Meg turned off the tap and plugged in the kettle. Still without a word, she went to the cupboard and pulled down two cups.

"Meg?"

"No, i-it's not that," she assured him brokenly. She spooned ground coffee into the plunger.

"I don't really believe you, but I'm craven enough to feel relieved. Especially when I know how hard it must have been for you, raising him alone."

The spoon dropped from her fingers to clatter onto the counter, and she pushed a long strand of blond hair away from her face. He wished he could still feel angry with her for deceiving him all these years. But her blue eyes were filled with anguish, and her mouth was working—as though there was something she badly wanted to tell him but couldn't.

"I find it hard to talk about him with you, too," he said quietly. "But that's something we're going to have to get over." Spencer's voice turned husky. "After all, he's...our son."

Not looking at him, she nodded, her clenched knuckles white.

"I...don't know what's going to happen," he continued, each word hard to say, as if he had to push it out. "I just want to do the best for Davis as...I'm capable of."

Which might not be very bloody much.

This time she glanced his way with weary eyes. "It might be best if you do nothing."

Her words stung. He was worse than useless; he was dangerous to his son's well-being. He swallowed hard.

"He's really a wonderful kid when you get to know him," she said, smiling tremulously.

"You could bring him out to the cottage next week during midterm break," Spencer suggested. "Ray would like to meet him."

"Would he?" Her smile became steadier. "I guess we could. I mean, as long as Ray didn't say anything..."

"He won't if I ask him not to."

"Okay, then. I'd like to see Ray again, too."

Spencer's answering smile faded. "Ray's still going through his crisis, whatever it is. Don't expect too much." He shoved a hand through his hair. "In fact, he's pretty much a mess."

Her big eyes clouded and she put a comforting hand on his chest. "Oh, Spencer, I'm sorry."

Warmth spread beneath his shirt where her hand lay. His teeth ground with the effort of not reaching for her. "Don't. Don't be, I mean." How could she feel sympathy for him after he'd let her down? "I'd better go. Why don't you and Davis come on Tuesday? We've got the *Cape Beale* booked Wednesday and Thursday."

"I remember. Don't you want your coffee?" She gazed up at him, her lips half parted.

"No. Thanks." What he wanted, badly, was to taste her lips and feel the warmth of her skin. He had to get away. Away from those eyes that were too forgiving and those soft curves that were too enticing. Away from the memories and the what-ifs and the coulda-beens. Away from the evidence of his failure.

She snatched her fingers away, curling them into her palm. "I'll walk you out."

"NO SOONER WAS DINNER over than Davis went berserk," Meg said to Patrick over a late-night cup of coffee. She knew she'd regret the caffeine when she was still awake at 2:00 a.m., but she suspected she wouldn't get much sleep tonight, anyway.

"What triggered it this time?" he asked.

"I don't know." Meg tucked her legs up on the sofa. "It wasn't the bedtime routine. He hadn't eaten anything sweet. He hardly ate anything at all, except an orange Spencer peeled for him."

"Maybe that's it—not enough food."

"Maybe," Meg said doubtfully. The pediatrician had told her that food, types of it or lack of it, made little or no difference to the behavior of A.D.H.D. kids.

"Or maybe it was just having a stranger to dinner,'' Patrick suggested. ''You know how he acts up whenever someone new comes around.''

''Lots of kids do.'' Meg tried, unsuccessfully, to keep the defensiveness out of her voice even though Patrick knew all of Davis's faults and had seen him at his worst. Patrick, who only wished for tolerance from others and gave it back in abundance.

But Patrick also never let her get away with wishful thinking. ''Yes, Meg,'' he said gently, ''but not to the same extent.''

She fell silent. Patrick leaned over and put his arm around her. ''What is it, sweetie?''

''I didn't tell Spencer about Davis's A.D.H.D.''

Patrick shook his head. ''Isn't it better to tell him than have him think Davis is simply a badly behaved child and it's all *your* fault?''

Meg winced, remembering some of her mother's comments before Davis had been diagnosed. ''I *want* to tell him, I really do. But what if it turns him against Davis?''

''I don't think you're giving him enough credit. But if he does turn against Davis, then he's a total jerk and you're better off without him.''

Meg sighed. Patrick was right.

CHAPTER ELEVEN

"HI, RAY. It's so good to see you again. You're looking great."

Davis heard the bright inflections in his mom's voice, the way she spoke when she started acting like Grandma. He stared at the man she was hugging. He didn't look great at all. His skin was kind of gray and he had big bags under his eyes. If Patrick looked in the mirror and saw those on his face, he'd moan about it for hours.

"And this is Davis." His mom was tugging on his hand, urging him forward. He dug in his heels and stared mutinously at the ground. "Davis, say hello to Dr. Valiella's father, Mr. Valiella."

"Hello, son. You can call me Ray."

The man had a booming raspy voice and a handshake that hurt. For a moment Davis was confused to be called "son." Could this be… No, he was too old, more like a grandpa. But what kind of grandpa had a ponytail? Davis reached out and touched the man's pants. They felt like his mom's purse. Weird.

Ray chuckled. Davis felt everyone's gaze on him and he ducked behind his mom. The man Mom called Dr. Valley-Alley-Something, the man whose name Davis thought was really Spencer and who peeled an orange so the peel was all in one piece, crouched to look him in the eye. "Would you like to walk on the beach?"

Davis hesitated. He loved the beach, but... "Is my mom going to go?"

"We'll all go, honey," Mom said, and then it was okay.

"Let me get my camera," Ray said.

They walked over the cobble and the coarse sand, down to the waterline. The tide had gone out, leaving a broad strip of hard-packed muddy sand strewn with tangled clumps of brown kelp and ridges of shells and tiny stones.

Davis stomped in the shallow water till his runners were wet and squishy, then ran off before his mom could yell at him to stop. Slowing, he saw sunlight glint off a trickle of water spouting from a small hole surrounded by a mound of sand squiggles. He crouched beside it. While he watched, a noodle of sand was ejected onto the pile. He patted the squiggles with his finger, feeling how smooth they were, then flattened them with his palm.

A shadow crossed the sand in front of him. He glanced up. Uh-oh. Dr. Valley-Alley. Was he going to yell at him? Davis wasn't sure what he'd done wrong—except for the shoes—but somehow he was *always* getting in trouble.

But the man just crouched beside him and cleared away the sand grains from the hole. "A worm lives in here. *Abarenicola pacifica.*"

Davis relaxed a little. "Mom said it's a lugworm."

"That's what its friends call it. This worm is special. It introduced your mom and me."

Davis stared at the hole, disbelieving. Then he

tilted his face up, squinting into the sun and laughed. "Worms can't talk!"

The man laughed with him and told him some more things about the worm and the other animals that lived in the mud. It made Davis feel warm and good inside. Mostly adults just talked to other adults. This man knew lots of stuff, just like his mom, except he didn't try to make him remember everything. Also, he'd taken off his shoes and rolled up his pants and didn't seem to mind when they got wet, anyway. Davis decided he liked him. It would be neat if he was his dad, he thought wistfully.

"What's this?" Davis asked, pointing to the sand noodle.

"That's a fecal casting," the man explained seriously. "The worm ingests sand and mud. As the material passes through the digestive tract, the worm digests the organic detritus before ejecting the mucus-encased casting."

Totally lost, Davis scrunched up his face. "Huh?"

The man shook his head at his own foolishness. "It eats and poops. Eats and poops."

Davis giggled at a grown-up saying "poop." "What else does it do, Dr. Valley...Valley..." He stumbled over the long name.

The man reached out and brushed a clump of sand grains from Davis's cheek. "Just call me—" He stopped and blinked, like he was going to cry, except that grown-up men didn't cry. Then he took a deep breath. "You can call me...Doc."

"Okay." That was easier, Davis thought. But for some reason he felt disappointed. He jumped to his feet and ran back to his mom.

Her arms went around him in a hug and his vague

sadness was chased away by her warm voice saying, "How you doing, guy?"

"Good." He clung to her for a moment. Then a large shaggy golden dog went rollicking past, chasing seagulls off a sandbar and into the sky. Davis ran after him, laughing for no reason except that it felt good.

Spencer fell into step beside Meg. "He's a nice kid."

She nodded, wondering what had passed between him and Davis that had sent her son running for a hug. "You didn't..."

Understanding warmed his gaze. "No."

Farther up the beach, Ray trudged over the sand, hunched in his sheepskin jacket, occasionally stopping to snap a photo.

Spencer strode at her side, loose-limbed, lean and strong, as much a part of the beach as the sea and the sky. His arms and feet were bare, even though it was mid-October and the air was crisp; like Davis, he was impervious to cold. Meg breathed in the fresh salty air and felt the gritty sand beneath her bare toes. Autumn always brought out a wild nostalgia in her, full of unfulfilled promise and yearning and regret. Now it tugged at her so strongly it was almost unbearable.

"I'm going to run," she said, loping ahead. And although partly she was running away from him, another part of her hoped he would follow.

He did. And then he was passing her, splashing through the shallows, kicking up spray to wet her jeans, laughing and reaching out to touch her arm. "You're it."

She chased after him onto the sandbar. Around in circles they went like a pair of puppies. Davis ran after them, shrieking with delight, the dog barking joyously at his heels.

Davis and Dog ran off at a tangent. Meg finally caught Spencer. Or was it the other way around? She'd lost track of who was chasing and who was running. Together they slowed to a laughing, panting halt, hands loosely touching each other's arms, waists.

Spencer's kiss seemed as natural as the day. A mere touching of salty lips, warm in contrast to the coolness of the air and water. Tingling where they touched. Kindred spirits communicating simple profound pleasures. Brief; too brief. Eyes full of yearning and unfulfilled promise. But no regret. Not yet.

Smiling, she touched his hair, tangled and tossed by the breeze. "You need a haircut. I could do it for you."

"No way, Delilah. Remember last time?"

Seven and a half years ago he couldn't afford a professional cut and she'd offered to do it for him. That day had been her first visit to the cottage. She'd adored its simplicity after her parents' huge house and envied Spencer his freedom and knowledge of the world. While she clipped his hair with kitchen scissors to the sounds of Ray and the Brass Monkeys, they'd talked about traveling and philosophy, evolution and the stars. And all those things she'd hoped to discuss at university but hadn't because she hadn't found anyone who shared her interests—till she'd met him. That day had marked the beginning of their friendship—and almost ended it the moment he'd looked in the mirror.

She laughed at the memory. Spencer's smiling eyes reflected the thoughts that flowed through her mind. Remembering time spent together strengthened the bridge from past to present. But how were they to cross the gap from the present to the future?

"I've had a lot of practice since then on Davis," she said.

He slid his hand down the length of her thick blond braid to tug on the end. "Thanks, we'll see."

The sound of splashing made them look around. Davis was sitting in the shallows, his arms dug into the sand up to his elbows, excavating a channel to the castle he'd built on the sandbar. The splashing came from the dog, who was helping dig and in the process sending a spray of water and muddy sand straight onto Davis. Who was, of course, oblivious.

"Man, is he a mess!" Spencer said.

"Don't worry," Meg said, resigned. "I never go anywhere without a complete change of clothing. Let's get him back to the cottage before he freezes to death."

They found Ray sitting on a log, staring out to sea. He chuckled when he saw the muddy bedraggled mess that was Davis. "Reminds me of another kid I used to know," he said with a wink at Meg.

"How on earth did you survive?" Meg murmured.

His smile faded. "Lorrie did most of the coping."

Back at the cottage, Spencer ran a bath for Davis and got him a towel and shampoo. Meg hovered outside in the hallway. It felt strange for someone else to be caring for her son when she was there.

"I usually wash his hair for him," she said when Spencer simply handed Davis the bottle and left. "He can't rinse it properly himself."

"Time he learned," Spencer replied, maddeningly unconcerned, and started back toward the kitchen.

"But...but..." Meg glanced from the bathroom,

where she could hear Davis happily talking to himself in the tub, to Spencer's retreating back.

Spencer paused and turned. "Come and talk to me while I make dinner. Ray's not too good at playing host these days."

"I'll help with the food, if you like."

"Thanks. I'm going to barbecue."

"Barbecue? It practically feels like winter."

"So?"

Meg shrugged. Maybe she was getting too rigid in her old age. Why *not* barbecue if that was what he felt like doing? "Okay."

She made a salad while Spencer dragged a rusty hibachi from under the house and cleaned it at the outside tap. Ray was working on his second drink and propping up the counter. Making conversation with him wasn't easy. She couldn't ask him what he was doing now because it was painfully obvious he wasn't doing much of anything. She couldn't speak of the future because he didn't seem to have one. And talk of the good old days seemed to depress him.

Ray's guitar stood in the corner of the small living room. Spencer had whispered a warning when she and Davis had arrived not to mention the guitar or to ask Ray to play. He was sensitive about it, apparently, and still angry at Spencer for getting it out of hock and thereby inadvertently putting pressure on him. Privately, Meg thought if he just tried to play, he might recover his spark, but you couldn't make that decision for another person, and she liked him too much to risk upsetting him.

Davis came into the room with his hair undried and dripping down his inside-out T-shirt. "Hey, Mom, look at the shell I found in the bathroom," he said, holding up a conch. "I'll bet Doc found it on the beach."

Doc? It took her a moment to realize he was talking about Spencer.

"As a matter of fact, young fella, *I* found that shell. We were doing a gig in Mexico—" Ray broke off and took a swig of bourbon.

"What's a gig?" Davis asked, unaware the subject was closed.

Ray's face shut down and he curled his arms protectively around his waist.

"Davis," Meg said, dropping the tomato in her hand and coming around the counter. "Please go back to the bathroom and dry your hair properly. Is it even rinsed?" She did the squeak test on a strand of hair as she gently steered him toward the hall, and surprisingly it passed.

Resisting her manipulations, Davis craned his neck around to ask again, "What's a gig?"

Meg cast about for a better diversion. Once Davis got going, he clung to a subject tighter than a limpet to a rock until his curiosity was satisfied. "Why don't you go see if you can help Dr. Valiella?"

But Davis pulled away from her to stand in front of Ray. "What's a gig?"

Ray stared balefully back at Davis. "It's when a band plays a concert."

"Are you in a band?"

"I was." Ray went to the fridge for more ice cubes, Davis on his heels.

"Why aren't you in one now?"

"Don't ask."

"Is that your guitar out there?" Davis asked. "Can I try it?"

Ray spun away from the freezer, a scowl on his face. "No."

"Meg?" Spencer called from outside the back door. "Can you bring me the barbecue scraper? It's under the sink."

Davis edged closer to Ray. "Please? I won't hurt it."

"Don't pester him, honey," Meg said. She poked about in the cupboard under the sink for the scraper.

"Only *I* touch that guitar, son," Ray said.

"You play it, then."

"Davis!" Meg said.

"Sorry, Mom. I mean, *please* play it?"

Ray's face grew tight and dark.

"Meg?" Spencer called again.

Damn. "Coming."

Meg forced herself to turn her back on the pair and shut the back door behind her. Sooner or later Davis was going to have to learn not everyone was as accommodating of his demands as she was.

"What's going on in there?" Spencer asked as she handed him the barbecue scraper.

"My son and your father are having a battle of wills."

"So Davis inherited the Valiella stubborn streak?"

"To put it mildly." Meg hesitated, hating to risk destroying the fledgling connection Spencer and Davis had forged today on the beach. But the risk of total alienation by *not* speaking out was greater.

"Davis is *very* stubborn," she said. "Also impulsive and unpredictable and, as you've seen, hyperactive. And although he's brighter than average, he finds it hard to concentrate, especially when it comes to learning to read and write."

Spencer tossed aside the scraper and started to pile charcoal briquettes into the base of the hibachi. "He's only six."

"He's got A.D.H.D."

Spencer frowned. "What?"

"Attention Deficit Hyperactive Disorder. No one knows exactly what causes it, but they think it's an imbalance of the neurotransmitters that send messages between brain cells—"

"No," Spencer broke in forcefully, "I've heard about A.D.—whatever. I just don't see what that has to do with Davis. He doesn't have a...a *disorder*. He's just your typical kid."

Meg's heart sank at the denial in Spencer's harsh voice. She'd been afraid of this reaction. "He's been diagnosed by a pediatrician in consultation with his kindergarten teacher," Meg said. "And me, of course."

"I had trouble learning to read and write," Spencer said. He crouched to pour lighter fluid on the briquettes and lit a match.

"It's often carried through the male genes."

Flames flared over the charcoal. "Now you're suggesting *I've* got it!"

"No." Meg wanted to warm her cold fingers at the fire, but Spencer's angry glare made her turn away. She hugged her arms around her waist and walked over to the ramshackle wooden fence where the tattered white blooms of a climbing rose clung to the boards. "But maybe you had it as a child. The fact that you've done so well gives me confidence Davis will outgrow it and won't always have to take the medication."

"You've got him taking drugs?" Spencer exclaimed.

"Please keep your voice down," Meg said, glancing at the open window into the kitchen. "His is only a mild case and he's on a very low dose. There's nothing to be alarmed about."

"I don't believe this."

"Well, you'd better start believing it, because this is your son. A.D.H.D. is part of his reality. And mine."

"I think this whole A.D.H.D. thing is way overblown," Spencer said, poking the coals into place. Gray tips had sprouted on the corners. "I don't believe in giving kids drugs. And I don't want my son growing up thinking they're the answer for every little setback in life."

"*Your* son?" Meg said in a harsh whisper. "Excuse me, but you're in no position to make pronouncements on what you want or don't want for Davis. You haven't been around."

Spencer got to his feet to return her whispered shout. "If you'd told me I *had* a son—"

"You haven't had to deal with his behavior. The medication makes a real difference."

"Keeps him doped up so he's easier to handle."

"It allows him to concentrate so he can learn. And anyway, what's wrong with me keeping my sanity? You don't know what he can be like." Tears of anger and frustration pushed at Meg's eyelids, threatening to spill.

Spencer rammed a hand through his hair. "I'm trying to learn."

"What's the point? You're not going to be around in the future."

"You don't know *what* I'm going to be doing in the future."

"Exactly!" Meg took in a ragged breath. "I resisted the pills for a long time. I felt the same as you. But being on medication is better for Davis's self-esteem than constantly failing or being yelled at by the one person who loves him just as he is, not for who he should be."

"I lo—" He stopped abruptly.

He couldn't say it, she thought bitterly. She'd accepted that he couldn't say he loved her. But if he couldn't even say he loved their son... She bowed her head.

Spencer stepped forward and wrapped his arms around her. "I'm sorry, Meg. So sorry."

She burrowed her head in the hollow of his neck. "Sorry doesn't help."

"You're right to blame me." His arms tightened.

Oh, how she'd craved the warmth of those arms. The feel of his strong body next to hers. The love and support, the passion and tenderness. All this she missed and longed for. All this she felt in one simple embrace.

All this was false.

Spencer had never lied, never promised more than he could give. She'd be a fool to start lying to herself. With effort, she pulled away. "Please don't—"

She broke off, hearing a sound from the house. "What was that?"

Spencer lifted his head, his hands falling away from her. The vibrating thrum of a guitar chord filtered through the window. "Ray got his guitar out," he said in amazement. "He's playing for Davis."

Spencer moved quickly toward the door, then

paused on the threshold with a triumphant grin. ''There can't be very much wrong with Davis if he's gotten Ray out of his slump, can there?''

Meg rubbed the heel of her hand across her eyes. The momentary lift she'd felt at Spencer's happiness faded. He didn't truly understand Davis. If he didn't understand, he wouldn't accept. And if he didn't accept him, nor the way she raised him, her job became that much harder.

Spencer walked softly through the kitchen so as not to disturb Ray and Davis. They sat side by side on the shabby couch, Ray showing Davis where to put his fingers and Davis's small hand stretching across the bridge of the guitar. Neither noticed Spencer.

''The strings hurt my fingers,'' Davis complained, even as he stubbornly tried to press the wire down to the frets.

''You've got to toughen them up, get callouses on your fingertips,'' Ray said. ''Okay, now hold the pick in your right hand and pull it down the strings. Over the hole. That's right.''

A faint twang was plucked from the strings. Brimming with excitement, Davis gazed up at Ray. Ray smiled back. Spencer blinked, an unexpected lump forming in his throat. *That's my son.*

Davis glanced over. ''Hey, Doc! Ray is going to teach me to play the guitar. Listen.'' He strummed again, his splayed left fingers slipping on the frets and delivering a discordant twang.

''You won't find a better teacher than Ray. Did he tell you he's almost a rock-and-roll legend?'' Spencer said, grinning at his father.

''What do you mean 'almost'?'' Ray flipped his ponytail indignantly over his shoulder.

Spencer laughed, he was so pleased to see Ray's spirit returning. But the adoring expression on Davis's face sent a fearful pang through him. "You realize it takes a long time to learn how to play the guitar," he said to his son.

Davis shrugged. "That's okay."

Okay as long as you didn't have a teacher who changed cities with as little thought as he changed his underwear. Spencer wanted to warn Davis not to expect too much. Not to get his hopes up in case they crashed. Not to count on his grandfather to be there for him. He shook his head, trying to clear the emotional confusion. And experienced a staggering empathy for Meg, knowing what she must feel in relation to himself and Davis.

SPENCER WALKED along the path from the faculty parking lot just as Meg was hurrying toward the biology building. Her long blond hair streamed out behind her, her cheeks were rosy with the cold and the blue of her eyes was intensified by the bright cobalt blue of her wool jacket. Her smile gave the jolt to his system that three cups of coffee at breakfast hadn't been able to accomplish.

"Do you have the tapes?" he asked when she'd caught up. Their field trip aboard the *Cape Beale* the previous week had been more than successful. It had taken a whole day to locate the killer whales, but once they had, they'd gotten enough hours of recordings for Meg to complete the research for her thesis.

"Yes, although I had to make copies, because listening to them once wasn't enough for Davis. I can't wait to start analyzing these new recordings of Takush and her calf."

"By the time you're finished you'll be hearing whale calls in your sleep," Spencer said, holding the door for her.

"I already am." She glanced at her watch. "I'd better run or I'll be late for my class. See you later." She started off, then paused. "Would you like to come for dinner again on Friday? Davis has been asking when we're going to see 'Doc' again."

Spencer was surprised at how good that made him feel. "Thanks. I will."

"Great. Six o'clock. Bye." She hurried off.

Whistling, Spencer moved along the hall to his lab. He inserted the key in the lock. The door swung open—good, Lee was here already. He entered and stopped short. Coming from behind the partition was the sound of a very distressed Lee speaking on the phone in Cantonese. His voice was high-pitched and strained, alternately defiant and diffident.

Spencer cleared his throat. Even though he couldn't understand a word, he didn't think it polite to listen without announcing his presence.

Lee broke off abruptly and poked his head around the partition, his dark eyes wide and worried. He put his hand over the mouthpiece and uttered a single word in English. "Help."

Spencer strode across the room. "What can I do?"

Lee jammed the receiver against his chest. "My father is very angry. He found out I dropped out of economics class. He demands to talk to the professor. Wants to know why his son failed the exam." Lee thrust the phone at Spencer. "Please. You talk to him."

"What? Me? What can I say?"

But suddenly the phone was in his hand and Lee's

beseeching gaze upon him. If Lee had failed his exam, it was probably because Spencer had given him the extra lab work he'd begged for.

"Hello, Mr. Cheung? This is Dr. Valiella, Lee's...professor."

Without actually saying so, Spencer let Cheung Sr. think he was Lee's economics professor. He reassured him that Lee was indeed a good student and was doing well in all his subjects. The failed exam was a fluke caused by fatigue and overwork. Spencer said he was certain it wouldn't be repeated. Lee would make up for the bad grade at Christmas....

"You're welcome, Mr. Cheung," Spencer said, winding up at last. "You know, Lee is also very interested in marine biology—" A barrage of excited Cantonese forced him to temporarily hold the receiver away from his ear. "I understand...yes...I know... Yes, it *is* possible to make a living as a marine biologist. No, not a lot, but he'd be doing something he loves. Isn't that important?"

Cheung Sr. then proceeded to tell Spencer what *he* thought was important—family honor, tradition, carrying on the business he'd worked many years to build. Spencer couldn't find a lot to disagree with. Yet he knew Lee was right, too.

Finally he said goodbye, handed the phone back to Lee and walked into his office. The leather seat let out a sigh as he slumped into it, head pounding. It was only Monday morning.

He pulled out a batch of essays he was grading and tried to concentrate. A few minutes later Lee appeared in the doorway.

"Thank you, Dr. Spencer."

Frowning, Spencer leaned back in his chair and

toyed with the red marking pen he held. "Don't do that to me again."

"I won't. Very sorry, Dr. Spencer." Lee hung his head.

Spencer rocked forward. "Lee, look at me."

Lee peered between the strands of black hair that had fallen over his eyes. "Yes, Dr. Spencer?"

"You've got to decide, you know, whether you're going to be a businessman or a biologist." Damn Ashton-Whyte for being right.

"You think I should be biologist?" Lee asked eagerly, his smile resurfacing with the smallest encouragement.

"I think you'd make a fine biologist—if that's what you want to do. But I can't make that decision for you. Neither can your father." He paused to let that sink in. "But if you decide on marine biology, you're going to have to tell your father. This pretense can't last. You know that."

"I know. Thank you, Dr. Spencer."

FRIDAY AFTERNOON, Meg spotted Davis through the crowd of parents and children milling in front of the school and hurried over. Shoulders slumped, jaw set obstinately, he stood kicking the metal base of the bicycle stand. Her heart sank. Of all days for Davis to be in a bad mood...

"Hi, honey. Everything okay?" She brushed the hair out of his eyes so she could see his face. Traces of dirt-smeared tears were visible on his cheeks.

Davis shrugged, dropped his head and resumed kicking the bicycle stand.

"I guess you've had a bad day," Meg said sympathetically, and took his hand to lead him to the

Toyota. "You can tell me about it on the way home. We have to hurry. Spen—, er, Doc is coming for dinner tonight."

As she edged into the traffic, Meg asked, "What happened?"

"Nothin'."

"Come on, Davis, I know something happened. What is it?"

He stared out the window. "I got sent to the principal's office."

"Why was that?" Meg hid her shock by keeping her voice neutral. It was the best way she'd found to prevent whatever the crisis was from escalating.

"...hit Tommy," Davis mumbled.

"You hit Tommy? Why?" This time she couldn't stop her voice from rising. One eye on the road and the other on her son, she navigated a left turn across an intersection and turned down their street.

"He was mean." Suddenly Davis blurted, "I'm *glad* I hit him. I *hate* him. He's always annoying me."

Meg breathed deeply. "What did he do that was so annoying?"

Davis turned away again. "Dunno."

"If you don't know, then why did you hit him?"

"I forget."

"Davis, we've talked about hitting. You know it's not right. No matter what someone does, they don't deserve to be hit. Did you say you were sorry?"

"No. That's why I had to go to the principal's office."

"Well, Davis—" Meg gripped the steering wheel "—when we get home you're going straight to your room."

"But, Mom! Doc said he was going to play catch with me next time he came over."

Meg would have liked to say, *You should have thought of that before you hit Tommy,* but she didn't. Kids didn't always think before they acted, especially kids like Davis. But she couldn't let him get away with bad behavior just because she wanted him to look good in front of his father.

"Then I guess you'll both be disappointed."

Davis burst into tears. He kicked the glove compartment. He yelled at Meg that she was the meanest mom in the whole world.

By the time she pulled up in front of the bungalow, he'd worked himself into a full-scale tantrum. Great. Spencer's black Camaro was parked across the street. Meg didn't wait for Spencer to get out of the car; she didn't even look his way. She hauled Davis out of the car and carried him kicking and screaming into the house and down the hall to his room.

"Time out, buster. Ten minutes—fifteen if I hear one single peep. Maybe, just maybe, you'll be allowed to play catch with Doc before supper. *If* you behave yourself."

She went back to the front door and greeted Spencer with a weary smile. "Sorry about that. Davis had a fight at school."

"What about?" Spencer asked, moving past her into the house. "Is he hurt? Where is he?"

"He's not hurt, but the other kid is. Davis was sent to the principal's office."

Spencer put an arm around her shoulders. "I'll talk to him."

Oh, the seductive power of a comforting embrace. Of shared responsibility. Meg shook her head and stepped away. "I sent him to his room. He's being punished."

"Were you ever sent to the principal's office?"

"Of course not!"

"Well, I was. I know what it's like. Let me talk to him." *He's my son, too.* Spencer didn't say it aloud but his intense gaze communicated the message loud and clear.

"Oh, all right. Second door on the left down the hall."

CHAPTER TWELVE

DAVIS SAT ON THE FLOOR, his knees up around his ears, and moved his toy cars in ever-tighter circles, crashing them into each other in head-on collisions. Stupid old principal. Stupid old Tommy. Stupid old Mom. They didn't understand him. Nobody understood him. *He* didn't even know why he acted so badly sometimes. That was hardest of all. *Crash. Crash. Crash. Crash.*

There was a knock at the door. Davis ignored it. It would just be Mom come to tell him again why he shouldn't hit. He knew he shouldn't hit. His hand had just flown up and smashed into Tommy's shoulder before he knew what he was doing.

Knock, knock.

"Go away!"

"Davis? It's me."

Doc. Davis brought the little red sports car to a halt before it smashed into the four-wheel drive. "What do you want?"

"I just want to talk."

Talk. Davis knew what that meant. All the things he'd done wrong and how he should try and behave better. But somehow Doc seemed different. He hadn't said anything about his wet clothes that day at the beach. "Okay."

The door opened and Spencer came in. He sat on the floor beside Davis. "Which is your favorite?"

"This one," Davis said, holding up the red sports car.

Spencer picked up a white Camaro and ran it across the floor in front of him. "I'll bet you a doughnut my car can annihilate that old Jeep real easy."

"What's annihilate?"

"*Destroy!*" Spencer said and smashed the Camaro into the Jeep with a force that sent it flying across the room.

"Cool!" Davis said, and ran to retrieve it. "Let *me* try."

Mom hated it when he crashed his cars and lectured him about damaging the cars and the walls. But Doc didn't mind. He even liked it, too, Davis could tell.

After they'd thoroughly annihilated the Jeep, they lined up all the cars and set up a ramp to do an Evil Knieval-style jump. While they worked they hardly needed to say anything. Doc seemed to know just what to do. Davis laughed when his sports car crashed down in the middle of the row of cars and quickly set them up again.

"I used to get in trouble at school," Spencer said, holding his white Camaro by the roof and moving it toward the ramp.

Here it comes, Davis thought.

"You know, Davis, there are a lot of people out there who want you to be just like them. They don't understand that it's your differences that make you special."

Mom was always saying he was special, but Davis hadn't heard anything quite like this before. He wasn't sure he understood. "Tommy laughs at me when I have to read out loud."

"Tommy's a jerk. Was that why you hit him?"

Davis shook his head. "He tells lies about me."

"What kind of lies?"

Davis's heart started to pound. He was scared to tell Doc what Tommy said about him not having a father in case it settled things once and for all—and not in the way he hoped. Making a *vroom*ing sound in his throat, he pushed his car down the ramp and sent it flying up and over all the cars.

"Good one!" Spencer straightened the lineup of cars. "If *you* know the truth, does it really matter what Tommy says?"

Davis shrugged. "I dunno."

"I guess other kids listen to Tommy and believe him."

Davis nodded. *Everybody* listened to Tommy, instead of him.

"That kind of thing makes you hurt inside. When I was a kid my dad and mom went away for a long time. I told everyone my dad was the leader of a rock band and he was playing in Europe. Nobody believed me. They didn't like me because I didn't fit in. I wasn't good at games. I didn't know how to make friends."

"Did your dad come back?" Davis found he couldn't take his gaze off Doc's face. *Doc.* That wasn't his right name.

Spencer's straight dark brows pushed together, making a wrinkle above his nose. "Yeah, he came back eventually."

"Tommy says I don't have a dad." Davis looked

Doc straight in the eye. "I *know* I have a dad. His name is Spencer."

Davis held his breath while he waited for Doc to say something. Would he tell the truth? Would he lie? Or would he say something stupid like "Everybody has a dad"? The small bump in Doc's throat slid up and down. Davis felt his hands grow clammy and he gripped the sports car till the tires dug into his palm.

"*My* name is Spencer," Doc said at last. His voice was low and raspy. "I'm your father. But I think you already know that."

Davis blinked. His throat closed up and he couldn't speak, so he nodded. He waited for Spencer to hug him or something, but he didn't. He just put a hand on Davis's shoulder and gave it a squeeze.

"Hey, do you want to go kayaking sometime, just the two of us? I've got a kayak that seats two people."

Davis nodded again. "S-sure. Thanks..." He wanted to say "Dad" but couldn't.

"Great." Spencer unfolded his legs and rose to his feet. "And, Davis? I don't believe in violence, but sometimes the Tommys of this world need to be reminded they're not the boss of you. You're a great kid. You do what you think is right."

"Okay." Davis felt better than he had in a long time. His father *liked* him. He hadn't gotten mad at him for hitting. He *understood*. And he was taking him kayaking.

Happily, Davis started to line up his cars again. This time the sports car was really going to kick some butt.

Meg was putting out the plates when Spencer came

into the kitchen. Her questioning glance sought his across the table.

"Davis wasn't very happy with himself for what he did, but he's okay now." Spencer hesitated. "I told him."

Her eyebrows rose further. "I thought we'd do it together when the time was right."

"It just came up." If the situation had been reversed, he would have wanted it to be a joint effort, too. But he didn't think it pure conceit to believe he'd made a difference to the boy today. He *knew* how Davis felt in this situation, probably better than Meg.

He walked around the table and put his hands on her waist where it curved into her hips. *Mother of his child.* He couldn't be angry with her anymore. Not now that he knew what it was like to feel protective of Davis. "He knew already. I don't know how."

Meg's gaze shifted from his mouth to his eyes. "More goes on in his head than I sometimes give him credit for because he doesn't always express himself well."

Her eyes were so blue they made him dizzy, as if he was looking up, up, up, into a summer sky. "I said I'd take him kayaking one day soon."

The tip of her tongue touched her lower lip as she held his gaze. "He'll like that."

"Can he—" He forgot what he'd been about to ask. He just wanted to bury his hands in her hair, to kiss her sweet mouth.

Her shallow breath was audible. "Swim? A little."

Spencer was drowning. He bent to kiss the corner of her smile. She turned her head so their lips met full-on. Meg—soft, warm, infinitely desirable. He pulled her to him, molding her body to his. Their mouths opened to each other and their tongues met. Suddenly he was so hard he ached. His hand slipped inside her sweater, skimmed upward across heated skin to cup her breast. His thumb brushed her nipple and she moaned, her hips pressing into his. *Oh, Meg. Oh, Meg.*

"*Vrooom, vrooom, vrooom.*" The sound of a toy car being driven along the wall heralded Davis's approach.

Meg's lashes swept Spencer's nose. She pushed him away, fumbling to pull down her sweater. "Oh, hello, Davis. You can come out of your room now."

Dazed, Spencer let her go only to be confronted by Davis's curious gaze. The boy looked at him, then said to his mom, "Spencer's my dad."

Spencer listened for anger or resentment. After all, they hadn't been straight with him. There was nothing but quiet pride in the boy's voice. Pride in having him as his father. Spencer hadn't considered that possibility. Or how good it would feel.

"That's right." Meg pushed back her long hair. "I didn't tell you before because I was waiting for the right time."

"What time is it?" Davis asked, glancing at the wall clock.

Spencer chuckled and caught Meg's eye. She smiled back and a feeling of warmth stole through him, catching him off guard. This was what belonging to a family felt like.

"Time for dinner," she said, and pulled her son into a hug. "Go wash your hands."

He didn't move. "You two were kissing. Are you going to get married?"

Meg's gaze darted to Spencer's and back to Davis. "Married? My goodness, no!"

Spencer didn't know what to say. Marriage had never been in his plans. "Better go wash your hands, Davis."

He stayed till Davis was tucked into bed. Before he had a chance to take up with Meg where they'd been interrupted, she said, in her bright false voice, "Wow, look at the time. It's been a really nice evening, but I've got homework to do. Some slave driver of a prof assigned the class three chapters to read *and* a ten-page essay due next week."

"You'll ace it." He reached for her but she slipped away.

"If I do, it'll be because I work like a dog. Not everyone is naturally brilliant." She continued toward the front door, forcing Spencer to follow.

"You're kicking me out. Why?"

She dropped the pretense. "Because of Davis, of course. He saw us kissing and jumped to the conclusion we were going to marry. What would he think if he found you in my bed?"

Spencer opened his mouth to protest.

"You *know* that's where we were headed," she said.

"It's what I wanted." He stepped closer, tucked a strand of hair behind her ear, his eyes searching her face. "I could leave before he gets up."

She shook her head, her gaze never leaving his.

"I think about making love to you." His voice came out low and husky. "All the time."

Meg shut her eyes, swallowed and stepped back. "It's too soon."

"You mean, it's seven years too late."

She wrapped her arms around herself. "No."

Spencer took a deep breath and got hold of himself. It wasn't going to happen. At least not tonight. He took his jacket from the rack and put it on before opening the door and stepping out onto the stoop. "Davis took the news very calmly."

Meg came forward to lean on the door frame. "I know, and it worries me. We haven't talked about the future. He may be expecting more than you're willing to give."

She seemed to be waiting for him to say something. But at this point, the future was too uncertain for him to make pronouncements on it. "One day at a time, Meg. But no matter what happens, I'll always be his father. I won't forget that fact."

He leaned forward, unable to leave without one more kiss. Her lips felt lush and warm, but her mood was cold. "What's wrong, Meg?" he murmured.

"Nothing. Everything. I don't know. Maybe I'm just tired." She pulled away and retreated into the warmth and light of the house leaving him on the step with the cold wind seeping through the seams of his jacket.

He jammed his hands into his pockets. "I'll see you tomorrow. No, wait, not tomorrow. I've got a field trip with my first-year class. I'll call you, okay?"

"Sure." She gave him a small sad smile. And shut the door.

SPENCER DIDN'T SEE much of Meg the next week; they were both in and out of the lab, busy with classes, but he arranged to take Davis kayaking the following Saturday. On that morning, Spencer was awakened by an unfamiliar sound outside his window.

A metallic *click-thwack, click-thwack* underscored by a *swish, swish, swish.* What the hell?

He sat up in bed and pushed the dark blue curtains aside to see Ray walk past pushing...*a manual lawn mower?* That was strange enough but...*Ray had cut his hair.* Gone was the ponytail he'd worn for as long as Spencer could remember. His black hair with its frosting of silver had been cut in a short spiky style, and his chin was shadowed by the bristly outline of a future goatee.

Ray turned the corner at the end of the patch of lawn, glanced up and saw Spencer staring at him. He smiled, his eyes crinkling at the corners, and waved.

Spencer twisted the latch and shoved on the window to push it open. "What's going on? Where'd you get that contraption? What'd you do to your hair?"

Ray stopped pushing the mower. "The old boy up the road had a garage sale. He gave it to me for a dollar. How many things can you get these days that are so useful for only a dollar, eh?"

"And your hair?"

Ray grinned and shrugged. "Felt like a change, is all."

Spencer shook his head, unable to come up with a coherent response. Dropping the curtain, he pushed himself out of bed.

By the time he'd washed and had breakfast, Ray had finished cutting the lawn and was stripping the peeling paint off the front of the cottage. Spencer took him out a cup of coffee and sat on the step to drink his own. His feet were bare and his toes curled against the cold, reminding him that it was already November and the end of term wasn't far off.

"What brought on this surge of activity?" he asked Ray.

"Can't sit around doing nothing forever," Ray said, scraping energetically. "It's not right the boy should come here and see us living like pigs."

Well, well, would wonders never cease? "Isn't this the wrong time of year for painting exteriors?"

"Just getting it ready for next spring. The whole place could use some sprucing up."

"You planning on being here next spring?"

Ray paused to reach for his coffee. "I might."

They eyed each other for a moment in silence. Finally, Ray said, "I called my agent last night. Told him I'm going solo. I've been working on a couple of new songs. Whole new style."

Spencer nodded. Once or twice he'd heard his father playing late at night in his room. What he'd heard he'd liked, although he hadn't said a word for fear of jinxing it. He was just glad to see his father happy again.

"Comes a time when a man's got to reinvent himself," Ray went on as he resumed scraping paint. "If what you're doing isn't working, you've got to change."

"Are you really going to give Davis guitar lessons?"

Ray squinted over his shoulder. "Afraid I didn't mean it?"

Spencer shrugged, not saying anything.

"*I'm* not going to be the one to disappoint that kid," Ray said, shaking his scraper at Spencer.

Finding the wooden porch suddenly uncomfortable, Spencer got to his feet. The wind coming off the beach carried the iodine scent of seaweed, and far out over the water it was already starting to rain.

"I gotta admit, it was a shock to find out I'm a grandfather," Ray said. "But now that I'm used to the idea, I kinda like it. It's a chance for me to make up for screwing up as a father."

"Forget it, Dad, you didn't screw up." Spencer drained the last of his coffee.

Ray glanced down at the scraper in his hands. "I always felt bad about that year and a half we left you with Bob and Julie."

"Yeah, well." Spencer set his gaze on a distant freighter.

"We were still struggling then. Going to Europe was the chance of a lifetime."

He shouldn't let his father get into this. There was always a justification. Still... "How could you abandon me to strangers?"

Ray glanced at him in surprise. "Bob was my cousin. I hadn't seen him in a few years, but at one time we were very close. They had kids, animals. I thought you'd like it there. And I wasn't abandoning you, I was protecting you."

"From what?"

"Life on the road. It was bad enough taking you that summer you were thirteen, but as a five-year-old? No way. You would have missed your first year of school, seen and heard things no child should see or hear. And who would have looked after you? Your mom was part of the band."

Spencer hadn't thought of it that way. Odd how childish feelings of rejection could color adult perceptions. But he was the last person to suggest Ray ought to have compromised his career for someone else's sake.

"Yeah, well, maybe you're right." He glanced at his watch. "I've got to go. I'm taking Davis kayaking."

"Say, Spence," Ray called after him.

Spencer turned and waited.

"All that boy wants is someone to look up to."

Spencer nodded, but he knew better. Davis wanted a father to be there and to love him.

MEG PEERED FRETFULLY through the kitchen window at the rain and, shivering, wrapped her royal-blue robe around herself more tightly. On the radio the weatherman announced light winds increasing to strong later in the day.

She wished Spencer hadn't said he'd take Davis kayaking today.

She was still upset with Spencer. She'd given him a clear opening to say he'd be around for Davis in the future and he hadn't taken it. Well, it was no more than she'd expected. He'd never been able to commit himself. She supposed she should be grateful he wasn't making promises he couldn't keep.

Patrick's humming baritone and light step made her turn. "You're up early for a Saturday," she said.

"Couldn't sleep," he replied, making a beeline for the coffeepot. "What's with Davis? He almost knocked me over racing for the bathroom to brush his teeth. Is he sick or something?"

"Spencer is taking him kayaking."

Patrick folded his arms and gave an exaggerated shiver. "You wouldn't catch me on the water today for love or money."

"Patrick, you're in the navy. You're supposed to *like* the ocean."

"Yes, love, but we're on those great big boats, high above the actual wet stuff." He sipped at his coffee. "The north Pacific is damn cold. You fall in, you can die within thirty minutes in these temperatures."

"Thank you so much for reminding me." Meg had awakened in the night from a dream of Davis falling out of the kayak and floundering and sinking, hampered by heavy clothing. When he reached out to Spencer, his father wasn't there.

She snatched the phone off the wall and punched in Spencer's number. "I'm going to call and cancel. It's too nasty a day."

As she picked up the receiver, Davis raced into the kitchen. "Is he here yet?"

"Shh, I'm on the phone. Oh, hi, Ray. Is Spencer there?" Her shoulders slumped. "Thanks, anyway. No, no message." She paused, listening. "How about next Saturday? He's really looking forward to learning to play. Take care. Bye."

She hung up and bent to put an arm around Davis's shoulders. "I don't know if you'll be going on the water today, honey. It's wet and miserable outside and—"

"Mom!" Davis wailed. "I wanna go kayaking."

"Weather conditions aren't very safe. And not much fun, either. Spencer will tell you the same thing."

"But you *promised!*"

She hadn't, but Meg wasn't about to engage in a session of "Did too" "Did not"—a battle she never won. Instead, she removed herself to the laundry room to throw a load of wet clothes into the dryer.

Charlie the lizard slithered out from behind a rock and flicked his tongue at her.

She heard the doorbell ring and hurried back out, but Davis had already run to answer it. Spencer entered, his hair beaded with water, his shoulders damp.

Davis tugged on his jacket. ''We're still going kayaking, aren't we? It's not too wet, is it?''

Spencer reached out and ruffled Davis's hair. The simple gesture stabbed at Meg's heart. ''Of course we're still going,'' he said. ''What kind of marine biologists would we be if we let a little rain put us off?''

''You won't be kayaking among killer whales, I hope,'' Meg said, twisting the cord on her bathrobe into a knot.

''Oh, boy, I hope we do!'' Davis exclaimed.

Over Davis's head, Spencer lifted his eyebrows and Meg was marginally reassured. The gesture told her that he wasn't planning on pursuing killer whales and that if he encountered any, they would keep a safe distance. But he wasn't going to say so aloud and spoil Davis's excitement.

''Well, if you're really determined to go, I'll get the lunch I packed for Davis.''

''I brought sandwiches.''

''But you don't know what he likes.''

''Peanut butter and jam.'' He glanced down at Davis. ''Right?''

Davis smiled up at him. ''Right.''

''Have you got drinks?''

''Hot chocolate for Davis. Coffee for me.'' Spencer plucked Davis's raincoat off the coatrack and handed it to him.

''What about a life jacket?'' she said, more to detain them than because she thought he wouldn't have one. Unfamiliar panic was overtaking her. Spencer had opened the door and Davis was slipping away.

"I borrowed a child-size jacket from the neighbors."

"The wind is freshening."

"I checked with the Department of Meteorology this morning. The wind's from the southwest, gusting up to twenty knots. I'll take him to Pedder Bay—it's very sheltered." He stepped onto the porch. "See you later this afternoon."

"Wait!" Meg cried. "Davis's medication." She ran back to the kitchen to dig the plastic pill container out of Davis's lunch bag. Patrick spooned branflakes into his mouth and shook his head in amusement. She started back, then grabbed the lunch, as well. Davis was already in the Camaro, his face a pale blur behind the rain-streaked glass.

"One tablet after lunch," she said, handing Spencer the vial. "But he's got to eat first."

Spencer held the vial up to the light and frowned. "There's half a dozen pills in here."

"Just in case." She thrust the plastic bag into his other hand. "You might as well take the sandwiches, too."

His dark green gaze softened. He laid his palm against her cheek and smiled. "I'll look after him as if he was my own son."

"I know," she whispered, her eyes shutting briefly. His touch made her weak. She'd been alone so long and the illusion of partnership, of love, was so strong, so tempting.

And then his hand was gone and he was pulling an envelope from an inside pocket of his jacket. "If you're going near a post office today, would you mind mailing this for me?"

She glanced at the address. Bergen, Norway.

"I've decided to defer the fellowship for a year. Get to know my son. See what happens. But maybe you shouldn't tell Davis just yet."

Meg searched his eyes. She saw confusion and the willingness to try. He'd accepted fatherhood, if only temporarily. Slowly she reached out and took the envelope. Now, more than ever, she had to hold on to her heart.

She gave him a little shove out the door. "Go."

MEG HAD A TON OF HOMEWORK to do, but although she spread her books over the kitchen table and sat herself down, she couldn't get her mind to focus.

"Why don't you come to the art gallery with me and Douglas?" Patrick suggested, checking his hair in the hall mirror.

"Thanks, but no. I might go visit my mother."

"Now *there's* a fun way to spend a Saturday afternoon. Give the Dragon Lady a big kiss from me. Ta-ta, sweetcheeks," he said, and waggled his fingers in farewell as he went out the door.

"Bye. Have fun."

Meg put Spencer's letter in her purse and drove across town. He was only staying out of a sense of duty, but that was better than nothing. Maybe. As she passed the post office she slowed, but the traffic light was about to change so she sped up to catch it before it turned red. Plenty of time to find a mailbox later.

The situation with her mother had improved in some respects and deteriorated in others. Helen no longer shunned Davis or refused to talk about his

A.D.H.D. Instead, she spent hours at the library and on the Internet researching the subject—and coming up with reams of unsolicited advice for Meg.

By the time Meg turned into the long curving driveway, the rain had stopped. She drove slowly past the rosebushes, stripped of blooms but strung with spiderwebs beaded with water droplets. Helen was kneeling on an old cushion and digging in the garden bed. When she saw Meg, she brushed the dirt off her gloved hands and rose stiffly to walk over to the car. Her gray sweatpants were damp at the knees, and she wore a yellow silk scarf around her neck above the matching top.

"Hello, dear." Helen glanced at the empty back seat. "Isn't Davis with you?"

"Spencer took him kayaking." Okay, so maybe she had another reason for coming by today—to let her parents know Spencer was taking a genuine interest in his son.

"Is that safe?" Helen asked, frowning.

"Perfectly," Meg replied blithely. "What are you planting?"

"Hyacinth and daffodil bulbs. Come and talk to me while I carry on. I want to finish in case it starts to rain again."

Meg glanced at the lowering clouds. They would be out on the water by now. She hoped Spencer made sure Davis wore his hat.

She took a handful of bulbs from the burlap sack lying by Helen's cushion and crouched to dig a hole in the soft, loamy soil. She had to admit digging in the dirt held a certain sensual enjoyment. Davis apparently thought so; he liked to get right down and roll around in it.

"So Spencer has acknowledged Davis as his son?" Helen's acerbic tone grated on Meg's nerves.

"He never denied it, Mother. That day on the boat when he left so abruptly he was just shocked by the news. He likes Davis. Likes him a lot."

"But is he going to be a real father to him or just drop in whenever he's in town?"

Something, some doubt or fear, stopped Meg from telling Helen that Spencer was opting out of Norway to stay in Victoria. "Wherever he is, he'll be Davis's real father."

"Now, Margaret, you know what I mean. I only have your and Davis's interests at heart."

Meg rammed the hyacinth bulb into the hole she'd dug. "For six years *you* barely acknowledged Davis's existence. Now suddenly he's the flavor of the month and you're blaming Spencer for not immediately knowing how his son is going to fit into his life? Give the guy a break."

Helen's lips pressed together as she stabbed at the earth with her trowel. "How can you defend him after all he's done to you?"

"He's done nothing to me."

"Then what has he done *for* you?"

"He gave me Davis."

"He ruined your life."

"*Mother.* My life is what I make it."

"He won't marry you."

Meg put down her trowel. *Damn Helen for saying that.* All the hurt and fear and confusion she was feeling welled up. She fought back the tears. "I know," she said quietly.

"Oh, Meggie." Helen moved across the grass and put her arms around her. "You love him."

Meg nodded against Helen's shoulder. It seemed years since her mother had embraced her. Heedless of her dirty hands, she clutched Helen's back. Before she knew it, her tears were flowing.

"Does he love you?"

"I don't know."

"Have a good cry—you'll feel better." Helen rocked Meg as though she were a little girl and not a full-grown woman.

Meg abandoned herself to being comforted, soaking up her mother's love and support. But when finally she got herself under control, she wished she hadn't broken down in front of Helen. Slowly she lifted her eyes. Helen's gaze was sympathetic rather than judgmental. It almost made her cry again.

"Thanks, Mom," she said, sniffing. "I needed that."

Helen smiled and patted her on the back. "I understand your attraction to him."

Meg pulled back, surprised. "You do?"

Helen nodded. "He's good-looking and sexy and intelligent. But it's the attraction of the unattainable, darling. Not a good bet in the long run."

"I DREAMED ABOUT THIS," Davis said from the bow of the kayak, awkwardly wielding the heavy paddle with his small arms. His stroke fell into the water with a splash that would have sent the boat sideways had Spencer not anticipated the movement and compensated with a stroke of his own.

"About kayaking?" The boy hadn't stopped talking since they'd left the house. Spencer hadn't realized there were so many questions in the world.

The red bobble on Davis's knitted hat bounced as

he nodded. "I dreamed I was in a kayak with my dad behind me. And you are," he added happily. "Wait'll I tell Tommy."

Spencer paddled closer to the rocky tree-lined shore, not knowing quite what to say. Davis seemed to accept his sudden appearance so matter-of-factly and to take for granted Spencer's continuing presence in his life. Spencer almost felt he should warn the boy, but couldn't bring himself to damage the bond forming between them.

"Do you have a lot of dreams?"

"Oh, yes," Davis said, and went on to describe in vivid detail his latest.

Spencer listened in wonder. Until Davis, he'd had no idea children led such complex inner lives. To the boy, everything was a source of intense interest, from the row of long-necked black cormorants perched on a log to the whiskery splash of a sleek brown head as a harbor seal slipped beneath the water.

With Davis, Spencer felt as if he was experiencing being on the water for the first time. The splash the paddles made as they dipped, the cool wetness on their cheeks as the breeze blew the spray back into their faces. When Davis was older and a more accomplished paddler, Spencer would take him out on open water—

Spencer chopped his thoughts short. He'd put off going to Norway for the moment, but just how long was he planning on staying here? One year? Two? It was almost impossible to imagine.

Would he be around to teach Davis how to paddle properly? Or how to swim and use a snorkel? The boy needed someone to play catch with, too. Sure, he had Meg's father, but Roger was, well, Roger. Ray was teaching him guitar—until he got a hankering for different scenery and took off.

Spencer decided he'd leave this kayak behind when he left so Meg could take Davis to see the killer whales.

The decision made him feel only slightly better.

WEEKS FLEW BY, and suddenly Meg noticed that Christmas decorations had gone up in stores. It was early December and still she hadn't mailed Spencer's letter. It weighed on her conscience. She thought of it whenever she passed a mailbox. Once she even went so far as to push it halfway through the mail slot. But at the last minute she pulled it out again and stuffed it back in her purse.

For regardless of all Spencer's efforts to be a dad, she knew he wasn't fully committed to staying in Victoria. Oh, he saw Davis regularly and she could tell he enjoyed their son's company. But there was an air of impermanence about him that she couldn't pin down, but couldn't entirely dismiss, either. Maybe it had something to do with the fact that ever since the night Davis had caught them kissing, Spencer hadn't tried for a repeat performance even though the sexual tension between them had heated unabated till the pressure was almost unbearable. If he really intended to stay, he would have pursued an intimate relationship.

What she'd admitted to Helen was true—she loved Spencer. But it wasn't enough that he should stay for Davis's sake. She wanted him to stay for her, as well. She wanted them to marry so they could become a real family. But unless and until he wanted that, too, until he *spoke* those very words, Meg wasn't going to burn his bridges. The time might come, sooner than he thought, when he'd decide to leave, after all. If that happened, she knew she'd want him out of her life as fast as possible.

So the letter sat in her purse in a tangled nest of grocery-store receipts and tissues, its edges curled and worn, a constant reminder of how her life could change on a whim.

And then one day while she was working in the lab and her eyes were starting to cross from staring too long at spectrograms and her brain was turning to mush from hearing the same *weeoaws* over and over again, she heard a slightly different sound. She played it again just to make sure. She peered at the accompanying spectrogram, and excitement started to build. She'd have to analyze it statistically to be certain but...

"Spencer!" she shouted, leaping to her feet. "Come and see this!"

CHAPTER THIRTEEN

"I'M GOING TO RUN the program again to double-check," Meg said to Spencer from her seat in front of the computer. Spectrograms of Takush and her calf etched themselves across the monitor screen.

Spencer glanced at her tired intent face as she punched in the commands, and wondered if she was taking care of herself. Wondered what she'd say if he put his hand on her cheek and brought her mouth slowly around to meet his lips...

Who was he kidding? He didn't even kiss her casually hello and goodbye anymore. Every time he so much as brushed her lips with his, he became instantly aroused. He thought about her every second of the day and night. He wanted her so badly he could taste it. Sometimes he caught her looking at him, and knew she wanted him just as much as he wanted her. But he didn't pursue a physical relationship. It wasn't fair when he knew she wanted more from him.

Meg was being cautious and he didn't blame her. He was beginning to think he shouldn't have canceled Norway so hastily. The tighter the bonds of responsibility and commitment became, the more he wanted to run.

"If this test confirms your results—"

"Don't," she said quickly. "Because if it doesn't, I'm going to shoot myself. I should have been studying for Christmas exams this week, instead of spending all my time on my project.''

''A little sleep wouldn't have hurt, either.''

''Sleep? What's that?''

''How's Davis?'' Ever since their kayaking trip Spencer devoted Saturdays to his son. They went beachcombing, to a movie, and once they went on the ferry to Vancouver and visited the aquarium in Stanley Park. And he always made sure he was home when Meg brought Davis out to the cottage for a guitar lesson with Ray. When they weren't together, Spencer thought about the boy and wondered what he was doing and how he was feeling.

''He's supposed to be a reindeer in the school Christmas concert, but he refuses to wear antlers.'' Meg's voice held exasperation and a touch of motherly indulgence.

''I'd feel silly in antlers, too.'' Spencer was tolerant of Davis's quirks, but maybe that was because he didn't have to deal with their consequences on a daily basis. He knew now how frustrating the boy's unpredictable and sometimes difficult behavior could be. Yet also how rewarding his quick intelligence and huge capacity for affection were.

Meg flashed him a wary glance. ''He's hoping you'll come to the concert.''

''When is it?'' he asked, equally wary. Appearing in public as a family was something he had trouble dealing with. He was trying hard to do and be everything a dad was supposed to, but he hadn't been able to perform one essential task—making a commitment to Meg and Davis in his heart. Norway was always at the back of his mind as an escape hatch. With one call to Bergen he could be gone. There were days when his hand itched to pick up the phone.

"Next Wednesday night," she said. "At the school."

"That's the night my Philosophy of Science class is sitting their exam."

"Can't you get someone else to supervise?"

"I promised I'd buy them all a beer afterward."

Meg turned back to the computer, her lips compressed.

"I'm sorry, Meg. It's not something I can get out of."

"Don't worry about it. I understand how a bunch of students could be more important than your son."

What might have developed into an argument was cut short by the sound of voices in the corridor. Voices speaking Cantonese. A moment later Lee entered the lab with a balding man in a well-cut business suit.

Lee glanced nervously at Spencer. "Dr. Spencer, this is my father, Cheung Yau."

"Hello, Mr. Cheung." Spencer rose and extended his hand, hoping this wasn't what he thought it was. "Welcome to the lab. Have you come to see where Lee works?"

"I have come to take my son back to Hong Kong," Mr. Cheung replied, courteously dipping his head. "Pack your things, Lee."

"Yes, Father." Lee cast a dejected glance at Spencer as he slipped past him to the desk behind the partition. In a few seconds they could hear the sounds of him emptying his drawer. Mr. Cheung waited silently, hands clasped in front of him.

Spencer pushed his fingers through his hair. He

couldn't believe Cheung was going to take Lee away. He had to do something, or Lee would lose all he'd worked for. He glanced at Meg. White-faced and anxious, she'd risen from her chair, her spectrograms and the new stats program forgotten.

"Mr. Cheung," Spencer began, "Christmas exams start soon. If Lee leaves now, he won't get credit for the term."

Cheung Yau bowed his head again. "Lee will stay to write his business exams, but I do not wish him to be distracted by working in this laboratory. As for biology exams, they are irrelevant."

"But what will he do back in Hong Kong?"

"He will go to work in my office until he can enrol at a local university. In the business school."

Lee reappeared, his ordinarily smiling face set in gloom. All his energy and exuberance seemed to be packed into the briefcase that weighed down his right arm. "I am very sorry, Dr. Spencer, to leave so suddenly. Please tell Doc I will finish the journal article and send it e-mail…" His voice trailed off, his Adam's apple bobbing.

Spencer stepped between Lee and his father. "Lee, you've worked hard to accumulate your biology credits. If you went to summer school, you could probably start an honors project next year. And after that, a master's degree."

An agonized expression appeared on Lee's face.

"Lee, come," his father commanded.

Lee hesitated, then started forward.

"Wait a minute," Spencer ordered. "Mr. Cheung, Lee has what it takes to be an excellent biologist."

"Lee also has an aptitude for business."

"What do *you* think, Lee?" Spencer demanded.

Lee glanced at his father and shifted his briefcase to his other hand. "I could do biology *or* business."

"But marine biology, you love. What about your passion for killer whales?"

Lee hung his head.

"Imagine what it would be like to spend the rest of your life doing something you don't enjoy. Living somewhere you don't want to be." *Stuck in Victoria, under Ashton-Whyte's thumb.* Just the thought made Spencer start to perspire. "*Think,* Lee. What do *you* want?"

Slowly, Lee raised his head. Conflict raged in his tortured eyes. Tension pulled the skin taut around his unsmiling mouth. He looked at Spencer. He looked at his father. "Family honor comes first."

His father nodded approvingly.

"Nothing is impossible if you want it badly enough," Spencer said, refusing to give up. "You can write your own story."

Lee stared at Spencer, his gaze opaque now. Cheung Yau barked out a few sharp words in Cantonese. Lee's shoulders stiffened and he moved toward his father and the door. "Goodbye, Dr. Spencer. Thank you for all you have done for me."

All he'd done wasn't anywhere near enough. Spencer's gaze darted to Meg. "You can jump in anytime."

She gave her head a tiny shake.

She hugged Lee, blinking hard. "Good luck," she said, a catch in her voice. "Come back as soon as you can."

And then Lee and his father were gone. Just like that.

Spencer turned on Meg. "Couldn't you have said *something* to try to get him to stay?"

"Do you think he'd listen to me with his father right there?" she shot back. "People do what they have to do. You should know that better than anyone."

"But he's just thrown away years of study. Hell, he's thrown away his future. Don't you care about that?"

"Of course I care. But you can't interfere. You want him to choose biology because that's what *you* see as most important. Maybe he's just dabbling. Maybe this isn't the big crisis of conscience you think it is for him."

Spencer shook his head. "Doc doesn't waste time with dabblers. Look what Lee's already gone through to work with killer whales. He deserves a chance to study marine biology if that's what he wants. He could have told his father he wasn't going back to Hong Kong. Maybe he would have if he thought more people were on his side."

"I *know* what it's like to want and wait and sacrifice to get an education," Meg said forcefully. "It's worth almost anything. But I'm afraid I don't agree with your individual-is-all stance." She jumped up and pushed past him to her desk, returning with her backpack and purse. "I've got to get out of here."

She was out the exit door and halfway down the steps when Spencer caught up with her. "Why are you running away?"

She strode on. "*I'm* not running away."

"Then maybe you're on your way to my car."

"I'm not going anywhere with you."

"Have you forgotten?" he said. "We're visiting Doc today."

Meg strode on. "I'm not in the mood for visiting."

Spencer grabbed her arm and made her stop. "Don't you want to tell him your results?"

She clapped a hand over her mouth. "My results!"

Together they hurried back into the lab.

The computer had finished running the new stats program, and the results she was hoping for stared up at her from the monitor screen. Meg shrieked and threw her arms around Spencer's neck, their heated words forgotten. "It's true! Oh, Spencer, we did it!"

He picked her up and swung her around. "*You* did it."

Laughing, Meg said, "I couldn't have without your help."

Spencer set her back on her feet, his eyes locked with hers. "We make a helluva team."

Meg's breath caught in her chest as his intense gaze dropped to her mouth and his lips parted. She pushed herself out of his arms. "If only Lee could have stayed just a little longer, he would have known about this, too."

"There'll be a lot of things he won't learn about now."

"Oh, Spencer, I do feel badly about Lee." She laid a hand on his arm. "I'm sorry."

"Hell, it's sure not your fault." His hand closed over hers and squeezed. "Let's go see Doc."

While Spencer got his things from his office, Meg hit the print button and waited impatiently for the sheets of data. Spencer came out, one arm in the sleeve of his jacket, a sheaf of papers stuffed in his briefcase. "Have you got the tapes?"

"Never go anywhere without them," she said, patting her backpack.

When they were in the car, Meg took his briefcase and tried to shuffle the crumpled pages into order. "These are student essays you've messed up. Do you have any idea how much care these kids take to make them perfect?"

"Since when did you become a neat freak?" He took the briefcase away from her and tossed it into the back seat. Then he started the engine and squealed out of the parking lot.

"You know what your trouble is?" Meg said, stabbing the air in his direction. In spite of Lee's departure, getting the results she'd hoped for had put her on top of the world, and she was more than ready to take Spencer to task. "You think you can have it all your own way."

One hand draped over the wheel, he squinted sideways at her. "*What* are you talking about?"

"You're just like your father—afraid of the future."

Spencer snorted disparagingly.

"It's true," she said. "You're treading water, refusing to acknowledge it's time to move on to another stage of life."

"Just what am I supposed to metamorphose into?" Spencer flattened a hand against his chest. "This is it, baby. What you see is what you get. My father's problem is that for years he's been living in the past and he's only just realized it."

"It would help if you weren't so critical of him. But I guess I shouldn't be surprised," she said, turning away and putting her nose in the air. "According to you, family obligations are subordinate to individual desires.''

"Oh, no, you can't throw that back at me. I've given him money, listened to his drunken ramblings…'' Spencer pushed a hand through his rumpled hair. "He's trying, I guess, to bring himself up to date. Look at the haircut.''

"The haircut is nothing. Don't you know Ray is *that* close to signing a new recording contract?'' She held up two fingers almost touching.

Spencer turned to stare at her. "Are you kidding me?''

"Watch out!''

He straightened the wheel, narrowly missing an oncoming delivery truck. "Why didn't he tell *me* that?''

She shrugged. "Maybe he wants it to be a sure thing first. For some strange reason he values your opinion of him.''

"Well, I'll be damned," Spencer said, grinning proudly. "This will be a solo album, right?''

She nodded. "Did you know he's seeing a woman?''

"The painter who lives a few cottages down from us? Yes, I know about her. I'm not totally out of touch.''

Meg turned sideways in her seat to face him. "Ray is doing just fine. What are *you* doing to step out of the past?''

His smile faded. "I'm moving forward all the time.''

"Right," she muttered. "So fast no one can keep up.''

Spencer turned onto the short gravel road that led

to Doc's Panabode house overlooking the ocean. "Here we are."

Marjorie Campbell, a tall strapping white-haired woman in a handknit sweater and skirt of russet wool, opened the door. "Spencer, Meg!" she boomed. "Angus is waiting for you. I've got hot griddle scones and a pot of tea ready. Come in, come in."

"Thank you, Mrs. Campbell," Meg said, stepping inside.

"Call me Marjorie, my dear."

They followed Marjorie through to a light-filled living room with floor-to-ceiling windows where Angus Campbell, leaning on a walking stick, was squinting through a telescope.

"Hello, lad," Doc said to Spencer as he straightened. "Meg, you're a sight for sore eyes."

"Hiya, Doc." Spencer clasped Angus's good hand.

"Hi, Dr. Campbell," Meg replied. "See anything interesting?"

He grinned evilly. "There's a couple sunbathing in the nude down the beach."

"In the middle of winter?" Marjorie scoffed. "Do you think we're all daft? You can't believe a word he says," she told Meg and Spencer as she bustled over to help her husband back into his reclining chair. "Look at you, man, you're supposed to be resting."

"Rubbish. Go fetch the tea and scones like a good wee wifey." He waved Meg and Spencer over to the sofa. "Sit down."

Meg intercepted a worried glance from Spencer as they took their seats side by side. She knew what he was thinking. In spite of Dr. Campbell's bluster, he still walked with a limp and didn't appear to have full use of his right hand. Both those things would likely come right with time and physiotherapy, but there was no escaping the fact Doc was a lot frailer than he used to be.

"Heard from Ashton-Whyte lately?" Spencer asked.

Doc waved his left hand in disgust. "Aye. He ferreted out my true age, Lord knows how. But I don't want to talk about that ratbag. Meg, how's your project coming along?"

"Wonderfully," she replied, digging in her backpack for her preliminary results. "I've identified calls from Takush's calf, as well as interactions between the mother and baby. And—" she glanced at Spencer and the look of pride in his eyes intensified her excitement "—I've identified a call used by those two that isn't used by the rest of the group."

Doc pushed his chair to an upright position. "Isn't that interesting. Are you sure about that?"

"Spencer helped me design a statistical test to determine if it is, in fact, distinct from a call made by all the whales in Kitasu's group," Meg said. "And I'm running a literature search to see if anyone else has recorded similar results."

"So far, it looks like a first," Spencer said.

Doc's eyes gleamed. "What were the whales doing when they made the call? Did you get any direct observations?"

"The call appears to be associated with the calf nursing from its mother," Meg said. "It makes some sense when you think about it. After all, nursing is something these two share that the others don't."

"This is thrilling news, Meg," Doc said. "You're taking it calmly."

She shrugged modestly but knew her face must be

glowing. If her results proved correct, it was a very big deal and would gain her recognition in certain scientific circles.

"Until I double-check all the stats and get the results of the literature search, I'm keeping a rein on my excitement."

"Very wise," Doc said. "Keep me posted."

"Of course. You're still on my supervisory committee."

Doc's bushy dark eyebrows pulled together. "Not if Ashton-bloody-Whyte has anything to do with it." Spencer started to open his mouth but Doc held up a hand. "No, don't talk to me about that man."

Marjorie Campbell returned with a loaded tray, which she set on the glass-and-walnut coffee table. "Has Angus been telling you about his plans for retirement?"

"Retirement?" Spencer exclaimed. "Is Ashton-Whyte forcing you out? You can fight it, Doc. There must be an appeal process."

"Calm down, lad," Angus said quietly. "I don't want to fight it, though I do want to see Meg's thesis through." Marjorie had gone to stand behind his chair and now he reached up to grasp his wife's hand. "I'll go on my own before I let that hamster handler push me out. The stroke was a warning to slow down. We're going to take an Alaska cruise—"

"We're going to the *Caribbean*," Marjorie interjected. "I fancy a little warm air and sunshine. And you're not going to spend your holiday looking for killer whales. Before we knew it, you'd be lowering a lifeboat into the water to get closer to the wretched beasts and having another stroke."

Doc scowled up at her. "We're going to Alaska, woman, so I'll hear no more of your nonsense."

Behind his head, Marjorie mouthed, "Caribbean" to Spencer and Meg.

Meg suppressed a smile. She'd lay money the Campbells ended up in Jamaica. "Er, when are you planning this trip to...Alaska?"

"As soon as the physios will let me go. I'll be back in time for your thesis defense," Doc assured her. "And I daresay these new cruise ships have facilities on board for e-mail. You can post me your thesis and I'll post back my comments."

"But when did you decide all this?" Spencer asked, getting up to pace the room. He clearly wasn't happy with the situation.

"We've been talking about it for some time, but we only made the final decision when you told us you weren't going to Norway. I wouldn't have wanted to leave Meg without one of us to supervise her thesis." He glanced at Meg. "With Spencer as your adviser, you can't go wrong."

Meg nodded. And thought about the letter.

Doc turned to Spencer. "Ashton-Whyte will be calling you any day, no doubt, to offer you my position."

Spencer turned to gaze out the picture window. Silence filled the room. Then his face angled toward the light and Meg caught his expression in profile. *Trapped.* There was no other word to describe the look of his downturned mouth and drawn features. One way or another, she was responsible for him being stuck in Victoria.

Finally, with a grim smile, he turned back to her

and the Campbells. ''I guess it's me and the hamster man.''

MEG FOLLOWED SPENCER down the Campbells' winding front path to his car. Dead leaves littered the lawn and skeleton twigs reached across the paving stones to scrape her cheek. ''You don't have to do it, Spencer,'' she said. ''You don't have to stay.''

He put the key in the lock and turned to look at her. ''What choice do I have? I canceled Norway in that letter. Even if I hadn't, I couldn't leave you without a supervisor.''

She shrugged, pretending his presence or absence didn't matter one whit. ''I've already got most of my results and, like Doc said, we can correspond by e-mail. As for Norway—'' she reached into her purse and withdrew his letter to Dr. Henrik Jorgensen ''—I'm sorry, I just never got around to mailing it.''

Slowly he reached for the envelope. ''I'll mail it.''

But just for a second his eyes had lit up and she glimpsed his true feelings, the elation and the relief at knowing the bridges he'd thought were burned were suddenly whole again.

Something died inside her. Hope. Funny, she thought she'd lost that a long time ago.

CHRISTMAS EXAMS came and went and Spencer still hadn't mailed the letter. Mail it and he was stuck in Victoria, playing a role in which he felt increasingly uncomfortable. Tear it up and he could go on to Norway as planned. Spencer hadn't told anyone in the department he was thinking of staying in Victoria. As far as they all knew, he was still leaving at Christmas.

Getting the letter back was a reprieve, as though

the past two and a half months of playing at being a father had been a dream and he could wake up if he chose to. Moving on tempted him every waking moment and at night he dreamed his Camaro had sprouted wings.

The biology building was silent when Spencer let himself in late one morning two days before Christmas. The students had all gone home and only a handful of die-hard professors and research assistants beavered away quietly in their labs. Spencer didn't have any real work to do, but Ray was out with his girlfriend, Linsey, and Meg and Davis were at her parents'. It seemed a good time to tidy up loose ends.

He put the key in the lab door and found it already open. *Strange.* He came around the lab bench and stopped short.

Lee was seated at the computer.

"Lee!" he said, coming forward with a glad smile. "I thought you'd have left for Hong Kong by now."

Lee jumped up, a huge smile on his face. "I write my own story, as you say. It is about killer whales, not business. I told my father, no business degree for me!"

"Good for you!" Spencer clapped him on the shoulder.

"You think I will be able to write make-up exams for biology?"

"Absolutely. I'll help you explain the situation. This is fantastic."

Lee's smile widened. "I am glad you are happy."

"It's more important that *you're* happy." Spencer threw his briefcase down on the lab bench. "Wait till you hear about Meg's results with Takush and her calf.'' He went on excitedly, telling Lee all about her findings.

Suddenly he stopped. Something was wrong. Lee wasn't really paying attention. He wasn't smiling and getting excited. And then Spencer noticed the dark circles under the young man's eyes and his drawn face.

"What is it, Lee? What's wrong?"

"Nothing is wrong."

"Was your father okay with your decision?"

Lee's face crumpled and he seemed to shrink from within. "No, he is not okay with it. He is very unhappy with me. He cut off my money, for one thing."

Spencer dropped into a chair. Foreign-student fees were high. This was serious. "Maybe we can squeeze more hours out of the grant budget for you. Have you thought about moving into shared accommodation? It's often cheaper."

"Money is not the real problem," Lee said, blinking rapidly, his eyes very black in his pale face.

Oh, no. Spencer's heart sank. He had a bad feeling about this. "What *is* the problem?"

"Father says—" Lee swallowed, his bony Adam's apple bobbing "—I am no longer his son."

Spencer pulled back in stunned disbelief. "He *disowned* you?"

Lee nodded then quickly averted his head. "He says if I stay in Victoria I am not welcome back to the family home."

Guilt propelled Spencer to his feet and sent him pacing across the lab. It was his fault. He had prodded Lee into choosing biology. Lee had followed his advice and now he was miserable. Meg was right. He had no right to interfere.

"He'll forgive you. You're his son." He was ashamed to realize he was asking Lee for reassurance.

Lee shook his head. "He is a proud man with big hopes for his only son. He will not forgive." His mouth tugged into a wan smile. "I am very fortunate to know you, Dr. Spencer. You are very kind, helpful. You are like family to me."

Every word of praise and regard stabbed like a knife. The unspoken message that now Spencer was *all* the family Lee had put the twist on the blade. His chest tightened as though he were being squeezed by a giant vise. It was too much responsibility. He'd never wanted it, never asked for it. He wasn't worthy of trust. He wasn't dependable. He'd failed Human Relations 101 and now he was screwing up people's lives.

An awful thought occurred to him. What if it had been *Davis's* life he'd screwed up?

He really ought to do them all a favor and leave. Just go to Norway as he'd planned. The thought of leaving the entire tangled mess behind brought a sweet rush of relief. A lifting of an insupportable burden.

He made the decision on the spot.

"Uh, Lee, I guess you didn't know—I'm going to Norway, after all."

White-faced, Lee stared at him. His voice sunk to a whisper. "When?"

"Tonight. Or maybe tomorrow." Whenever he could get a ticket.

"Tomorrow is Christmas Eve," Lee said. "My father flies out tomorrow, too."

Spencer fell into an agonized silence. He was afraid to say anything in case he made matters worse, but

Lee looked so miserable he had to do something. "Maybe you should go with him, Lee. Doc's retiring, I'm leaving. Sort things out with your father and when you can come back to biology I'll do whatever I'm able to help. We'll stay in touch through Meg."

Lee nodded sadly. "Why do you not stay for Christmas with Meg? I thought you and she make romance."

They'd told no one about their personal history, not even Lee, so he had to be guessing. "No," Spencer said, "there's no romance between Meg and me."

And now that he was going to Norway, there never would be.

But he couldn't leave without saying goodbye to her. He'd promised he wouldn't do that to her again. Nor could he do it to Davis.

"I—I've got to go, Lee. I wish I could stick around but...I've got to go." He grabbed his briefcase and headed for the door. "Got to go."

He pushed through the lab door and headed toward the exit.

"Spencer!" Dr. Ashton-Whyte's voice boomed down the empty corridor.

Spencer groaned. Ashton-Whyte was absolutely the last person he wanted to see right now. Reluctantly he slowed his headlong flight. "Randolph."

Ashton-Whyte caught up with him and flung an arm around his shoulders. "Looking forward to the holidays, my boy?"

Spencer glanced with distaste at the beefy hand clutching him in fake camaraderie. His intense dislike of Ashton-Whyte bordered on the irrational, but dammit, the man stood for everything he'd avoided all his life—small-minded adherence to regulations, mind-numbing routine and rigid thinking. He stepped away, regaining his personal space. "I'm in a hurry."

"This will only take a moment. It's come to light that Dr. Campbell is well past the age of retirement. The situation I alluded to some time ago has come to pass, and we need a permanent replacement. Naturally the position will be advertised, but your application could be fast-tracked should you choose to submit."

"Took you a while to get to me. Did you already have a look around and not find anyone to take the position on short notice?"

"Well, humph, ah…" Ashton-Whyte pulled on his mustache. "Just answer the question—do you want the job or not?"

Spencer started for the double glass doors that would take him out of here. "I've got a research position in Norway. I'm leaving on the next available flight."

Ashton-Whyte followed him outside into the frigid December air. His phony smile turned to a frown. "This is a good opportunity. Assistant professorships don't come up every day."

"Sorry, I can't help you out." He lengthened his stride down the path to the faculty parking lot.

The last thing he heard was Ashton-Whyte calling, "The keys to your office and lab. Dammit, Valiella, *give them back!*"

CHAPTER FOURTEEN

BLACK THOUGHTS crowded Spencer's inner vision like the dense forest that encroached the winding road back to the cottage. It was only four o'clock and already darkness was falling.

He didn't *have* to go to Norway. No one was forcing him. He had a job he was a fool to leave, in a part of the world he'd always loved. Leaving Meg and Davis would tear him apart. Part of him longed to stay, to slip into a life of love and companionship.

But every time he thought about Lee, his hands started to tremble and he had to grip the wheel. He'd let that kid down badly. The scary thing was he still didn't quite know how it had all come out so wrong. His take on the world was obviously faulty, his judgment too different from the norm for him to be a good influence on others.

What kind of father would he be to Davis? Meg was doing a great job raising him. Who was he to barge in and screw it all up? Davis was too important to be at the mercy of someone like him. He'd tried to be a part of their lives, but it wasn't working. His father hadn't been able to stick out domestic life and he couldn't, either. Sometimes he had visions of marrying Meg. Of the two of them living, working, loving together. Until he thought of all that went with that scenario—mortgage, routine, boredom. Sooner or later he'd leave again. Run, like the coward he was. Like he'd run from Lee today.

Oh, God, *Lee.* Spencer groaned. How could he have just taken off from the lab that way? No explanation. No advice or provision for the future. He hadn't thought; he'd just acted. But maybe it was better. Make a clean break. Yes, that was the only way. For *all* concerned.

A few thick flakes of snow were beginning to fall as he turned in to the cottage driveway. But lights were on, which meant Ray was home. Good. He wanted to get all his goodbyes over with tonight.

Spencer heard the shower running and Ray singing above the sound of the spray, so he went straight to his room to pack. Some of this stuff he'd have to have shipped on to him, such as his books and equipment from the lab. He crammed as much as he could into his suitcase. Then from the closet, he took a large package wrapped in Santa Claus paper. Davis's Christmas present.

He was staring sadly at it when Ray appeared in the doorway, dressed and toweling dry his short hair. "You're back early. Want to grab a meal with me and Linsey at the Metchosin Inn?" He noticed the suitcase. "Hey, what's going on? I thought you'd decided not to leave."

"Changed my mind." Spencer set the Christmas present aside and pushed down hard on the suitcase to pull the zipper closed. "I'm heading out tonight."

"What about a ticket?"

"I'll get one at the airport. Or go standby if I have to." He heaved his bags off the bed and walked to the door.

Ray stood in his way. "Do you want to tell me what this is all about? Did Meg give you the boot?"

"No, and I'd rather not talk about it. Can you pick up my car from the airport after I'm gone? You can use it while I'm in Norway. That van is just about to crap out on you."

"I'll drive you to the airport."

Spencer glanced at Ray's freshly pressed shirt and best leather pants. "I thought you had a date."

"Linsey will understand. She can come with us."

"Thanks, but it's starting to snow and the forecast is for a heavy fall." He was going to miss Ray, he realized suddenly. These past few months he'd spent more time with his father than he had in years. They'd gone through a lot of changes together in a short time.

"Well, okay. Give me your extra set of keys. But with the snow, and Christmas, I might not get out to the airport until Boxing Day."

"That's okay." Spencer put down his suitcase to dig in his briefcase for the keys. "What will you do Christmas Day? Spend it with Linsey?"

"Meg invited us to Christmas dinner at her parents' place."

Spencer almost dropped his briefcase. Meg had invited him, too, but he'd waffled, planning to deliver presents in the morning before making himself scarce. "Roger and Helen *agreed? You* accepted?"

"Hey, I'm not so bad," Ray said cheerfully. "I'm almost respectable these days."

"God forbid," Spencer said, laughing. He picked up his bag again, not sure he liked the idea of Ray cozying up to Roger and Helen. And Meg and Davis. What was missing from this picture?

Ray walked him to the front door. "I hope you intend to say goodbye to Meg and Davis."

"I'm going over there now, on the way to the airport." He fought the sadness that welled up in his chest.

"I gotta tell you, Spence, I think you're making a mistake. You leave now, and Meg isn't going to welcome you back the next time you feel like dropping in."

A muscle in his cheek began to twitch from the effort of holding his jaw tight. "Let me know when your next CD is out."

"Send me your address and I'll mail you one just in case they don't play music above the Arctic circle."

"It's not *that* far north," Spencer said. It might as well be Timbuktu for all the real contact he was going to have with the people he cared about. He put down the suitcase and embraced his father. Ray hugged him back tightly.

Blinking, Spencer stepped back. "Ray— Dad, let's keep in touch this time, okay?"

Ray smiled his crinkly eyed smile. "You know where to find me. Take care of yourself, son."

"Will do. Goodbye."

Snow came down all the way to Esquimalt, splatting against the windshield to be swept off in melting drops by the wipers. By the time he pulled up in front of Meg's house, a thin layer had accumulated on the grass.

Spencer's footsteps lagged on the path. A warm glow shone from the kitchen windows, and the colored lights of the Christmas tree twinkled through the open living room drapes. Saying goodbye was the hardest part of any journey. One he usually avoided.

He tucked Davis's present under his arm and rang the doorbell. Muted footsteps approached from within. His heart beat faster. The door swung open... He was glad to see Patrick's smiling face. A few more minutes' grace.

"Hey, Patrick, what's cookin'?" Spencer asked over the now familiar sound of Gilbert and Sullivan. *The Mikado,* if he wasn't mistaken.

"Come in, dear boy. We finished dinner ages ago but I'm sure I can find you something." Patrick bustled around, taking Spencer's jacket and hanging it on the coatrack beside the door.

"Thanks, but I didn't mean that literally. Is Meg here?"

"She's putting Davis to bed. A glass of wine, perhaps?"

"Not right now, thanks. I'll say good-night to Davis."

First he went into the living room and put Davis's parcel under the tree. What he had for Meg he wanted to give to her personally.

His heart weighed heavily in his chest as he moved down the short hallway. Outside Davis's door he paused, listening to the indistinct murmur of voices inside. He touched the ceramic nameplate on the door. It had originally said David, but someone, Meg, presumably, had obliterated the *d* with white paint and replaced it with an *s,* using a black felt pen. As the rest of his legacy to his son, nothing was straightforward.

He was about to knock when he heard the faint

creak of Davis's captain's bed and a moment later, Meg opened the door.

"I wasn't expecting you." Fine lines creased her eyes. Lines that only appeared when she was tired or strained.

There was so much he wanted to tell her. And so little he could actually say. "I know I haven't been around much lately."

She shrugged. "I've been busy, too."

"Can I say good-night to Davis?"

"Yes, but please don't get him excited. He had another trip to the principal's office today. He seems to think you told him it was okay to punch people."

"I said it was okay to stick up for what he believed was right."

"Well, I guess he translated that differently from the way we would. The trouble is, Tommy's twice as big as he is. When Davis hit him, Tommy belted back. Your son got a bloody nose and a black eye, thanks to you."

Thanks to him, his son had gotten beaten up. If Spencer needed confirmation he was doing the right thing by leaving, this was it. He touched Meg's hair, missing her already.

She shook his hand off. "Go on. Before he falls asleep."

She shut the door behind him as Spencer walked over to the bed. Davis, realizing who had arrived, was up on one elbow, looking more wide awake than a small boy had a right to be at nine o'clock at night.

"Hi, guy." Spencer sat on the edge of the bed and ruffled Davis's hair, smiling at the boy's eager expression. How on earth was he going to say goodbye?

"Hi." Davis threw his arms around Spencer's neck

in a spontaneous hug. Spencer felt an intense painful stirring in his heart. He hugged Davis as tightly as he dared, careful not to crush his small bones, and for a few precious seconds savored the warmth of his son's love. If only he was a different kind of person. If only his life was set on a different course.

Spencer eased Davis back onto his pillow. "That's quite a shiner you've got there."

"I punched out Tommy." Davis looked pleased with himself.

"I thought you'd worked out all that stuff about having a father."

"Oh, it wasn't that. He was picking on a little kid. Calling him names, making him cry. He wouldn't stop, so I popped him one."

Spencer suppressed a proud smile. "Listen, Davis, it's great that you stuck up for the other kid, but hitting isn't an acceptable way to do it. You know that, don't you?"

Davis shrugged and squirmed, his lower lip jutting obstinately.

Spencer sighed quietly. He didn't want his last conversation with Davis to take the form of a lecture. "Never mind. I guess Tommy won't mess with you again."

"Can we go kayaking again?"

"Davis, there's something I have to tell you." Spencer paused, searching for the right words. There were none. He took Davis's hand in his. In the low light of the bedside lamp, his son's dark eyes looked huge and solemn, as if sensing something important was coming. "Someday I hope we can go kayaking again. But right now I have to leave. I'm going on a plane to Norway."

"Why?"

"I have another job there. I'm going to study Norwegian killer whales."

"Why can't you study the killer whales here?" Davis sounded hurt and bewildered.

"I could…but I arranged to go to Norway way before I came to Victoria. I only came here as a favor to my old professor."

Davis's lower lip began to tremble. "I thought you came to be with Mom and me."

Dear God. How could he have said that? The hurt in Davis's eyes flashed him back to the day his father and mother had left him weeping and struggling in the arms of a caretaker he barely knew. Pain constricted his heart and he didn't know if it was a response to his son's loss or his own.

"Spending time with you and your mom is one of my favorite things. I'm going to miss you." Just how much he was only starting to realize.

Tears in his eyes, Davis threw his arms around Spencer's neck again. "I want to go with you."

Spencer held him tightly, feeling the moisture and heat prick his own eyelids. "You've got to stay here for your mom," he said, his voice husky. "She loves you. She needs you to love her."

"Don't *you* love me?" Davis sobbed.

The tightness in Spencer's chest made it almost impossible to speak. Somehow he got the words out. "I do love you, son."

Davis's arms pulled tighter. "I love you, too, Dad."

Wet-cheeked, he held Davis to him, silently rocking him back and forth. Love and loss. Love and loss.

"I'll write to you," he said at last. "And you can write back."

Davis sobbed harder. "I can't write. I can only print."

Spencer hugged him closer, laughing through his tears. "You'll learn. You're going to learn so many things. And when I come back, we'll go kayaking."

Davis pulled away. "Promise?"

"Cross my heart and hope to die," Spencer said, sketching a cross over his chest. "I'll leave the kayak for you and your Mom so you two can practice while I'm gone."

"No," Davis said impatiently, scrubbing away the tears, "I mean, do you promise to come back?"

One way or another he would always be a part of this boy's life. "I won't ever be able to stay, but I'll come back for visits. Okay?"

Davis shrugged and dropped his gaze, his small face bleak. Spencer felt a pain in his stomach. Davis was already learning to do without the love to which he had every right.

"I brought you a present. It's under the tree."

Davis's face brightened. "What is it?"

"You'll find out on Christmas morning." He tweaked Davis's nose gently between two knuckles. "No peeking."

"I got a present for you, too," Davis said. Pushing back the covers, he went to the bookshelf and returned with a clumsily wrapped parcel. "I made it myself." He smiled wanly. "No peeking till Christmas."

Spencer would be on a plane come Christmas morning.

"Come here, you." Spencer grabbed him and tickled him till he giggled. Then he picked him up and wrestled him into bed, joking and teasing till Davis shrieked with laughter. Laughter, not tears, that was how he wanted to exit.

From the living room, Meg heard the shrieks. For crying out loud. Was she dealing with *two* A.D.H.D kids? Dragging herself off the couch, she stalked down the hall and pushed open Davis's door. Her frown turned to a resigned smile when she saw two faces illuminated by lamplight, flushed with pleasure and so alike.

"What a pair," she said. "But now it's time for bed. Not you," she added to Spencer, who was gazing at her from under his lids.

She tucked Davis in again, folding back his covers just so, arranging his toys just so and smoothing his hair off his damp forehead. "Good night, sweetheart."

"Good night. Mom?"

"Tomorrow," she said firmly, and turned out the lamp.

In the dark she bumped into Spencer. She let him take her hand and lead the way toward the thin rectangle of light coming from the hallway. At the doorway he paused and looked back.

"Bye, Dad," came a small voice from the darkness.

"Goodbye, Davis."

In spite of the warmth of Spencer's fingers wrapped around hers, Meg felt a whisper of cold steal over her. Those goodbyes sounded final.

"Is Patrick still here?" Spencer asked as they walked back to the living room.

"He's gone out with Douglas. Third time this week."

"Must be serious."

"I think it is and I'm glad. Douglas is nice."

They paused in the hall between the living room and the kitchen. Spencer glanced toward the front door.

"Would you like a glass of wine?" she asked.

His face showed a brief struggle. "Better make it coffee. I can't stay long."

Premonitions of grief clutched her heart. "Going somewhere?"

He held her gaze. "I'm leaving for Norway as soon as I can get a flight."

She would *not* cry. "So you *are* going. I thought you would have waited until after Christmas. Davis is going to be so disappointed."

"You can usually get a cheap ticket on Christmas Eve."

Her fist clenched around the kettle as she filled it, anger chasing away thoughts of tears. "*Cheap ticket.* Is that more important than seeing Davis's face on Christmas morning?"

"You know I don't think like that."

She knew, all right. She could read him so well he never had to try very hard to communicate with words. But there was more in his gaze than he meant her to see. She plugged in the kettle and stalked back to him.

"You love me," she declared, "and you love Davis. You're just too scared to admit it. The thing I'd like to know is, do you admit to yourself that you care? Or have you brainwashed yourself so thoroughly that you believe your own lies?"

"This isn't easy for me, Meg. I'm thinking of you and Davis."

"You're not thinking at all. What are you going to do in Norway on Christmas Day not knowing a soul?" She pushed past him to the pantry for the coffee.

"Do you want to get married?" he demanded. "If that's what you want, okay." He flopped down on one knee and spread his arms. "Meg McKenzie, will you marry me?"

Tears started in her eyes. "Don't be a jerk."

"I'm serious."

"You're feeling guilty. And you're proposing in such a way I couldn't possibly accept even if I wanted to. You don't want Davis and me dragging after you around the world. Or worse, dragging you to a standstill in one small corner of the globe."

Spencer rose to his feet.

Her hands shaking, Meg scooped coffee into the plunger, and grounds spilled over the counter. Then she set the canister down and took a deep breath. "You love me but not enough. I don't like it, but I can accept it. Just don't pretend otherwise."

"I'm not pretending," he said. "I would marry you—"

"—if you had to marry someone."

He threw up his hands. "What do you want, my soul signed over in blood?"

"I don't want *anything* from you." She turned away, knuckles pressed to her mouth. *Don't cry, don't cry, don't cry…*

"Now who's fudging the truth?"

Silence filled the kitchen.

Spencer came closer and put an arm around her.

"You're right, I was being a jerk. I'm sorry. Sometimes I say dumb things. You've been very understanding. *Too* understanding, according to Ray."

She brought her head up and her forehead bumped into his chin. "Do you talk about me with Ray?"

"Only when he's giving me hell for screwing up my life."

She sniffed. "So why *are* you screwing up your life?"

"I'm trying to prevent *your* life from being screwed up."

"There you go again with your ridiculous excuses." She pulled away. Reaching into the cupboard, she took down two coffee mugs. "Have you eaten?"

"You don't have to feed me all the time. You're not responsible for me."

Surprising how much the little things hurt. She'd *happily* be responsible for him. Now she wanted to hit back. "I only asked because I've got leftovers and I want to get rid of them."

He grinned, disarming her. "You're all heart."

Would she ever get over that smile? She poured boiling water over the coffee and the aroma of cinnamon and hazelnut rose on the steam. With so little time left, she ought to be practical. "Is there any medical history in your family I should know about?"

"You mean, like diseases and stuff?" He thought a moment. "Not that I know of. I could ask Ray and e-mail you at the university."

"Never mind. I'll talk to him myself."

Spencer frowned, as though that hadn't occurred to him.

"You surely don't think that just because you're going away Davis won't see his grandfather, do you?'' Meg pushed the plunger on the coffee, then poured out two cups and handed one to Spencer. He was feeling uncomfortable. So he damn well should.

Spencer added cream. ''What's all this about Ray and his girlfriend going to your parents' for Christmas?''

''Why not? It solves the problem of dividing time between grandparents. Davis is very excited about it.'' She glanced at him over his cup. ''You were invited, too, you know.''

''Maybe next year.''

''Sure.'' She sipped her coffee. ''Ray told me he got Davis a guitar for Christmas. He thinks Davis has real potential.''

Spencer frowned. ''I don't know that I want to encourage a musical career for him. I mean, look at my father.''

Meg smiled. ''Ray's all right. He just had some things to work through.''

Spencer took Meg's cup and placed it on the counter next to his. He took her hands. ''I want to stay in touch this time. I want to know how you and Davis are doing. Can we do that?''

''Yes,'' she whispered, clenching her jaw to stop her mouth from trembling. Whatever it cost her, for Davis's sake she would do it.

His arms went around her, holding her tightly. ''No matter where I am, I'll think of you,'' he murmured into her ear. ''I'm going to miss you. Like I always do.''

Then why don't you stay? her heart cried. But pride sealed her lips. In the circle of his arms she vacillated between wanting him and wanting to hate him. She could push him away or she could hold him one more time.

She wound her arms around his neck, pulling his head down. "Make love to me," she whispered against his lips.

"It's not what I came for," he protested, his eyes searching hers. But his hands slipped beneath her sweater and her skin rippled in response to his touch. His gaze turned dark and hungry.

"I want tonight with you, Spencer," she said, abandoning pride along with hope. "Give me one more night of memories, and I'll never ask for anything else."

He pulled her hips in tight to his and his body hardened against her as he pressed kisses over her face. "Forgive me, Meg, I can't say no. I've wanted you so badly for so long."

They stumbled to her bedroom, loosening buttons and pulling down zippers. Half-clothed, breathing hard, they fell across the bed. Still kissing her, Spencer rolled her onto her back, his leg between her thighs. Her muscles tightened against him. It wasn't enough. Nothing would ever be enough. But she wanted him. Oh, how she wanted him.

"Up," he panted, helping her to a half-sitting position to tug her sweater over her raised arms. Her long blond hair fell in a silky curtain around her bare shoulders and down the swell of her breasts above the lacy top of her black bra.

He unclasped the bra and tossed it aside. Then plunged his hands into her hair, sifting it through his fingers, glorying in it, spreading it across the curves of her breasts. "You're so beautiful, Meg."

His burning gaze made her throb and tingle. She

wanted to feel his hands on her. To see them move over her body. Reaching back, she lifted her hair away, raising herself toward him. "Touch me, Spencer."

With a groan he took her breasts in his hands. His palms, his fingers, felt wonderful, warm and rough against her tender skin. And when he dipped his head and sucked one tingling nipple into the hot wetness of his mouth, she thought she was going to die of pleasure. "Spencer."

The years and the months of wanting him burst forth, making her hot and wet and aching to feel him inside her. She pushed his open shirt off his shoulders, running her hands over his hard muscles and smooth skin. So hot, his skin, almost burning. When her bare breasts grazed his chest, she gasped. He pushed her back onto the pillows and she pulled him with her, unwilling to let him go.

Her jeans were already unzipped and his tongue laid a swath of moisture across her lower belly from hip to hip above the bikini line. Then his hands were tugging her jeans off and she was lifting her hips and feeling frantic and urgent because nothing was happening quickly enough.

Spencer stood and dropped his own jeans while she flicked hers away from her ankles. She lay there, flushed with desire, her gaze riveted to his naked body. The killer whale tattoo on his biceps gleamed in the light of the table lamp as he sheathed himself. And then he was on her again, pushing her legs wide and sliding between them. Her eyes closed as sensation took over. Hot. Hard. Sliding into her wetness. Filling her. Giving her what she craved. Deep thrusts that stoked her body into a sexual firestorm.

"I need you, Meg." His kisses claimed her mouth, her neck, her breasts. "I need you, baby. I need you, need you..."

MEG STARED AT THE CEILING in the dim glow of the streetlight outside her window. It was very early, maybe five or six in the morning. Spencer lay asleep beside her.

He needed her. He hadn't ever said he loved her.

But he cared about her. And their son.

She turned on her side and watched the slow rise and fall of his chest, the movement of his eyes beneath the lids, the twitch of a brow, the flash of a smile. A deep sigh. His hair lay tousled on the pillow. Her pillow.

She loved him. She would always love him.

He was hers. And he was not.

Hers to love forever, but she couldn't hold him. Nor should she try. If she tried to bind him with duty or even love for his son, he'd chafe at the bonds and eventually grow to resent her, then maybe even hate her. She couldn't bear that.

She sighed, not wanting to think of the future. All she had was this moment, replete with the contented aftermath of loving, of happiness hard-won and treasured all the more because it was fleeting.

Meg breathed lightly, careful not to disturb the silent space where love had blossomed in the night. Beneath her sheets, Spencer's warmth mingled with hers. His scent marked his place in her bed; his smile, a place in her heart. After the wild abandon of the first lovemaking, his touch had turned tender. Without words he'd told her how much she meant to him. It was enough. It had to be.

Dreamily, Meg yawned and shut her eyes. And slept.

When she opened them again, Spencer was lying on his side and watching her.

The light had changed subtly as darkness melted away. He gazed at her in silence, his eyes full of the feelings she longed to hear from his lips but never had and never would. Wordless and breathless lest the slightest movement break the connection, she held his gaze. Memories, thoughts and feelings drifted between them, full of silent laughter and unspoken sorrow.

Into this deep dear silence came the first faint twitter of birdsong. Dawn had arrived. And with it, Christmas Eve.

Spencer pulled a hand from beneath the quilt and touched her cheek lightly with his fingertips. Meg stayed frozen in place, unwilling to move past this moment into the inevitable future.

But it was already too late. It had been too late before they'd even started. She knew the look that came into his eyes—she'd seen it before—the distant gaze of a man who in his mind was already halfway to where he was going. Where neither she nor Davis could reach him.

He pushed back the quilt. "I've got to go."

Not trusting her voice, she nodded. Then shut her eyes as he rose from bed, shedding the covers like the past, stepping into the future. Without her.

She waited till he'd dressed, then rose and put on her dressing gown. "Do you want some coffee?"

Shaking his head, he pulled her into his embrace. Buried his face in her hair. She felt him breathe in, knew he was memorizing the scent of her just as she was him.

Say it, Spencer. Just once, say you love me.

Wordlessly he pulled away again. Reached around his neck for the thin leather thong that held the killer whale tooth. He took it off and hung it around her neck, pulling out thick swathes of blond hair till it settled against her skin. "It's been my good luck charm. I'd like it to be yours."

He was severing the last tie.

She touched the ridged cone of ivory and willed the tears to stay behind her eyes. There must be an ocean of them back there by now, enough to flood the world if she let go.

They went down the hall, stepping quietly so as not to wake Davis. Spencer paused outside his son's room. Meg stopped and glanced back. His hand was on the knob as if to open the door for one last look. But he didn't, and then he moved on.

At the front door he put on his jacket. She stroked the soft leather, savoring the feel. His eyes met hers, then darted away. From an inside pocket he pulled a thick envelope stuffed with badly folded papers.

"I've opened a bank account for Davis," he said, handing it to her. She started to say no, but he stopped her. "I'm not asking. It's done. I'll make regular payments into it. If it's not enough, or if you need extra for something, just let me know. I've filled out the forms to make it a joint account. All you have to do is sign the papers and return them to the bank and you'll be able to make withdrawals."

Numbly she nodded. It was too hard to do anything else.

He wrapped his fingers around a thick lock of her

hair and held on. "Meg, I hate the thought of you struggling. If you need something for yourself, just tell me."

I need you.

She nodded, knowing she would never ask him for anything.

He glanced at the door. His fingers slipped away from her hair.

"Wait!" she cried. And hurried into the living room to the Christmas tree. She found the small parcel she'd wrapped for him and brought it back to the front door. She handed it to him, worrying he would see the photo as an attempt to remind him of his ties to her and Davis, yet silently daring him to deny those ties existed. "Be careful. It's glass."

He felt the outer edge of the thin flat package through the red and green paper and his lips flattened as he guessed what it was. Meg felt her heart constrict as he tucked it in his inner pocket without opening it.

When he stepped outside, snowflakes blew inside. The snow was coming down in dense flurries from an opaque white sky. Overnight the air had cooled and now a thick layer of snow blanketed the yard and street.

"I bet you don't have snow tires," she said.

He grinned. "I bet I do."

"Spencer..."

His expectant gaze rested softly on her face.

She took a huge breath. "I—I want you to know I'm glad about last night. It's what I wanted and I'll always treasure the memory of being with you. But next time you're passing through...well, you can see Davis. You can see Davis anytime you want. He's your son. You have the right to know him. But as for me—" she paused and met Spencer's now-troubled gaze full-on "—I don't want to see you again. No more than necessary, at least. Certainly not like last night. I love you. I'll always love you. But I just can't..." She bit her lip hard, unable to go on.

Spencer reached for her. Took her into his arms and held her close till she heard the beating of his heart, felt his warm breath on her temple. Her own breath was tight in her chest. He was holding her for the last time. The final embrace. If this felt so right, why was he leaving?

When he pulled away at last, she let him go. She'd promised herself she wouldn't cling. "Goodbye, Spencer."

He nodded, his eyes infinitely sad. With one last touch of her cheek, he turned.

She watched him go down the path, get into his car and drive away.

Meg closed the door, went back to her bed.

And wept.

CHAPTER FIFTEEN

SPENCER WAS ABLE TO BUY a ticket to Norway, but he was ten hours early for his flight. After he checked in, there was nothing to do but wait. God, he hated airports. The framed photo burned next to his heart, but he didn't have the nerve to open it. He was still too close and it would be too easy to turn back.

He wandered around. He browsed the bookshop, fingered the souvenirs and checked out the duty free. He stood and gazed at a row of phone booths for minutes on end, Davis's image before his mind's eye. He shook his head clear and forced himself to walk away. His course of action was set. He couldn't afford doubts at this stage. This evening he would board a plane that would take him half a world away. In Bergen an office and lab space awaited him. In his brief-case was his research proposal to study the killer whales of the fjords.

Yippee.

He found a coffee shop and had a late breakfast, lingering over three cups of coffee and two newspapers. Restless and bored and sick at heart, he went and sat in the waiting lounge in one of a row of plastic seats facing the runway and stared out the window. Lousy weather, but not bad enough to cancel flights. For a while he slept, sitting up.

When he awoke he remembered Davis's present to

him. And found he didn't want to wait till Christmas to open it. He pulled it out of his briefcase and tore off the wrapping. Inside was an envelope, which he opened. What met his eyes almost made him cry.

It was a huge cardboard card, hand-printed and colored, that read, "Merry Christmas to the World's Best Dad!"

Spencer pictured Davis sitting at the dining room table laboriously printing the letters in his childish uneven hand, waiting for Meg to say each letter in turn so he could write it down. Underneath the lettering were crude branches of holly hung with gold bells that looked like dirigibles. Below that Davis had drawn a picture of himself and Spencer in a surprisingly accurate kayak. They were crude block figures, one small, one tall. The tall one's paddle looked about to take off the small one's head.

Spencer chuckled quietly to himself. A chuckle that turned into a sob. Tears escaped and wet his cheeks. He started to his feet. He would call Davis, after all. Thank him for his gift, tell him—

He stopped. Tell him what, exactly? That he'd see him soon? Spencer wasn't the world's best dad. He wasn't any kind of dad at all.

Sadly he put the card back into the envelope, being very careful not to bend the corners. Then he sank back into the chair, blanking his mind. He fixed his gaze on the world outside and watched the sky go from white to gray to black as darkness descended. He'd send a postcard from Norway. Yeah, that was it.

Finally he boarded his plane, an old DC-9 that inspired no confidence, and they made the short hop to Calgary. There Spencer spent the hour-and-a-half stopover pacing the transit lounge in front of the floor-to-ceiling windows, glancing worriedly at the thickly falling snow. Now that he was irrevocably on his way, he wanted nothing to detain him.

At last the flight attendant made the boarding call and Spencer headed back to the jetway behind a thickset middle-aged woman burdened with several plastic duty-free bags. Her wrinkled cotton slacks looked as if she'd slept in them, and her hair was flattened at the back from too long against the head-rest.

A smiling flight attendant in a brown-and-orange uniform checked his boarding pass, and Spencer returned her smile automatically. As he stepped on board, he glanced down through a gap between the jetway and the plane. Snowflakes whirled in the frigid air and gave him a momentary feeling of vertigo. He quickly brought his foot inside and, shaking off a sense of unease, moved down the aisle, glancing over-head for his seat number.

On the first leg of the journey he'd had all three seats to himself. Now the woman with the wrinkled pants and plastic bags was settling into the aisle seat in his row. "Excuse me," he said, and stepped past her to the window seat. He tucked his briefcase under the seat in front and avoided eye contact. He'd trav-eled enough to recognize a talker.

Eye contact or not, she started right in.

"My word, quite a blizzard out there," she said in a strong Australian accent, and leaned over the empty seat between them to peer through the tiny window. "M'name's Joyce. What's yours?"

"Spencer." He didn't want to be rude, but lack of sleep was catching up with him and he couldn't contain a yawn. "Pardon me," he said, and closed his eyes.

"I'm visiting my son in Montreal for Christmas," she confided relentlessly. "He and his wife just had a baby. Nine pounds, five ounces. A whopper for a first child, doncher think?"

Spencer nodded and said something vague about it being nice she could visit at Christmas.

"Never been this far north before," Joyce rambled on. "Is it always this cold?"

"Only in winter," he murmured. The thrum of the engines lulled his fatigued brain. In the middle of last night he'd woken to the feel and scent of Meg lying next to him, and they'd made sweet sleepy love. Thinking about it made him hard. And sad. He missed her already. The erection faded but the sadness lingered as he dropped into the hazy zone between consciousness and sleep. He should have told her how he felt....

Spencer heard the clatter of the dinner cart moving down the aisle and opened his eyes. Turbulence slowed the attendant's progress and his stomach was rumbling by the time the cart stopped at his row. The attendant passed over a tray just as the plane lurched. He grabbed it in midair and brought it to his table.

He glanced sideways. Joyce was looking pale.

"I'm not a great one for flying," she said apologetically, opening the foil cover on her dinner.

Spencer gave her an encouraging smile and hoped for the best. Braised beef undoubtedly looked even worse when recycled.

Dinner came and went, thankfully without incident. He sipped a brandy, hoping it would help him sleep again, and thought ahead to his arrival in Norway.

He'd been to Bergen for a conference once and had always wanted to go back. But so far he was hating this journey. It had none of the excitement, none of the anticipation he usually experienced when moving to a new place.

He dozed again in spite of the erratic lurching motions of the plane. And again, he awoke, this time to a pinging sound and the flash of the seat-belt light coming on. An attendant's calm voice came over the loudspeaker explaining that more turbulence was expected and all passengers were requested to please remain seated and to have their seat belts securely fastened.

Spencer checked his belt and glanced at the woman next to him. Her garrulousness had vanished behind tightly compressed lips and her eyes were squeezed shut. She clutched the arms of her seat with white-knuckled hands.

"Are you all right?" he asked. The bumpy, jarring ride seemed rough even to him, a seasoned traveler.

"Fine," she said flatly. "Couldn't be better."

He nodded and glanced at his watch. Still an hour to go till Montreal. There was nothing any of them could do but endure.

DAVIS CARRIED the plate of cookies to the coffee table along with a carrot for the reindeer. "Can you pour a glass of milk, Mom?"

"Coming right up." Meg brought the milk into the living room and placed it next to the cookies they'd made that afternoon.

Davis, fresh from his bath and dressed in his new Christmas pajamas, knelt beside the coffee table. His cheeks were flushed and his eyes were bright with excitement. Meg forced herself to put on a bright smile. She was tired from lack of sleep, and her limbs still ached from last night's lovemaking. But it was the sense of loss and hopelessness that sucked the energy out of her. If it wasn't for Davis, she would have curled up in a ball and put herself to bed till New Year.

How many more Christmases would he believe in Santa? Meg wondered. She wished Spencer could seen his son now. She wished he could be here, holding her in his arms. She wished—

"I wish Dad was here," Davis said wistfully. "Where do you think he is right now?"

Her heart ached for her son. Davis hadn't stopped talking about Spencer all day. He hadn't yet taken it in that Spencer was really gone, if not forever, then for a very long time. Longer than a small boy could comprehend, at any rate.

"Well, most flights to Europe go the polar route."

Davis turned anxious. "You mean, the *north* pole? What if his plane crashes into Santa's sleigh?"

"Your father's plane is *not* going to crash," Meg said reassuringly. But a shiver crossed the back of her neck. She was so tired. Hugging her sweater closer, she rose. "Bedtime, honey. The sooner you get to sleep, the sooner it will be Christmas."

This was the one night of the year Davis went willingly to bed. She tucked him in and together they sang, "'Silent night, Holy night, All is calm, All is bright....'"

Outside the window, snow continued to fall. And the wind began to howl.

SPENCER CHECKED HIS WATCH. They should be landing in Montreal shortly. There he would change planes for London and Oslo. The cabin lights had been dimmed, and most of the other passengers, including Joyce, were asleep. He was wakeful, thinking of Meg.

He wished he *had* told her how he felt. He'd thought it would make it harder to leave, and probably it would have. But still, some words were meant to be spoken.

He didn't blame her for not wanting to see him again, but it hurt. Badly. His heart was so swollen with pain and love and guilt it felt as though his whole body ached with it. He'd spent his life avoiding emotional ties and he didn't know how to deal with being separated from Meg and Davis. He *had* done the right thing by leaving, hadn't he?

Spencer held his watch up to the dim light and frowned. They should have landed half an hour ago. He glanced around for a flight attendant to ask how late they'd be. A group of them were conferring near the galley. Before he could press the call button, the cabin lights came back on. A bell sounded, alerting passengers to an announcement from the captain. At last, he thought, settling back in his seat. They were going to land.

"Good evening, ladies and gentlemen. This is your captain, Tony Melville, speaking."

Beside Spencer, Joyce awoke with a grunt. "What's going on?"

"Preparation for landing," Spencer said.

But the captain's words proved him wrong.

"We're experiencing some difficulties with the landing gear," Captain Melville said in a bored, relaxed tone of voice. "For the past thirty minutes we've been circling Montreal International Airport while attempting to engage the landing-gear locking mechanism—thus far, unsuccessfully. Despite blizzard conditions, the control tower was able to inform us that the landing gear has extended. However, our instrument panel here in the cockpit indicates the wheels are not locking into place. This could be due to failure of the locking mechanism or simply that a warning light is out in the instrument panel. Rather than risk a belly landing on an icy runway, I've decided to go on to Halifax, where current weather conditions are clear. En route, we hope to ascertain the extent of the malfunction. On behalf of the airline I would like to apologize for the inconvenience.'' The captain paused briefly and began again in French. *"Mesdames et messieurs..."*

"Halifax!" Joyce turned indignantly to Spencer. "My son's waiting at the airport in Montreal!'' Her hair stuck out in all directions, and her mascara was smudged where one eye had pressed against the pillow.

"The airline will fly you back, I'm sure," he said calmly. The word *malfunction* buzzed around in his brain.

"They'd darn well better."

A few minutes later she'd woken fully. "How can we land if the locking whatchcallit is broken?'' she demanded in an alarmed whisper. "We're going to crash!"

"No, we aren't." Spencer refused to even consider the possibility the situation wouldn't be fixed before Halifax.

Joyce gave him a skeptical glance and ordered a

gin and tonic. "Make it a double, darl'," she said to the flight attendant. "Don't you want one, Spencer?"

He shook his head. Joyce wasn't the only passenger availing themselves of false courage, but his stomach was churned up enough without adding alcohol.

For a long time there was no sound but the steady drone of the DC-9's engines as it pushed on through the night to the east coast and Halifax. Maybe it was just his imagination, but he thought the engines sounded overworked. He tried listening instead to the headphones, but the music was elevator fare and the comedy channels irrelevant and irritating. He tried to doze, but was too tense to relax. Everything was going to be all right, he told himself. It had to be.

An hour out of Montreal the captain came back on the loudspeaker and this time he sounded neither bored nor relaxed. "Good evening, ladies and gentlemen. This is Captain Melville again. We've been battling a head wind on our eastward flight and the plane has used more fuel than expected. We don't have enough fuel to reach Halifax, so I've made the decision to turn back to Montreal. The light on the instrument panel still indicates a malfunction in the landing gear. Chances are there's nothing to be concerned about. However, flight attendants will now instruct you in emergency landing procedures."

"Oh, my God! We *are* going to crash," Joyce wailed. A jerky movement of her hand sent the little plastic gin bottles on her tabletop scattering. She began to weep, causing what was left of her mascara to smear along the tops of her puffy cheeks.

"We're not going to crash." Spencer didn't much care for touching strangers, but he reached out and patted her arm. It felt soft, almost squishy. Panic fluttered deep in his stomach.

His thoughts, never far from Meg and Davis, turned to the framed photo she'd given him. He pulled it out of his briefcase and ripped off the foil wrapping paper.

The five-by-seven-inch photo was an enlargement of one Ray had taken that day on the beach out at Sooke. Spencer was holding Meg in one arm and Davis in the other, their laughing faces turned into the sun. The tip of a furry tail could just be seen curling up to Davis's waist.

Spencer dropped the photo on his lap. He fought back the choking sensation of too much emotion. Emotion he hadn't allowed himself to feel. It surged forth, drowning him in love and regret. If only he could see Meg one more time. And his son. *Oh, Davis. Oh, Meg.*

He shut his eyes and let his mind go, running over all the times they'd shared. He felt automatically for the killer whale tooth and found it missing. Panicky loss crashed down on him. Then he remembered he'd given it to Meg. His luck had run out. At least if anything should happen to him, she would have it to remember him by…

Angry at himself, he blinked away tears of self-pity. *Jerk.* The killer whale tooth was *all* he'd given her to remember him by. Whether he lived or died.

She deserved better. So did Davis.

"Is that a photo of your family?" Joyce asked, her words slightly slurred. "Can I see?"

Reluctantly he showed her.

"Aren't they gorgeous? Your wife's a real looker, and what a beaut boy. You must be proud."

His fears tightly held in check, he nodded.

"Are you traveling to meet them?"

"I just left them." He turned to the window. There was nothing there but blackness. Meg was right; he wasn't doing this for her and Davis, only for himself. Because he was a coward. Who was he kidding? Davis would be far better off with a full-time father, no matter how flawed, than with some jerk who sent postcards from Norway.

The bell sounded again and the flight attendants moved into position, going through procedures Spencer had witnessed during countless plane rides but never encountered in a real emergency. New instructions were added to the familiar repertoire. Hands over the head. Head down between the knees.

And kiss your ass goodbye.

Spencer watched the demonstration as though his life depended on it. His palms began to sweat. Beside him, Joyce was going quietly hysterical, whimpering and moaning.

When the attendants had finished, the captain came on again. In clipped, anxious tones he informed the passengers they were beginning their descent into Montreal. Emergency vehicles were standing by.

Spencer took a last look at the photo of Meg and Davis and placed it in his briefcase. He knew what was wrong with him now. It wasn't about mortgages or picket fences or the fear of routine. The terrified five-year-old inside his brain screamed out the truth. *He always left first so no one could ever leave him again.*

Yet Meg had loved him all these years even though he'd left her. Even though when he'd come back he'd given her no real encouragement. How could he not

believe she would continue to love him? She would.
He knew she would. She'd said so. Oh, why hadn't
he trusted in her love? He would make it up to her.
He would make her so happy...

If it wasn't too late.

Spencer bent over. He crossed his hands behind his
head. Beside him Joyce whimpered. A few rows up,
a baby was crying.

One more chance. That was all he wanted, one
more chance. He would never deny Meg and Davis
their place in his life again. He wouldn't deny himself
their love. He'd already missed too much.

He wanted to see Davis grow up. He wanted to
make love to Meg. Over and over. To make her pregnant with another child. To care for her, to share sun-
sets and sunrises, and killer whales and laughter
and...

Tears ran freely down his cheeks. His ears popped
as the plane lost altitude. His stomach was free-
floating.

Stop the cycle of connecting, then running.

Against the burning blackness of his tightly
squeezed eyelids he saw a grown-up Davis walking
away from a woman he loved. He saw another small
child crying for his dad.

Meg was the key, the link between himself and his
son. Meg was the link between himself and humanity,
himself and love. She was the key to his becoming a
whole person.

He had to get over his fear of commitment.

Stop the cycle before he infected Davis.

Stop the plane, I want to get off.

Just before the DC-9 hit the ground, his entire being was flooded with love—bright, blinding love,

pure and unselfish. For Meg, for Davis, for the husband and father he could have been.

MEG AWOKE in the middle of the night with a jolt.
Chill air poured over her exposed shoulders where the
quilt had slipped off. With icy fingers she tugged it
up around her neck. Then she lay in the dark, eyes
wide open, filled with an inexplicable sense of fore-
boding. Had she heard a noise outside? She listened
hard. Nothing but silence. But the silence was thick
with dread. Finally she pushed back the covers and
went to the window. With the palm of her hand she
wiped the condensation off the glass and peered up
into the blackness of the midnight sky.

There was nothing out there but a billion tiny
snowflakes.

Falling. Falling. Falling.

THE PLANE HIT the ground with a bone-shuddering
thump. Joyce screamed. Spencer's head knocked hard
against the seat-back in front of him. With a screech-
ing of tires the plane skidded down the icy runway,
bounced back in the air and landed with a second
spine-jarring jolt. Then the plane evened out and began to slow. They were back on terra firma.

Seconds passed with no more bumps. No tearing
of metal.

Cautiously Spencer raised his bruised and aching
head.

They hadn't crashed.

The plane wasn't on fire.

The wheels *had* locked. And the DC-9 was slowly
taxiing toward the terminal, where lights could be
seen dimly through the blizzard.

They were safe. He was alive.

There was a moment of stunned silence in the cabin. Then a great roar of relief went up from the rows of passengers. People were laughing, crying, embracing each other.

The breath Spencer had been holding rushed out with a whoop of joy. He turned to Joyce. He grabbed her and hugged her, loving her squishiness and her smeared makeup and her faint odor of sweat and gin.

Someone shouted, "Three cheers for Captain Melville," and the roar echoed again and again, "Hip, hip, hooray!"

The flight attendants appeared, smiling, the naked relief shining from their faces belying the false calm they'd earlier projected to the passengers.

Captain Melville came on the loudspeaker, his casual drawl back in place, if a little shaky. "Ladies and gentlemen, we've just arrived at Montreal International Airport where local time is five minutes past 4:00 a.m. on December twenty-fifth. Merry Christmas." He paused. "God blessed us, every one."

FREE DRINKS were flowing in the special transit lounge set aside for passengers on Spencer's flight. The disparate crowd, silent and alone with their private fears such a short time ago, let loose with a vengeance.

Spencer edged to the bar. "I'll have a Wild Turkey, please. Double. No, make that a triple."

"Spencer!" Joyce flung herself at him with drunken abandon. "Isn't it wonderful to be alive!"

He grinned and held up his drink to avoid sloshing it over her head. "Can't think of anything better. Is your son here"?

"I called. He went back home when he found out the plane was delayed. He's on his way again, but I reckon I've got time for another drink. One humdinger of a hangover coming right up," she added happily.

"Didn't you say they had a new baby? Those things can howl." He felt like howling himself. With joy.

"Ooh, ha, ha. You're right. Who cares?" She lifted her drink.

"Say, where'd you find the phone?"

"Over there," she said, pointing. "By the washrooms."

Briefcase in one hand, drink in the other, Spencer pushed through the crowd to the telephones. He had to wait a few minutes till the woman with the crying baby, who was now sleeping peacefully on her shoulder, hung up.

Spencer dialed Meg's number, calculating too late, what time it would be on the West Coast. It rang and rang, and the pressure built in his chest. His words were all in his heart. Could he get them to come out?

"Hello, Meg?" he said when she finally answered. "Did I wake you?"

"Spencer? Where are you?"

"Montreal." Now that he had her on the phone he couldn't seem to speak. "I, uh, I forgot something. I'm coming back."

"You are?"

The noise of the partying passengers almost overwhelmed her soft voice. He cupped a hand over his free ear, listening hard and hearing her hesitation, her wondering. This was not the time or the place to explain. "There's a plane leaving for Vancouver in twenty minutes. I'll be there first thing in the morning.''

"We're having a white Christmas," she said.

"I'll see you soon."

MEG GLANCED at the digital bedside clock. It was only a little after one in the morning, but there was no way she'd get back to sleep. Shivering, she flung off her nightgown and pulled on a long burgundy velvet skirt, thick wool socks and her black cashmere sweater. She made herself a cup of tea, built up the fire in the living room and settled down in an armchair to wait for Spencer.

Why was he coming back? He said he'd forgotten something. It must be really important to fly all the way back from Montreal. Surely he could have just asked her or Ray to mail whatever it was. The whole thing was so unlike Spencer. He'd sounded different on the phone. And what was all that noise in the background? It sounded almost like a party.

Should she have said, "No, don't come here"? She hadn't been quite awake, certainly not enough to think clearly. Although she had to admit that hearing Spencer say he was coming back had given her a surge of hope. But coming *back* wasn't the same as coming *home*. And what would Davis think when he saw him?

Worry warred with hope, anger with love, sorrow with anticipation. All through the long hours of Christmas morning Meg paced and fretted, attempted to read and failed to concentrate, and ended up staring glassy-eyed into the flickering red and gold flames. Eventually her eyes became heavy....

When she opened them again, the fire had died to glowing embers and Davis was shaking her shoulder.

"Mom, Mom. Can I open my presents? Please, can I?"

Meg blinked and shook the hair out of her eyes. "Good morning, Davis," she said, pulling him into a hug. "Merry Christmas."

"Can I open them? Plee-ase, Mom?" Davis left her side and went to kneel on the floor beside the Christmas tree where presents were piled in colorful confusion.

She glanced at her watch—seven-thirty.

Davis picked up a box and shook it. "This is from Dad. I wonder what it is?"

Meg rubbed her bleary eyes. *Spencer was coming home.* She didn't want to believe anything less, but she couldn't tell Davis that in case it wasn't true. Still, she ought to prepare him.

"Davis, come here, please." She waited while he dragged himself away from the tree, then pulled him onto her lap. "Your father called last night long after you were asleep. He's coming back this morning."

Davis bounded off her lap and raced around the room. "Yippee! Daddy's coming home."

"Whoa!" She snagged him by his pajama top as he went by. "Don't get too excited. I don't know how long he'll be here. He said he forgot something. He'll probably just pick it up and be on his way again." It would always be this way, she realized, and almost wished she'd told Spencer not to come back. Davis would know enough disappointment in his life without the roller-coaster ride that would come from being Spencer's son.

"I wonder if he opened my present to him yet?"
Davis said.

"I don't know. But shall we wait till he gets here
to open yours? I'm sure he'd like to be part of your
Christmas morn—"

There was a knock at the door.

Meg froze, her heart pounding with sudden ur-
gency.

Davis's face lit up. He charged toward the door.
"It's him! It's him!"

Meg rose slowly, her limbs numb. In slow motion
she turned and watched as Davis flung open the door.

Spencer stood on the doorstep, his tousled hair
frosted with snow, his face tired but jubilant. With an
inarticulate groan of joy, he scooped Davis into his
arms, his eyes falling shut as he held his son.

Meg took a tentative step forward.

Spencer's eyes opened and they locked with hers.
She knew in that second he *had* come home. Tears
welled in her eyes.

Spencer swung Davis to the floor and stepped
toward her. He swallowed, as though he had something important to say. Meg could hardly breathe.
"Wh-what did you forget?" she whispered.

And then she was in his arms and his face was
buried in her hair. "I forgot to tell you I love you."

"Oh, Spencer." Now she was the one who
couldn't articulate her feelings. All she could do was
hold on to his jacket and blink back the tears that
were preventing her from seeing into his dear, dear
face.

"I love you," he repeated, kissing her cheeks, her
eyes, her nose.

"Don't say that unless—"

"I mean it. I really do." His voice was low and rough. "I want to marry you. Please say you'll marry me, Meg."

She smiled at him and blinked away her tears. "Well...okay." Then she threw herself into his arms again until Davis clamored to be let into the magic circle of love.

"Group hug," Spencer announced, and picked him up. Davis's thin arms wrapped around their necks, pulling them even closer.

"Why are you crying, Mom? This is happy."

"I know," Meg bawled. "I'm so happy I could die."

Spencer shuddered. "Don't say that, please."

"Can we open the presents now?" Davis demanded, already squirming to be let down.

"Sure thing, son." Spencer smiled fondly after Davis as he ran to the tree. "Son," he repeated softly, then sought Meg's eyes. There were tears in his.

She couldn't believe it was true except the evidence was right here in front of her. Later, she'd demand an explanation for his change of heart. But for now, she just wanted to bask in his love.

Davis ripped the paper off a box, uncovering a bright red remote-controlled sports car. "Wow! Thanks, Dad."

He came over and gave Spencer a big hug. Meg's heart filled to the brim with happiness at seeing the man she loved, laughing and holding their son.

"Thank you for the photo," Spencer said when Davis had run back to the tree. "It reminded me of what was important in my life at a moment when I needed hope. It brought me back to you."

"Are...are you sure?"

His smile faded a little as his intense gaze met hers. "I don't blame you for wondering or being skeptical. But I promise you, Meg, I'm here to stay. For as long as you'll have me."

He kissed her then. And when his lips found hers, Meg finally felt free to pour the love and yearning she'd had for him all these years into her response. *Spencer, I love you.*

After a minute Spencer pulled back a little. He fished inside his jacket for a small box. "I got this at the airport in Vancouver, but even if I'd gone to the finest jeweller I don't think I could have found anything more fitting."

A ring. She bit her lip in expectation and opened the lid.

A thick circle of carved gold lay nestled in black velvet. With trembling fingers Meg removed it and held the piece of Haida artistry up to the light. Two leaping killer whales rising from the waves, by their side a smaller whale.

"Oh, Spencer. It's perfect!"

He slipped it onto her finger and raised her hand to his lips to kiss the backs of her fingers. Meg thought she would burst with love and happiness.

Then Spencer's expression turned sheepish. "Would you mind very much if I took back the killer whale tooth? I really missed it."

"Of course." Meg reached under her sweater to lift the leather thong over her head and put it around his.

Spencer rubbed the ivory with his thumb before kissing it, too.

She laughed. "It looks better on you, anyway."

At the tree Davis shouted with delight. Meg and

Spencer turned to watch as he pulled the paper off a snare drum.

"Oh, no!" Meg cried. "Andrew. I'll kill him."

"Your brother? The one who freaked when you gave his three-year-old daughter two allegedly male white mice that later had babies? Looks like payback time."

Meg glanced up at Spencer from beneath a curtain of blond hair. "By the way, we *are* going to my parents' for Christmas dinner."

"Oh, *are* we? I suppose you expect me to sip Roger's Scotch and make small talk about the price of IBM shares."

"If you give me a ring and ask me to marry you, you accept the whole package, buster. All or nothing." She punched him jokingly in the shoulder, but a thin thread of fear ran through her. Maybe it was too much to ask right away.

Spencer tenderly brushed the hair from her forehead. "For you, Meg, I'll make any sacrifice. I'll work for Ashton-Whyte. I'll even be nice to your father."

And then she knew for certain that he loved her.

EPILOGUE

MEG'S GAZE DRIFTED away from the computer screen where she was typing up the last of her thesis. It was April and the university year was almost over. She glanced out the window to the beach below. Spencer and Davis had just dragged the two-person kayak onto the pebbles and were climbing the wooden staircase to their house of timber and glass.

Meg loved their waterfront home on the outskirts of Victoria. She'd worried a little that Spencer would balk at a mortgage, but he'd been the one to suggest buying rather than renting and he'd signed the deed without batting an eyelid.

A few minutes after they left the beach he and Davis came through the door, carrying the scent of the ocean with them.

Meg got up to kiss her husband and wrap an arm around her son's shoulders. "There's a postcard from Lee," she said, handing Spencer a card picturing the houseboats of Hong Kong. She turned to Davis. "Go get out of your wet clothes, honey."

Spencer read aloud. "'Father and I have made up now that I have returned to Hong Kong and finished my business degree. He tried hard to entice me to join the family company but he keeps to the bargain. This fall I will enroll one hundred percent in biology. See you in September, Dr. Spencer. And Mrs. Spencer.'

Signed, 'Lee. P.S. Maybe you need experienced research assistant?'"

Spencer chuckled. "Yes, Lee."

Meg searched his face. "Are you going to accept
Ashton-Whyte's offer of a renewed contract?"

Spencer tossed the card back on the desk and
pulled her into his arms. "Unless you have something
better in mind."

"Well," she said, planting kisses along his jaw, "I
hear Norway is a great place to do a master's degree
on killer whales. They might even take *you* back if
you ask real nice."

"Dr. Jorgensen *was* very understanding when I explained the situation. And he did say I could defer
the grant for a year." Spencer pulled back to look at
her. "Is that what you want to do?"

"I'm easy."

He grinned. "I know that." Then he stroked her
hair back from her temples and planted a kiss on her
forehead. "What about Davis? Going to Norway
would really disrupt his life. Do you think he could
handle it?"

"There's only one way to find out. Besides, I think
as long as he has the two of us, he'd be just fine."

Davis appeared in the doorway, still in his wet
pants. "Are you guys talking about me again?"

Meg caught Spencer's eye and they both laughed.
Then she leveled a look at her son.

"Change. Now."

Spencer shook his head as Davis trundled off. "Is
that stare of yours an approved child-rearing tech-
nique?"

"Hey, you don't mess with what works. It took me
years to perfect it."

Spencer traced a finger over her lips. Meg shut her eyes. She never tired of his touch. Never took for granted his presence even though she was finally convinced he was committed to her and Davis, one thousand percent. Their wedding, and the sincerity with which Spencer promised to love and cherish, had removed all doubt. Ray had done them proud by playing one of his new songs, a romantic ballad, and Davis, as ring bearer, marched up the aisle on his best behavior. Even her mother and father were pleased with the way things turned out, although Helen complained at the whale recordings as they'd exited the church.

"You could do a master's degree here," he suggested. "I mean, we've got this great house, Lee's coming back, Ray's staying put...I like it here."

She studied his face. He really seemed to mean it. "I'd like to stay, too," she agreed softly.

"The real question is," he said, planting a kiss on the tip of her nose, "when are we going to produce a brother or sister for Davis?"

She smiled. "I think we ought to make up for lost time so the sooner, the better."

"Sounds good to me," Spencer said, and pulled her into his arms.

They were still kissing when Davis returned, dressed in clean dry clothes, and declared he was "starving."

"In that case, you can lend a hand making spaghetti while your mom finishes her work," Spencer said, reaching out to straighten his son's collar with a tender smile.

A while later Davis glanced across the table at his mother and father. It was kind of yucky how they got so mushy sometimes. But having his dad around was a dream come true. He'd even framed Davis's Christmas picture and hung it on the wall. That made Davis feel like the world's best son. Best of all, Davis knew his dad would always be there. He'd promised.

And Mom. Dad was always teasing her about something. Like now. Her cheeks were pink, she was laughing, and she couldn't seem to decide who she wanted to look at more, him or his dad.

There was no doubt about it.

He'd never seen his mom so happy.

HARLEQUIN®
SUPERROMANCE®

Three childhood friends dreamed of becoming firefighters. Now they're members of the same team and every day they put their lives on the line.

They are

AMERICA'S BRAVEST

An exciting new trilogy by

Kathryn Shay

#871 FEEL THE HEAT
(November 1999)
#877 THE MAN WHO LOVED CHRISTMAS
(December 1999)
#882 CODE OF HONOR
(January 2000)

Available wherever Harlequin books are sold.

HARLEQUIN®
Makes any time special ™

Visit us at www.romance.net

HSRAB

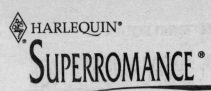

HARLEQUIN®
SUPERROMANCE®

By the Year 2000: *BABY!*

**What have *you* resolved to do by the year 2000?
These three women are having babies!**

Susan Kennedy's plan is to have a baby by the time she's forty—in
the year 2000. But the only man she can imagine as the father of her
child is her ex-husband, Michael!
MY BABIES AND ME by **Tara Taylor Quinn**
Available in October 1999

Nora Holloway is determined to adopt the baby who suddenly
appears in her life! And then the baby's uncle shows up....
DREAM BABY by **Ann Evans**
Available in November 1999

By the year 2000, the Irving Trust will end, unless Miranda has a
baby. She doesn't think there's much likelihood of that—until she
meets Joseph Wallace.
THE BABY TRUST by **Bobby Hutchinson**
Available in December 1999

Available at your favorite retail outlet.

HARLEQUIN®
Makes any time special ™

Visit us at www.romance.net

HSR2000B

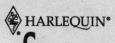

HEART OF THE WEST

Every Man Has His Price!

Lost Springs Ranch was
famous for turning young
mavericks into good men.
So word that the ranch was
in financial trouble sent
a herd of loyal bachelors
stampeding back to
Wyoming to put themselves
on the auction block!

July 1999	**Husband for Hire** Susan Wiggs	January 2000	**The Rancher and the Rich Girl** Heather MacAllister
August	**Courting Callie** Lynn Erickson	February	**Shane's Last Stand** Ruth Jean Dale
September	**Bachelor Father** Vicki Lewis Thompson	March	**A Baby by Chance** Cathy Gillen Thacker
October	**His Bodyguard** Muriel Jensen	April	**The Perfect Solution** Day Leclaire
November	**It Takes a Cowboy** Gina Wilkins	May	**Rent-a-Dad** Judy Christenberry
December	**Hitched by Christmas** Jule McBride	June	**Best Man in Wyoming** Margot Dalton

HARLEQUIN®
Makes any time special ™

Visit us at www.romance.net

PHHOWGEN